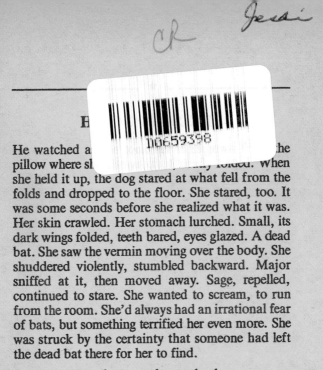

He watched a... ...the pillow where sh... ...folded. When she held it up, the dog stared at what fell from the folds and dropped to the floor. She stared, too. It was some seconds before she realized what it was. Her skin crawled. Her stomach lurched. Small, its dark wings folded, teeth bared, eyes glazed. A dead bat. She saw the vermin moving over the body. She shuddered violently, stumbled backward. Major sniffed at it, then moved away. Sage, repelled, continued to stare. She wanted to scream, to run from the room. She'd always had an irrational fear of bats, but something terrified her even more. She was struck by the certainty that someone had left the dead bat there for her to find.

Someone wanted to scare her to death.

★

SOMETHING TO HIDE

PATRICIA ROBINSON

TORONTO • NEW YORK • LONDON
AMSTERDAM • PARIS • SYDNEY • HAMBURG
STOCKHOLM • ATHENS • TOKYO • MILAN
MADRID • WARSAW • BUDAPEST • AUCKLAND

SOMETHING TO HIDE

A Worldwide Mystery/August 1993

First published by St. Martin's Press, Incorporated.

ISBN 0-373-28007-6

Printed in U.S.A.

SOMETHING
TO HIDE

ONE

SAGE WALKED OUT into the Charleston twilight, locked her huge front door, and went down the piazza steps with too great a sense of relief. She paused in the garden to glance up at the old house. The fading light was kind, obscuring the paint peeling from the line of tall pillars, momentarily restoring grandeur. She looked at it with love. She turned away from it with dread. Stop it, she ordered herself. You're being an idiot. Houses are only haunted in books or on TV.

An hour later, standing in her sister's crowded drawing room, she wondered if it wouldn't be easier to deal with the dread. She felt like a pigeon among peacocks. Seeking familiar faces and meeting the cool, superior glances of Elise's new northern friends, she tried for an air of detached amusement, listening to the cacophony of voices, then gulped down the rest of her second martini.

Why did she come? she asked herself. The answer stood directly across the room. David Raeburn. The Dark Prince from Away. He was the hero of all the old novels she'd found in the attic, the romances that ended with her mother's era. Aim high, she advised herself recklessly. Her sister, all that was left of her immediate family, was dying to see her settle down with some passable lawyer, doctor, or investment broker whom she'd known since dancing school. Why not surprise her with a brilliant conquest? A real surprise. Sage, unlike Elise, had never been a belle. Her grades had been too high at Sweetbriar. She'd escaped from her own debut party by lurking in the ladies' room. Many of the girls she'd grown up with were pursuing careers in business and the professions. One was running for the legislature. Because Sage had spent the last two years taking care of her ailing grandmother, she knew it was assumed, at least by the old guard, that she was destined to be single, leading "a useful life."

Aim high. Why settle for a dreary suitable marriage or a useful life? She looked again at David Raeburn, seeing a veiled tragedy in the dark eyes, an implicit chivalry in his bearing. She also saw how many other women were glancing in his direction. First, she must get him to notice her. After all, they'd met before. One could say he'd been attentive. Well, maybe not attentive but extra polite. She tried to strike an alluring pose, then slumped. As soon as she'd walked in the house she'd known she shouldn't have come. The big Louis XVI mirror in the hall had informed her that her dress, a hand-me-down from Elise, sagged at the neckline and hem. The heels of her shoes were at least two inches too sensible. What's more, Elise expected her to mingle with grace and élan.

The hell with it, she thought. It would be far more fun to get drunk, turn into a dancing maenad. She could stop the party in its tracks, mid drink, mid canapé. Even better, she could pass out and get a good night's sleep instead of lying rigid in her bed, listening to strange sounds. A glance in the mirror above the fireplace reminded her abruptly that she was ill-equipped for a dance of Dionysian frenzy.

She imagined the remarks. ''Who is that pitiful creature falling over the andirons?'' from a stylish newcomer to Charleston.

''That's the hostess's sister. Can you believe they're related?'' from her spiteful cousin, Corinne.

''Here, let me help you up,'' from the fascinating David Raeburn.

As if on cue he turned from a raven-haired beauty with a throaty laugh, and looked in her direction. Almost at once he turned back to the siren. With disgust Sage remembered that on her way to the party she'd detoured past the house he'd rented next to her Great-aunt Octo's. When she'd seen that his dark blue Mercedes wasn't in his driveway she'd decided, with a rush of anticipation, that she'd find him at Elise's. She lifted a drink from a passing tray and smiled apologetically at the waiter. Taking a hefty gulp, she stared again at David. I'll will him to look at me, she thought, to see through this drab exterior to the vibrant woman within. But instead of finding that perfectly sculpted face turning to her, she met the pale-eyed gaze of David's ever-present companion, Peter Larson. Their glances locked, then with the faintest smile he turned away. For some reason she shivered.

''I'm mad for Charleston,'' said a northern female voice behind her. ''As I said to Ogden and Carla, it may not be the Hamptons or Hobe Sound but it really is divinely quaint.''

Sage hadn't been to a bona fide party since the one Elise had given for her on her twentieth birthday, six years ago. She realized how much the scene had changed. Charleston not only had become a tourist mecca, but the now-yearly Spoleto Arts Festival had brought in coveys of the rich and chic who, enchanted with it, were buying up old houses at outrageous prices and settling in. The once-sleepy town was filled with tour buses, horse-driven carriages, and sleek foreign cars. Elise celebrated her new friends. "God knows they liven things up," she insisted. "We could become quite cosmopolitan. And it's about time!"

Sage imagined all the social gatherings held in that same eighteenth-century drawing room over the past two hundred years. The costumes changed, knee britches and panniers giving way to Confederate uniforms and hoopskirts and then to the shifting fashions of modern times. Until recently these rituals had been familiar, predictable. Now the room seemed filled with alien accents, strange new forces.

The thought of strange new forces reminded her jarringly of Roper Chalfont, who'd just rented her carriage house. She knew he'd recently returned to town, having left some years before under a cloud. He was a born Charlestonian but he'd no more fit into this gathering than would Genghis Khan. He was even more alien than the newcomers. He was too big. His voice was too deep, too strong. She was certain his dark tan didn't come from a sun lamp or a resort beach. His conversation was blunt, utterly lacking in grace. He'd stood in her garden, looked up at the house, and grinned. "I love it," he'd said, "a single lady left over from the nineteenth century, living in the crumbling family shrine, resolutely maintaining her standards. Now I know I've come home."

With an effort she thrust Roper from her mind and looked again at David Raeburn. He was surrounded by women. Why don't I go home? she wondered. It was an idle question. Even this Tower of Babel was better than sitting at home, growing more certain each minute that something very strange was happening in her house, that the soft but jarring night sounds were real and not imagined. She recalled her sister's warning. "Dammit, Sage, you're getting downright odd. Locked in that dismal house. Crouched over old diaries. You have no excuse now that Gran's gone. You have every reason to get out, do things, see people!"

She watched a clutch of Charleston men, barricaded in a corner, deep in a discussion of fishing and politics. Next to them was a portly man in a cream-colored suit of European cut, flanked by three scrawny women in ultrafashionable clothes. Sage listened to the olio of remarks from the locals and the outsiders:

"It was written for winds, strings, and piano but Stanley transposed it for sitar and drums."

"Bo an' me—hell, we been fishin' the Cumbee since we were kids but I've never seen one that big!"

"Frankly, I was turned off by those orange primal dream sequences."

"Will says we'll need more'n an indictment for tax evasion to get that turkey out of the statehouse."

The Charlestonians had an air of polite reserve. They wore it when they were outnumbered, when their code of manners was being ignored. The newcomers looked more affluent and spoke with louder authority but their faces, too, were wary, as if they expected at any moment to become victims of the legendary Charleston snobbery. She watched a big grizzled man who looked like a Levantine rug dealer and a wafer-thin woman with mauve hair skinned back from an avid face. The woman wore an elegant white wool suit, tinted glasses, and a look of practiced superiority. Sage had read an interview with the man, Alfred Freeman, when he first moved to town. He was a writer of novels, screenplays, TV scripts, and witty exposés in magazines like *Esquire*. He'd bought a house on South Battery, owned six Impressionist paintings, and had his caviar and smoked salmon flown in weekly from New York.

"Of course, it's a charming town, architecturally," he said to the tinted glasses, "but culturally these people are poverty-stricken. They're mired in the past, wallowing in the contrived glory of their ancestry. It's their whole identity. They don't dare leave because they'd have no cachet elsewhere. So, they sit in these beautiful drawing rooms, drinking themselves silly and reinforcing each other's prestige."

He chuckled. "I remember talking to Bill Faulkner one night—we were close friends—about the peculiar backwardness of the South, the insularity. Incidentally," he spoke with sudden slyness, "are you going to the Bailliards' on Thursday?"

Below the tinted glasses an involuntary twitch of the lip betrayed the fact that she'd not been invited. "I'm afraid we'll be out of town," she said in a Long Island drawl. "Pity," she added.

"I was going to regret," smirked Freeman, savoring the moment, "but since I've been told quite solemnly that the Bailliards are the absolute crème de la crème—I mean, strangers rarely get beyond those big Ionic columns—I decided that it might be amusing. I'm doing an article on Charleston tribal rites, you know. Isn't that naughty of me?"

Sage marveled at the effect of the town on newcomers. They seemed to suffer an instant identity crisis. Frustrated by the Charlestonians' antiquated sense of values, they insisted that the locals were a bunch of provincial snobs.

Her look strayed again to David Raeburn. David not only had found quick acceptance but was much sought after. His manners and appearance were faultless. He was widely traveled and appeared well educated. Most important, he was a bachelor in his early thirties and had fallen in love with Charleston. The fact that he had come south to recover from a serious but little discussed accident added to his allure. He was mysterious, he was devastating, and he was well beyond the reach of Mary Sage Eliot. At the moment he still was surrounded by women, including the raven-haired beauty and an upcountry bunny, Sally Doone Cavette. Sally was batting sky-blue eyes and tossing her curls in a gesture that had helped her become a runner-up in the Miss South Carolina contest and, over the protests of his parents, the wife of Adger Cavette IV.

She noticed that the soignée female in tinted glasses had disappeared. Freeman was looking down at stocky Bubber Latour with lazy indulgence.

"Yessiree," Bubber exhaled, mopping his brow, "Charleston's a great place to live but it's sure as hell changing." He caught Sage's wink, grabbed her arm in desperation. "Hey there, Sage! How you doing, honey?"

"Good to see you, Bubber. How're Della and the kids?" she asked.

"Right as rain." Bubber glowed with relief. "Dell's around somewhere. Maybe I better go check on her. Can I freshen your drink, Sage?" He didn't wait for an answer. "This is Mr. Alfred Freeman," he waved toward the big man. "Bought a house on South Battery. He's a writer. Miss Mary Sage Eliot, Mr. Freeman."

Freeman watched Bubber disappear, then openly culled the crowd for a likelier prospect than Miss Mary Sage Eliot. When his look returned to her she could feel him reviewing her lack of makeup, her hair twisted in unfashionable braids around her head, her dress hanging with all the flair of a dust cover.

"You live here?" he asked with no interest.

Sage looked at the arrogant face, the eyes blurred with boredom. "I'm a bird of passage, my dear." Her assumed Long Island drawl sounded pretty good; she pressed on. "Can you believe these people?" She waved her drink toward the clutch of Charlestonians, managing to spill several drops on Freeman, thoroughly enjoying herself. "Let's face it, Charlestonians aren't people, they're period pieces. Talk about backward!" She squinted at the Adam woodwork, the flow of Scalamandre silk and the tall windows, she bent toward him confidentially. "Do you realize," she whispered loudly, "they've only had indoor plumbing for five years?"

"Sage!" The hand on her arm was an iron clasp, Elise's smile a work of art. "Excuse us, Alfred, but my sister has a phone call." With the skill of a Sherpa guide Elise led Sage through the tangle of guests without bumping into a glass or stepping on a toe, dispensing gracious greetings as they passed, kissing a cheek here, pressing a hand there, until they were in the less crowded hall where, instantly, she turned from consummate hostess into avenging angel. "I suggest," she said, with formidable control, "that you go upstairs and throw cold water on your face."

Sage clung to the newel post, giving her sister what she hoped was an engaging smile. "Lise, you told me to make an effort."

"That doesn't include making fun of Alfred Freeman! He's an important writer."

"He's a pompous ass, Lise."

"That crazy sense of humor's going to get you in trouble, Sage. And that dress! When I gave you those things, I told you to have them altered."

Sage grinned at her sister. "Maybe you'd better hide me away, Lise, like Dilly Cheever's aunt. She's perfectly happy with her Ouija board and a bag of popcorn."

"I'll have Etta bring you some black coffee." In a flurry of pale chiffon, Elise swanned away to rejoin the party.

Sage started up the stairs, then, hearing the familiar voice, turned. David Raeburn, followed as always by Peter Larson, had come into the hall. With a spasm of hope, she decided he'd seen her after all, followed her from the room. Clutching the newel post, she stared, struck anew by his likeness to a Renaissance nobleman. She waited, expecting him to approach her, but he never glanced in her direction. "Dammit," he snapped, turning to Peter Larson, "it's none of your business!" He strode to the door.

Peter Larson offered a perfect contrast to David. Each of them stood an inch or two over six feet, but where David had a lean grace, Peter's body was overmuscled, almost crude. Next to him, even Roper Chalfont would look fine-boned. Under white blond hair his broad-featured face was impassive. "We have an agreement," he rasped. He'd caught up with David, seemed to loom over him. David gave him a quick look of fury. Then his gaze faltered, his shoulders sagged. Without another word or even a glance toward the stairs, the two men left the house.

Sage stared after them, thoroughly deflated. Besides being crushed, she was puzzled by David's anger. What on earth had prompted it? There had been widely divergent rumors about the two men since they'd arrived in Charleston six months earlier. No one seemed to know if Peter was a friend or an employee. At first there was some talk about whether or not they were gay, or as her grandmother would have put it, "light of foot." This idea seemed to have been discarded.

As she continued up the steps, she realized that she'd been silly to suppose that David found her interesting. The fact that he'd been attentive once or twice hardly indicated a fatal attraction.

She went to the second floor, passed the crowded library, and walked down the hall. She was still thinking of the odd exchange between David and Peter as she went by one of the guest rooms. She heard a sneeze, stopped, and then opened the door. Across the room a figure out of a Shakespearean play stood staring, totally absorbed, at a wall of old prints. Sage stepped inside.

"Amazing," said Beatrice Bonham without turning.

"Bea!" Sage greeted her with relief. "I thought you were Richard the Third." Bea, never given to conventional dress, was resplendent in a velvet suit of royal purple, a matching coif that covered her head, and a modified Elizabethan ruff.

"I'm mad for old eau fortes and mezzotints," she said, "and these are the real thing." She turned to

Sage at last, her face lit by a toothy smile. It was a hairless face, without eyebrows or lashes, the skin milky smooth. Her figure brought to mind Titian and Renoir, the word voluptuous. Bea, a writer of historical novels, appeared to be somewhere between forty and fifty.

"Late eighteenth century," marveled Bea. "All of St. Petersburg. The Hermitage, the Fortress of St. Peter and St. Paul, the bridges over the Neva. Extraordinary! Family heirlooms, Sage?"

"They were brought back from Russia by my great-great-grandfather's cousin, James Eliot. He was there on a kind of grand tour." Sage sank onto one of the twin beds, trying not to wrinkle the satin spread. "You might be interested in some of Elise's antiques," she offered, "like that Sheraton commode. It's supposed to be rare."

But Bea was riveted to the prints. "An embarrassment of riches," she murmured. "You people are surrounded by treasures that you no longer see."

"Not me," said Sage, thinking of her old house, stripped of any valuable pieces, filled only with dusty Victoriana. Watching Bea, she began to feel drowsy. The martinis were doing their work. Like her Aunt Octo, she was fond of Bea and found her not only amusing but stimulating. She'd enjoyed the lectures they'd attended together at the art gallery. Several times they'd gone out to dinner and then to symphony concerts. She couldn't understand how Elise could be taken in by that pompous Freeman and turned off by a newcomer as interesting and knowledgeable as Bea. She sighed.

"A touch of the doldrums?" Bea wheeled around, crossed to the bed opposite Sage, and sat. She slipped the magnifying glass she had been using into a lizard pouch and snapped the bag shut. Leaning forward, she looked at Sage with concern, waiting for an answer.

"Not really. I don't know. I—" Sage longed to have someone to talk to. She desperately needed a friend who would tell her that she was capable of handling her own life, that she could attract a man like David Raeburn, and that there was nothing abnormal about hearing odd sounds in an old house in the middle of the night.

"I guess it's just getting used to living alone," she answered uncertainly. "I don't sleep very well. I—"

"You hear gillies and ghosties and things that go bump in the night." Bea leaned back, tucked a red curl under her coif. "When my sister died back in Akron, I was alone for the first time in my life. I not only heard things, I began to see things. I even went to a shrink for a while." She laughed. "He advised me to move, take up aerobics, or have an affair."

Sage wanted to ask Bea some questions about David but she was beginning to feel dizzy. She stood up. "Bea, my sister instructed me to throw water on my face and lie down. I think she was right."

Bea rose with her, squeezed her arm. "Look, sweetie, why don't we get together this week, do something racy like feeding the gulls on the Battery."

"Sounds great." Sage tried to walk steadily across the room. When she reached the door, she turned to say good-bye but Bea was once again absorbed in scenes of St. Petersburg.

She headed back down the hall, then on impulse went into the nursery that Elise had furnished a year or so after she'd married Clay. Sage loved the room, with its *Wind in the Willows* wallpaper, its mobile of tiny shells, the white cradle that had held four generations of Clay's family. She noticed with a pang that since she'd last seen the room the blinds had been drawn and the furniture shrouded in sheets.

She continued down the hall, locked herself in Elise's apple-green bathroom and threw cold water on her face. She scanned her features for signs of debauchery but found as always a look of utter candor. It reminded her of her grandmother's attempt to teach her to flirt. On her fourteenth birthday her gran had explained the power of the sidelong glance, followed by a swift lowering of the eyelids. "Your eyes are your best feature, my dear. Wide-set, that soft gray green, and with those incredible lashes. But you mustn't use them like searchlights." Elise, at sixteen, had been more blunt. "For God's sake, don't stare. It puts people off, makes them uncomfortable, especially boys. Nobody wants to be gawked at."

Sage wondered now if there might be some truth in what she'd been told. Two days ago she'd had a discouraging interview for a job, an opening at the library. After she'd introduced herself, the man had never again regarded her directly. He'd gazed at his collection of ballpoint pens, at a stack of cards, and mostly at his watch. He'd fidgeted and sighed a lot. Sage didn't get the job. What's more, she'd never know if it was due to her lack of experience in library science or in the sidelong glance.

Thinking of the failed interview cut through the euphoria induced by martinis. She was reminded of her meager funds, her lack of skills, the dismal prospect for the future. By the time Gran had died she'd been able to leave Sage little more than the house. Sage kept envisioning sale ads for the place like those in the pages of the British magazine *Country Life:* "Superb antebellum residence in historic Charleston. Four floors and attic. Two apts on ground floor. Twelve twenty- by twenty-two-foot rooms, large entrance hall. Four baths. Double seventy-foot piazzas. Converted carriage house. Secluded garden."

She knew she spent too much time leafing through the magazines Elise had brought for Gran. She should have been reading the impassioned political tracts and searingly honest novels of the new feminists or at least rereading *War and Peace.* But during Gran's last days she'd had trouble concentrating. She'd sat for hours at the old lady's bedside and, when Gran dozed, had worked on deciphering and typing Charlotte Benford's diary. Lately she'd been taking afternoon naps, telling herself that the change of seasons always made her sleepy, but knowing full well it was the nights of broken sleep, the hours spent cowering in her bed, listening.

Awaiting the return of sobriety, she sat on the side of the tub where within easy reach she found a small table holding Elise's extra reading glasses, a pile of magazines, and a decanter of bath oil. Paging through a *New Yorker,* she found under the heading "Art Galleries, Uptown" several items marked for attention. She didn't like to think of her sister trying to impress celebrities and rich Yankees. She knew that since Clay was a prominent lawyer Elise had to entertain clients and business associates but surely not vipers like Freeman.

On the other hand it was evident why the newcomers appealed to the coming generation in town. It was a glamorous game. Suddenly the young Charlestonians were buying their clothes in New York or at least Atlanta; they were using caterers for even the smallest dinner parties. They were driving expensive new cars, something that would have been considered bad taste a generation ago. In a few years, thought Sage, the character of the town might be gone. Except for its treasure of eighteenth- and nineteenth-century architecture, Charleston could be indistinguishable from Akron or Dallas. Good Lord, she caught herself, I'm getting to be just like Gran. I'm a period piece, a twenty-six-year-old period piece. Maybe Roper Chalfont's right. Not long ago she'd had lunch with a friend from Ashley Hall school days who'd returned to town for a visit. Barbara Jane Thorpe had been voted the prettiest girl in the class and the most likely to marry first. Currently she was living in a Soho loft with a poet who had a knack for getting grants.

"Sage, you've got to get out of Charleston," she'd said. "My God, you're still singing on the beat. You'll rot here, believe me." She'd added that she hoped Sage wasn't still a virgin. She said that marriage was no longer relevant. She'd explained the difference between a meaningful relationship and a commitment.

Sage threw more cold water on her face, dried it with a tiny towel. It didn't help. She went to the adjoining room and lay down on the big bed where a number of her brother-in-law's forebears had been born, died, and undoubtedly between times passed out. She wanted to forget about Barbara Jane, forget about what was happening to the town. She felt drained, exhausted. And it wasn't just the drinks.

She gazed up at the pale lilac canopy and realized that, for the first time in a long while, she could doze off with a feeling of safety.

She thought of all the nights she'd lain rigid in her bed, waiting for the sounds, sounds that proved to be nothing when she dared leave her room to investigate, tiptoeing barefoot into the upstairs hall, once even venturing to the top floor. If she were to mention any of this to Elise, her sister would tell her she was getting kinky from being alone. Once again Elise would start pressing her to sell the house, despite the fact that she'd promised Gran to keep it in the family. Gran, Elise regularly reminded her, hadn't any idea of how little money she was leaving for maintenance and taxes.

Several times she thought of calling the police, then abandoned the idea, knowing they'd think her some kind of crackpot.

"Now let's go over this again, miss. You keep hearing sounds, books have been put back wrong on the shelves and the dust disturbed on the mantels?"

Finally, lulled by the momentary sense of safety, she slept. Two hours later she was awakened by Etta. For a moment she felt ten years old again, with Etta telling her to rise and shine and get ready for school. Etta had helped raise her and Elise, and when Elise married and moved into the Hillman house she'd insisted on taking Etta with her. The old lady's face, regal as an Angolan monarch, looked sternly at Sage. "Lise tell me you got tipsy this afternoon. That's not like you, child. Think how 'shamed your gran would be."

"Etta, leave me alone."

"What's more, you better do something about yourself. Go to the beauty parlor, like Lise, get yourself prettied."

"I'm not the pretty type."

"Don't tell me my baby's not pretty!" Etta softened, smiled. "Sugar, I know. You were just kissing your troubles good-bye, I know." She helped Sage off the bed, smoothed her hair, clucked over the ill-fitting dress. "One of these days," she crooned, "some fine young gentleman's going to come along and find you. He's going to say, 'Now isn't that the sweetest little lady I ever seen!'"

Standing, Sage looked down at Etta, sighed, then burst out laughing. "Etta, you sound just like Gran." She hugged her, headed for the door than turned. "Is Lise really mad at me?"

Etta chuckled. "Well, she got that look."

SEATED BY THE drawing room fire, Sage was offered a cup of black coffee and a thin crabmeat sandwich. After she'd taken one sip, one bite, Elise started on her. "Sage, is it true what Carol Whittaker told me tonight?"

Sage knew that no answer was yet required. She looked about, impressed by how quickly the room had been restored to its orderly perfection; no dirty glasses, no overflowing ashtrays.

"Roper Chalfont!" Elise's melodic contralto held a shrill note. She looked at Sage with considerable outrage. "You rented the carriage house to Roper Chalfont?"

"Why not?" mumbled Sage through a mouthful of crabmeat.

"Sage, I've got to agree with Elise." Clay Hillman picked up a poker, nudged the log he'd just added to the fire. Replacing the poker, he brushed invisible ash from his pants leg and lowered his narrow frame into a wingback chair. "Frankly, I'm surprised at you."

Sage wished she had some rapport with Clay. She'd always wanted a brother. Clay was polite and considerate, but she was sure he saw her as Elise's hopeless sister, something of a family problem. Observing her brother-in-law in motion, his slow grace accented by occasional darting gestures, she decided that if humans were indeed the descendants of fish and birds, Clay favored an ancestral egret. "I ran an ad on a Tuesday morning," she said, "and Roper Chalfont was the first one to apply. Oh, I know there's been some gossip about him but," she said, with a touch of malice, "you can't fault his Charleston connections. The first Chalfont came here around 1700."

"Seventeen-Twelve," said Clay with a pained look. "And that's not the point."

"I may be a little lax about the moral history of my tenants," said Sage loftily, "but I'm a real stickler when it comes to lineage."

"Sage, this isn't funny!" With a swish of chiffon, Elise was on her feet, her back to the fire. She looked all of a color, ecru dress, pale blond hair sweeping her shoulders, angry gray eyes. "You know damn well that people are going to talk!"

"Yes." Sage smiled at her coffee cup. "In Charleston, that's a dead certainty." She looked up at her sister, astonished as always by her beauty. She'd never admit it to Etta, but each time she saw her sister she had a fleeting impulse to do something about herself, apply hand cream, join an exercise club.

Clay rose, went to the mantel, and picked up a miniature of his great-grandmother. He looked at it for a few seconds, then replaced it, turned to her. "Maybe you don't know the whole story, Sage. It certainly was hushed up. People in town are loyal to the Chalfonts, and there was very little said at the time. Nowadays, of course—''

"You must have known who he is." Elise was almost glaring at her. "You grew up here, in the same town with him. You must have met him."

"I met him," said Sage.

"Roper Chalfont," said Clay in his courtroom voice, "served a jail sentence eight years ago. The authorities found a large shipment of drugs on his sailboat up in Bull's Bay. Apparently, he had quite an operation going. You never heard anything about this?"

Not I, thought Sage, stunned. That was the year of my debut. I was a freshman at Sweetbriar. After my disastrous coming-out, I went right back in.

"Sage, you've got to consider your position." Clay's voice was laden with sweet reason. He brushed a hand over sandy blond hair and for a few seconds his face lost its habitual reserve, seemed curiously vulnerable. "The point is that you are a single woman living alone in that big house—"

"You can hardly say I'm alone. Besides Roper I have my two tenants renting the ground floor apartments."

"About whom you know nothing!" Elise lashed out. "Flotsam and jetsam!"

Sage looked up at her sister. "I don't consider a medical student flotsam, nor an executive secretary jetsam."

"There have been break-ins all over the town," Clay continued. "Women have been robbed, beaten up, assaulted. You can't blame Elise and me for being worried about you."

"But what has any of this to do with Roper Chalfont? Do you really think he's going to slip in and steal the silver or ravish me during the first full moon?"

Clay rose, moved to the drink tray set out on a Sheraton drum table between the windows. His slight limp, due to a birth defect, seemed more pronounced. "I think you've got to begin thinking about the future, Sage. It's been two months since your grandmother passed away. Now I know you felt you had to keep the house going while she was alive and we're all grateful for what you did for her—"

"Gran should have been put in a nursing home years ago." Elise faced the fire. "Needing sitters around the clock, special medical care. If you ask me, it was sheer lunacy to maintain that house when she couldn't even come down the stairs, just so she could have an illusion of her old life-style."

"Elise," Clay stopped her with an inflection, returned to his chair with a balloon of brandy. "That's water over the dam. Frankly I think Sage did a wonderful job of looking after your grandmother, and at a considerable sacrifice." He leaned toward Sage, long fingers encircling the glass. "But now it's time for her to think about the future, a new life. A trip to Europe maybe, or at least a Caribbean cruise."

"Amy Bancroft is going to sell her little townhouse." Elise sat on the sofa next to Sage, a determined look in her eyes. "It's perfect, almost new, with wonderful planting in the patio. And inside, the colors are marvelous. Amy really has taste—"

"I'm not going to sell the house," Sage broke in. She stood, appalled to find that she was shaking. "Not now. Maybe never." She had plans of her own but she wasn't ready to discuss them. She intended to get a job, perhaps rent a few rooms in the main house. With the job and the rentals she might be able to save enough money for graduate school. She could imagine Elise's look of disbelief when she told her she was going to get a degree in clinical psychology, that she hoped to work with disturbed children.

"You're right, Clay." She straightened her shoulders, mustered an air of authority. "I do have to think about the future, but I'm sure you'll agree it's my future." Suddenly she was Gran, with a bosomful of pearls, an imperious eye. "You both are trying to be helpful but there are things I must decide for myself."

Elise was on her feet. "But Sage, you've simply got to—"

"I've got to go home." Sage headed for the door. "The plumber's coming at the crack of dawn and I've been waiting for a week." She turned back to her sister and brother-in-law, unable to resist a granlike exit. "It was a splendid party and you know I love coming here. This room—" her eyes moved over the muted Aubusson, the aged glow of Sheraton and Hepplewhite "—driving over here, I thought, each time I sit in that beautiful room with my beautiful kinfolk, I tell myself that the world still is a safe and civilized place. Bless you."

"Sage—" Elise was moving after her.

"I'll call you in a day or two, Elise. We'll have lunch. Maybe try that new restaurant on East Bay."

Clay, hand at her elbow, saw her to her car. The narrow street glowed with lights from the tall old houses. The air held the final chill of March, tasted of salt from the sea a few blocks away.

"Sage," he bent to look at her through the window of the battered Fiat, "I'm sorry if Elise and I came on too strong. It's just that we're concerned about you."

"I know, Clay."

"Right now you could get a good price for that house but this real estate boom may not last."

"I'll think about it, Clay. Believe me—" she stopped as St. Michael's chimes announced the hour, resounding in the quiet street, reminding them of the church of their forebears, where they had been christened, instructed, confirmed, where Clay and Elise had been married six years before. The chimes, which usually brought Sage a sense of permanence, sounded different tonight, as if they marked the passing of more than time.

TWO

As SHE pulled into her driveway, Sage decided that she must do something about installing more outdoor lights. A small Venetian fixture hung on the main piazza at the top of the double staircase. Under the piazza another light shone weakly above the door leading to the tenants' entrance hall. The glow from the carriage house barely outlined the four other cars in the parking area at the end of the driveway: Duncan's saucy MG, Franny Barth's conservative Chevrolet, Roper Chalfont's battered station wagon, and a svelte yellow Corvette. She wondered who had come in the Corvette.

A tall hedge separated the parking area and the carriage house from the garden. At first her grandmother had resisted putting in rental units on the ground floor, and renting the carriage house, but Clay persuaded her, making it clear that with dwindling finances, this was the only way to keep the property and finally leave it to Sage.

She got out of her car, stared again at the Corvette, then looked toward the carriage house. Light streamed from the windows on either side of the front door. Unable to resist, and telling herself that it was only practical to keep an eye on her tenants, especially if they had a criminal record, she moved to within a few feet of one of the windows. Suppressing the feeling that she was a nosy sneak, she peered inside.

Roper Chalfont, tall and weathered as Attila the Hun, his dark red hair tousled, stood holding a woman in close embrace. It was the woman she'd seen talking to David at her sister's party, the dark beauty with the throaty laugh. She wasn't laughing now. Her face was pressed to Roper's, her arms wound around his neck, her body tight against his. Sage couldn't tear her glance from this scene. She watched as Roper said something to the woman, saw her draw back, look up at him, then touch his face with a caressing hand. With an enormous effort Sage pulled herself from the window, her feelings sharp, jumbled. Walking away, she tried to think sensibly. What her tenants did was of no concern to her. She was their landlady, no more, no less. She wondered what had led Roper Chalfont into a life of crime. How could a man of his background turn into the worst type of degenerate, a drug smuggler? She wondered if he was madly in love with the dark lady or if it was a casual encounter. Illogically but resolutely she decided on the latter.

The pale light of the street lamps filtering through the trees flattered the old house as candlelight flatters an aging beauty. The seventy-foot-long piazzas, one above the other, glowed whitely. The brown rose bricks, made on her great-great-grandfather's plantation over a hundred and fifty years ago, clung to each other in comforting solidity. The house was scaled to a way of life, a naive acceptance of privilege that some might confuse with arrogance. The forebear who built it was a gentle man, if not enlightened. Whatever he was, thought Sage, he didn't think small. If was no effort to envision a carriage pulling into the drive, of an afternoon in 1850. It would have been waiting at the nearby dock on the Ashley River when the family alighted from the barge that brought them from the plantation. She imagined Thomas Benford in a frock coat leading hoop-skirted ladies up the sandstone steps, his soft-eyed wife, their older daughters, the exquisite Dorothea and plain Charlotte and the elderly twin aunts, Luna and Stella. They might be coming for a weekend of social events or to spend the summer, escape the dreaded swamp fever that threatened those who remained in the country during the hot months. Along with the younger Benfords, at least ten house servants would have arrived by an earlier barge, cleaned the house, laid fresh linen on the beds, stocked the ground floor rooms with provisions. Invitations would be neatly stacked on the table by the front door, each marked "delivered by hand." The house would pulse with activity, children's voices echoing, hands lighting lamps, setting the huge dining room table with silver, china, crystal, filling empty fireplaces with magnolia leaves. From the ground floor kitchen would come the smell of freshly baked ham, pies, a wild turkey roasting.

Sage took a step backward, trying to see all of the house at once. There were no satisfactory pictures. One needed a wide-angle lens. She'd backed straight into something. With a shock, she felt hands on her arms, a body against her own. She opened her mouth to scream, but too quickly he was in front of her, grinning.

"Oh! Duncan, it's you. You scared me."

"You bumped into me." He didn't appear in the least apologetic.

It took her several seconds to compose herself. She barely knew her tenant. He had a habit of appearing out of nowhere, which she found disconcerting. On

the other hand, she couldn't help feeling a bit sorry for
him. Hulking, overweight, he was already almost
bald. He peered at the world through small, watery
eyes. Each day he went to the medical university and
each night he sat in his apartment studying. She never
saw friends coming or going. Once a week he swept
the entranceway under the piazza. Several times he'd
offered to help with repairs to the house.

"I was just standing here, looking at the old place."
His grin seemed mindless, involuntary. Or nervous.

"It looks better at night," said Sage. "You can't see
the paint flaking." She smiled back at him, started
down the driveway toward the steps.

"You let me know now if anything goes on the fritz.
I'm a pretty good plumber and electrician."

"Thank you, I will." She moved faster but he kept
pace with her.

"You play chess?" he asked.

"No," she said.

"Look—" He darted almost nimbly in front of her.
"The next time my folks come over from Eutawville,
do you suppose I could bring them upstairs for a look?
They've never been inside a house like this."

"Of course. Let me know." She walked around
him.

"My grandmother, on my father's side, she was an
Eliot." His voice had a belligerent note, but he didn't
follow her. "She was raised in Augusta but her folks
came from Charleston. Maybe we're kin."

"That's interesting," said Sage over her shoulder.
She saw that he was lonely, that he wanted to prolong
the conversation, but her stamina was failing.

"Good night," they said at the same time.

As she went up the steps she noticed that Franny Barth's apartment windows were dark, but she heard strains of country music, a voice singing fretfully of love and deception. Something new had entered Franny's life. Like Duncan, she'd come to the city from a small upcountry town to better herself. She still went to the medical university every morning looking like the perfect secretary, the sexy figure obscured by a tailored suit, not a jet black hair out of place, but there was an added spring to her walk, a heightening of color in the magnolia skin. A few days before, Sage had seen her putting out her trash, wearing not the usual dingy corduroy bathrobe but a negligee the color of a bonfire.

Opening the big front door usually filled Sage with a sense of homecoming, thoughts of arriving from summer camp as a child, from trips to Flat Rock in the North Carolina mountains, from college at Sweetbriar and, in recent years, from an afternoon of errands to face the demands of her ailing grandmother.

"Major!" Her voice echoed in the hallway. The old basset hound rose drowsily from the rug by the wide stairway at the end of the hall. Sage bent and scratched behind his ears, grateful to feel the warm fur, the wet nose nuzzling her arm. "Need to go out, old buddy?"

As if stating his preference the dog turned and faced the dining room. "No late snack," Sage told him firmly. "You're beginning to run to fat. Remember what Gran used to say: 'You've got to have either looks or charm.'"

At the thought of her grandmother she glanced up the dark stairs, half expecting to hear that hoarse, authoritative voice: "Mary Sage? Is that you, dear? If you could come up for a moment." My God, Gran, I miss you, she thought. Full of airs and graces, pretending life hadn't changed, but so damn game, so much fun.

She looked at the big drawing room where a single lamp lent grace to the hodgepodge of Victorian furniture, undistinguished portraits of dead Benfords. She thought of sitting on that unyielding sofa one hot August afternoon when Gran had told her and Elise that their parents had drowned in a boating accident at Rockville. She had been four and Elise six, two proper little girls wearing their Sunday dresses because they had come to spend the day with their grandmother.

"Major!" The dog followed her through the door and she waited on the piazza while he went down to the yard. The coolness was deceptive. Any day now the town would quicken into spring. The air would be heavy with fragrance. Trees, vines, and shrubs would erupt with extravagant blooms. Tourists with guidebooks and cameras would crowd the streets, staring up at the old houses, peeking into gardens, looking curiously at the inhabitants of this Eden.

Sage shivered. She wondered if Elise and Clay still sat by their fire trying to decide how to handle her.

"God knows, Clay, I've tried to help, tried to get her to do something about herself. If she'd just make an effort—she's not all that unattractive. I mean, there are a few possible men."

"Talk to her tomorrow, Elise. She's got to make some decisions. The first step is to get her out of that house."

Major ran ahead of her back through the front door, waiting while she locked it, then he headed up the wide staircase. He stood patiently beside her while she undressed, brushed her teeth. He watched as she took her nightgown from the pillow, where she always left it, neatly folded. When she held it up, the dog stared at what fell from the folds and dropped to the floor. She stared, too. It was some seconds before she realized what it was. Her skin crawled. Her stomach lurched. Small, its dark wings folded, teeth bared, eyes glazed. A dead bat. She saw the vermin moving over the body. She shuddered violently, stumbled backward. Major sniffed at it, then moved away. Sage, repelled, continued to stare. She wanted to scream, to run from the room. She'd always had an irrational fear of bats, but something terrified her even more. She was struck by the certainty that someone had left the dead bat there for her to find. Someone wanted to scare her to death.

It was a wild thought. Paranoid. Who would want to scare her, and why? Besides, there had been bats in the house before. They'd come in through an opening between the roof and the eaves or down the chimneys. This one could have been wounded or diseased, crawled between the folds of her nightgown and died.

Fighting nausea, she threw the nightgown over the dead bat, carried it through the French door to the upstairs piazza, and flung both in the yard below. Back inside, she locked the door, leaned against it. Then with an effort she stood erect, made herself move. She put on a fresh nightgown, fetched another pillow from the hall closet, and climbed into the canopied bed. At once Major dropped to the floor and fell into a deep sleep. He didn't waken when she lifted her head, a few hours later, listening. She waited. For several nights the sounds had been coming not from the floor below but from overhead. Soft, dragging sounds, they barely cut through the silence. The next time you hear them, she told herself, for God's sake find out what it is. Then she lay without moving, telling herself it was all imagined, just as she'd imagined that someone had left the bat for her to find. A steady rain fell, announcing itself on the tin roof of the piazza. Major snored softly. Finally, her mind clouded by martinis and exhaustion, she lay back and slept.

Major graciously allowed her to sleep until eight the next morning, finally pressing his wet nose to her face. Sage fumbled into slacks and sweater, slipped on her worn sneakers, and walked gingerly after the dog, downstairs and out into a day the color of tarnished pewter. But the sky to the north was beginning to clear. She noticed that the dogwood at the far end of the garden was flecked with white buds. Camellias, offering the last winter blooms, rose from pools of dropped petals.

The yellow Corvette was gone. A tall extension ladder was braced against one side of the carriage house. Roper Chalfont sat astride the pitched roof, nailing slates into place. Every blow of the hammer resounded in Sage's aching head. Seeing her, he paused, waved. Sage had a sudden unwelcome idea of how she must appear, a gangling figure in shapeless garments, uncombed hair streaming down her back. She declined to wave back, whistled to the dog and started to go back into the house.

A shout from Roper stopped her. "Sage! Hold on."

Reluctantly she turned and watched him come down the ladder. He grabbed something from the hammock he'd hung between two pecan trees and strode across the patio. Looking like a longshoreman in a faded blue work shirt and jeans, he took the piazza steps two at a time, then stopped in front of her. His eyes shone topaz against the darkly tanned skin.

"I found this in the yard. Thought it must be yours."

His face was impassive, but his eyes were too bright. What he held out was her nightgown, the one she'd flung from the upstairs piazza with the dead bat. In silence they both stared at it, a nightgown Elise had bought for her grandmother, who'd never worn it. Plain white cotton, shapeless, its only decoration was a tiny pink rosette at the modest neckline. Sage felt a flush that seemed to begin at her feet and move upward like a red tide. She groped for a sassy comeback, a witty riposte. All she could think of was the dark beauty she'd seen him embracing, a woman who wouldn't be caught dead in such a nightgown, a woman who'd have a drawerful of wispy nothings, most of them black chiffon with marabou feathers.

She froze on the spot, still staring at the nightgown, longing to say something devastating. She felt short of breath, just as she'd felt when she'd peered in his window. He was too close, too big. He was using up all the air.

Gently he draped the nightgown over her shoulder. "I thought it must be yours." Though his voice was serious, she saw one corner of his mouth twitch. "Don't be embarrassed, Mary Sage. I never question what my friends do in the heat of passion."

His suppressed hilarity was more than she could bear. She turned and walked stiffly into the house.

Sitting on a stool by the kitchen window, she forced down a piece of toast and a cup of coffee. She tried to rid herself of the sense of mortification but she still writhed inwardly when she thought of Gran's nightgown. He undoubtedly assumed that she'd hung some laundry on the piazza to dry and that the nightgown had blown down into the yard. But he couldn't resist embarrassing her. She was glad now that she'd not spent the money to have the carriage house roof repaired. She hoped that last night's rain had leaked straight into Roper Chalfont's bed, soaking the raven-haired beauty. She wished it had drowned Roper Chalfont.

Hoping the roof would hold, she'd decided to use what money she could spare to have the washer-dryer repaired. In a moment of weakness she'd offered the use of it to her tenant, Franny Barth, mainly because Franny was such a busy woman and, after all, there was a door leading from Franny's bedroom directly into the laundry. If Elise knew, she'd call her an idiot for giving her tenant access to the main house. Fortunately Elise knew little about Sage's arrangements, especially the state of her finances. Just a few weeks ago she said, "Sage, why don't you remodel that nasty little kitchen, make better use of your space. You could panel the whole thing, maybe get one of those tabletop ranges—"

Sage rinsed her coffee cup. If Elise had an inkling of her bank balance she'd begin noticing that a lot of family antiques had been sold to pay for Gran's medical bills and sitters. Sage looked at the ancient gas stove and wheezing refrigerator, seeing them with Elise's fastidious eye. The room never had been intended as a kitchen but as a warming pantry. The original kitchen had been on the ground floor in Franny's apartment. Cramped and impractical as it was, Sage regarded her kitchen with stubborn fondness. Besides, there was little likelihood of a remod-

eling job. The carriage house was another matter. She
considered rechecking her budget, doing a little jug-
gling of funds, but it was an idle impulse. She would
pay Roper Chalfont for whatever materials he bought.
At any rate she was not going to think about that big,
muscular body astride the roof, the rough-featured
face under the bronze hair. There was too much to do.

She thought briefly of mopping the kitchen floor.
The drawing room and music room hadn't been dusted
since God knows when. The maid, a cousin of Etta's,
came once a week but Sage had been too embarrassed
to ask her to clean the chandeliers. With head still
throbbing she took pity on herself, rejected all do-
mestic chores, and went upstairs to take an aspirin and
type some more of her distant cousin Charlotte's diary.

Sage loved her workroom. She felt at home with the
sagging sofa, the sprung and lopsided armchair. She
didn't mind the paint flaking softly but steadily from
the walls and ceiling. She cherished the scarred table
where Charlotte's diary lay next to her typewriter. In
fact, she was almost certain that this room had been
Charlotte's. Surely it was here that the young girl had
written of the crumbling of her world during the years
of the War between the States. Charlotte often mentioned her view of the garden from the double French
doors that opened on the upstairs piazza, the glory of
the sunset over the Ashley River.

Two family diaries had survived, both written by
young women of unquestionable homeliness. Born
thirty years apart into a society that celebrated beautiful women, they stared from old pictures with the
same benighted look, sharing thin brown hair, protu-
berant eyes with scanty lashes, a distinct overbite. Not

destined to sit on piazzas, giggling and flirting with beaux, they'd found other consolations.

Auralee Benford, in the 1830s, wrote passionately of the world of nature, especially the sightings of various birds. She painted scores of timid watercolors, inspired by her naturalist friend. The friend's name was never spelled out, but apparently she was married to a clergyman, lived in a large house, and had a basement workshop where she and her husband collected bird specimens. It was obvious that Auralee found a place in M's lively household, which was bursting with children, relatives, guests, servants, pets, and often was graced with the presence of a visiting artist by the improbable name of Jostle. Auralee's scribblings could hardly be called a diary. Her entries were spasmodic and incomplete. She carefully identified birds but not people. Sage was the only family member who found it of interest.

It was Sage who had found the diary of Auralee's niece, Charlotte, in a trunkful of rusty hoops and old bustle pads, tucked among the folds of a yellowed petticoat. She'd been sorting through the staggering accumulation of chests, trunks, and boxes that jammed the top floor storerooms. With Charlotte she had lived through the cataclysmic events that began on an April day in 1861 when "at four-thirty in the morning, a star shell soared into the overcast sky and burst over Fort Sumter." Sage marveled at the scope of Charlotte's reporting, the detailed accounts of troop mobilizations, the building of fortifications, the recording of births, weddings, deaths, levees, balls, and picnics. She imagined Charlotte sitting in that upstairs room making her own chronicle of news

heard on the street, read in papers, or gleaned as she
stood on the fringes of social gatherings.

At first Sage had been shocked to read of the social
events that persisted through victory and defeat: an
outing at Ashley Hall Plantation the day after hearing of the bloody battle at Shiloh, the musical soiree
where everyone avoided mentioning the defeat at
Vicksburg. When Sage confronted her grandmother
with the record of this outrageous wartime party, the
old lady had looked at her with mild scorn. "Child,
you know as well as I that social concourse has always been a way of life here. In good times, it makes
life infinitely pleasanter; in bad times it's a way of
striking back at disaster, maintaining one's standards."

Sitting with the pages of Charlotte's diary spread
out before her, Sage thought suddenly of her last conversation with her grandmother. "What's the matter
with you, child? You look as if you haven't slept in a
week."

"I keep waking up, Gran. I know it's silly but
sometimes I hear sounds." As soon as she admitted
this she was ashamed.

Her grandmother had been unperturbed. "One always hears sounds, dear; pigeons on the roof, squirrels inside the walls, swifts in the chimney. The house
itself often shifts with a change in the weather." The
old lady had paused. "And of course there's the past.
A hundred and fifty years isn't old for a house but a
great deal has happened here. Think of the births and
deaths. Think of the times of happiness, grief, opu-
lence, poverty. This leaves a residue."

Weakened by her hangover, guilty at shirking
household chores, still chagrined by her encounter

with Roper, Sage sat motionless at the typewriter. She wanted to believe that Gran was right about the night sounds. The alternative was unthinkable. Either way she had a problem. One, she was suffering from a neurosis brought on by her grandmother's death and what Elise called an abnormal life. Her strained mind was inventing fantasies. Two, someone had left a dead bat on her pillow to scare her into leaving the house, someone who was going from room to room at night, searching. But for what? Silver? A few years back there had been a rash of silver thefts by professionals who broke into houses, grabbed their loot, and melted it down in the backs of panel trucks. But if a thief were prowling her house at night, why hadn't he taken the last remaining things of value, the silver service in plain view in the dining room?

What bothered Sage most was the idea that someone could have access to the house despite the iron grills at the windows, the dead bolts on the front door and the outside door to the laundry and back steps. It would take a twenty-foot ladder to reach the upstairs piazza. Only she and Elise had keys to the house. It didn't make sense. She'd better face the truth. She was displaying the worst symptoms of spinsterhood, though she was not quite twenty-six. Next, she'd suspect the mailman of looking at her with unbridled lust. She went back to Charlotte's diary.

She'd already typed out Charlotte's accounts of the first years of the war, the victories followed by terrible defeats at Shiloh, Antietam, the growing casualty lists, the fire of 1861 that swept through the town destroying many homes and public buildings, the fever that brought death to almost every household.

Fiercely optimistic, Charlotte didn't lose heart until the fall of Gettysburg. The Confederacy was broken, could no longer keep its shrunken army in the
field. Since spring, Charleston had been expecting
bombardment. Union soldiers were entrenched on
nearby Folly and Morris islands, and numbers of
Charlestonians had left for Columbia and Camden.
Some attempted to run the blockade and reach Can-
ada. But it wasn't until August 22 that the first
screaming shell flew over Charleston. The Union
forces had mounted a gun that could reach the town.
The southern end of Charleston was abandoned. Shell
followed shell. Many of those who stayed behind decided to join the refugees. It was just a matter of time.
But even during the last days before shutters were
closed, doors bolted, those still left came together for
farewell parties. Houses were in disrepair, clothes
shabby, and food scarce, yet the social gatherings,
though fewer and often without refreshment, continued to the bitter end.

It was in these particular pages that Charlotte became less a chronicler and more a young girl keeping
a diary. In scores of earlier entries she'd mentioned a
Reverend Gill. "I was conversing with Rosa Bridges
on Meeting Street today, when the Reverend Gill
stopped and greeted us. Teasingly, he asked if we were
having a gossip. When I replied that gossip was the
pastime of impoverished minds, he smiled most be-
atifically and exclaimed that I'd given him an excellent topic for a sermon."

Poor Charlotte, thought Sage. It was easy to imagine that ugly duckling worshiping from afar. One
could picture her in the corner of a crowded drawing
room, eyes fixed on the door, waiting for the rever-

end to appear, knowing she held no attraction for him yet hoping with the eternal hope of the young.

Too clearly Sage saw the Reverend Gill, trapped into talking to Charlotte at one of those final parties. He must have been both surprised and disturbed by her intelligence. Charlotte wrote:

"We discussed my favorite topic, the equality of the sexes, whilst sitting at the far end of Rosa's drawing room, quite unaware of the others. I marveled at his conversational powers, his rebuttals of my views, drawn from Bible and prayer book in such eloquent style and language and such honest seeking of my own good."

With considerable disgust, Sage typed, "He explained that he found me a person of exceptional intelligence and that I possessed an originally fine, noble character, but much warped." When she reached "He unconsciously revealed the native nobility of his soul with every word he uttered," she pushed away from the typewriter and went downstairs for another cup of coffee.

Before she reached the kitchen, there was a phone call from her sister. "Sage? What are you doing?" Elise always wanted to know what she was doing.

"Nursing my hangover. Reviewing my sins."

"I thought we'd go out to lunch. Then we'll take those clothes I gave you to Mrs. Helms to be altered."

"They're there already. She finished them several days ago."

"Including the dress you wore to the party?"

"That got left behind. I forgot it."

"I thought so. Sage, you looked—"

"Seedy but interesting?"

"Like someone from an impoverished parsonage on the English moors. I'll pick you up at twelve-thirty."

"I have to be at Aunt Octo's at three. The Readers and Writers Group."

"Oh, God! Why do you want to sit around with that bunch of old eccentrics? No, don't tell me. Anyway, you'll have plenty of time. Twelve-thirty, Sage."

Sage typed two more pages of Charlotte's diary, mopped the kitchen floor, and when the plumber arrived stood over him while he fixed the washer-dryer. She was ready to meet her sister at twelve twenty-five, wearing a raincoat to cover a college-vintage dress of which Elise was certain to disapprove. As she waited by the gate to the street, searching the oncoming traffic for Elise's white Jaguar, a deep voice spoke suddenly from behind her. "Can I drive you somewhere?"

Sage jumped like a startled hen, dropping her purse. She blushed hotly as she bent to retrieve it. Roper had already scooped it up and they managed to bump heads as they straightened.

"No. I'm waiting for my sister. I mean—thank you anyway."

"I thought your car might be out of whack." They both looked at the aged Fiat, huddling in the parking area.

"No, it's fine." For one blazing moment Sage longed to have Elise's flair and authority. She was determined there would be no further discussion of the nightgown. "Look, I'm sorry about the roof," she lied coolly. "I had no idea it was in such bad shape. Did you have a leak?"

One bronze eyebrow lifted in what might be amusement. "You could call it that."

"A bad leak? A torrent?"

"More of a slow, steady stream."

"I'm so sorry," she said with sweet insincerity.

"All fixed," he assured her. "Nothing but a few loose slates." He was observing her with what she considered undue concentration. "Sage, I appreciate your renting to me," he said. "No doubt there's been some flak from your family."

Sage had forgotten how tall he was. He reminded her of a statue she'd seen in the Vatican Museum, a barbarian bursting with vitality in a roomful of effete Roman busts. He exuded the same brute strength, raw sexuality. "No," she lied again. "No flak. They respect my decisions."

"Come on now, Sage. Haven't you set tongues wagging?"

"A few maybe. People are wondering why you came back to town, what you're doing here."

Roper stared at one big, square hand, rubbed his thumb against a broken fingernail. "If they press you," he said, "tell them I'm a double agent on the lam. The KGB has a hit man on my tail."

Sage saw Elise's car drawing up to the curb. "And if they don't believe it?"

Roper swung open the iron gate with the hint of a bow. "Tell them I'm a Peace Corps volunteer. I've been sent to help ease backward Charlestonians into the twentieth century before we reach the twenty-first."

Elise didn't speak until they'd ridden almost a block. "Who was that?" she asked. "The plumber?"

THREE

AFTER THEY'D PICKED UP the altered wardrobe from Mrs. Helms, Sage and Elise went to a chic new Italian restaurant near the old market. Sage was impressed by her sister's accent in ordering costolette di vitello alla Veronelli. They sat under striped umbrellas on a terrace that caught just enough sun to keep them from shivering. Elise, quite stunning in a suit the color of raspberry sherbet, seemed no more relaxed than she'd been the night before. Her monologue ranged from bits of gossip to complaints about tourists. Amory Seldes had deserted his wife of thirty years to marry his twenty-year-old secretary, and even worse, to move west of the Ashley River. Forty people had signed a letter to the mayor, complaining about tourists banging on their doors, wanting to go to the bathroom.

Finally Elise ran low on chitchat. She sighed, unbuttoned then rebuttoned her jacket. "Look, Sage, I apologize for fussing at you last night." She pushed away an almost untouched lunch, lit a cigarette. "I've stopped smoking at home," she said, "Clay hates it." Then she looked across the table at her sister. "I shouldn't tell you how to live your life."

"Lise, I understand. Really I do." Sage had cleaned her plate. She found the Italian bread delicious, buttered another piece.

"No, I know what you think of me. I know I come across as pretty shallow and materialistic. Always worrying about what people think, how the house looks, if my clothes are right. God, sometimes I revolt myself.''

"Lise—"

"Sage, remember when we were little and starting school at Ashley Hall? The way all the kids called us the grasshoppers because we were so tall?''

"I remember socking Cynthia Deveaux by the water cooler and being sent home with a note.''

"Those awful voile and pongee dresses Gran made us wear—"

"With bloomers to match and no belts!'' Sage laughed. "White silk socks and Mary Janes. Exactly like those old pictures of Mother. Remember what Gran used to say? 'Fashion is vulgar. Style is timeless.'''

"It never bothered you much, did it, the teasing? Remember when we were in our teens? The horrible clothes Gran bought us then? Lace-up oxfords and jumpers with box pleats! Everybody else had dates on Saturday nights and was invited to dances. No, of course it didn't bother you. You always had your face in a book.''

Sage was touched by the look on her sister's face, suddenly vulnerable, young. "It bothered me once,'' she said, wanting to share the pain of that look. "It was at my debut party. Remember how Gran insisted on dance cards, even though no one had used them for years? Anyway, after some of the boys had asked me for a token dance, I spent what seemed hours behind a potted azalea, wondering if I dared go hide in the ladies' room again. Then I saw this tall man watching me from the doorway. He wasn't just a boy like the others, but a real man. Nobody had ever looked at me like that. I prayed he'd ask me to dance, but I was terrified of being awkward. He came toward me with this wonderful smile. He took my dance card and wrote his name across every dance and then put the card in his pocket. I knew I wasn't going to be awkward at all. I was going to dance beautifully."

"Oh Sage, I'm sure you did!"

"Someone came over and told him he was wanted on the phone. He looked at me and said, 'I'll just be a minute. Promise you'll wait.' And I promised. I waited and waited. I stood there trying to think of some smart remark to make when he apologized for taking so long. I decided I'd lift one eyebrow and say, 'Was it long? I hardly noticed.'"

"Don't tell me—"

"He never came back."

"You never saw him again?"

"I've seen him."

"He's never apologized or explained?"

"He's completely forgotten. It was a long time ago, Lise."

"Sage—" Elise leaned toward her. "Oh honey, how awful! I should have helped you through that party. Where was I?"

"You were pretty by then. And popular. You'd found Clay."

"I was a selfish monster."

"You always were trying to help me." Sage grinned. "You still are."

"I'll try to be less helpful in the future. Except—" Elise paused, straightened the gold link bracelet on her narrow wrist. "Sage, about the house—"

"Lise, I don't want to sell it."

"Not even to Clay?"

"Clay? Why would he want it?"

Elise took a sip of her cappuccino before answering. "It would be a way of preserving it, Sage, keeping it from being remodeled beyond recognition. You see, Clay has formed this group of lawyers, investment counselors, realtors who are trying to bring more business into the state. Well, they need a base of operations, some place to entertain, put up prospective investors, a kind of club."

"You want to turn Gran's house into a club?"

"Sage, face it. You can't go on living alone in a house that size. It's ridiculous! Sooner or later you'll have to let it go. Clay wouldn't make any big structural changes. And it's perfect for what they need. There's plenty of space for a big dining area, lounge, and library downstairs, and with the upper floors, apartments, and carriage house there could be six or seven really handsome suites."

"The kitchen," Sage reminded her grimly, "is, in your own words, the size of a tool shed."

"Clay said something about enlarging it to take in the east side of the piazza."

Sage stared at her for several seconds. "My God, Elise, a club!"

"You know you'll have to give it up eventually."

"But to a family, someone with a lot of children! A family should live in it. It was built for a family." The minute the words were out she regretted them bitterly, especially when she saw the look on her sister's face. She thought of the nursery in Elise's house, the room furnished five years ago with such blithe expectations. She remembered the furniture now shrouded in dust covers. "Lise," she said quickly, "there are a lot of other houses Clay could buy."

Elise was looking carefully at a picture on the opposite wall. "Not that size. How often does a downtown house that size come on the market?" Elise looked at her squarely. "Honey, you've got to accept change. The whole town's changing."

As Elise drove her home, the warning sang through her head. On every side she saw that the narrow peninsula with its heritage of irreplaceable old houses and neighborhoods was being fragmented by motels, condominiums, parking garages. Once a quiet town that attracted a few visitors on their way north from Florida, Charleston had been discovered, had become a tour mecca. Developers and politicians, in their frenzy to cash in or, as they euphemistically called it, "raise the tax base," were running roughshod over the embattled preservationists.

"At least think about it," said Elise as she pulled up by Sage's gate. Sage didn't answer. As she opened the car door Elise stopped her. "Promise you'll think about it."

Sage saw more than concern for the house or concern for her in Elise's look. She knew her sister well and was certain something else was bothering her. Trouble between her and Clay? Clay fooling around with another woman? She leaned over and kissed her.

"It was a lovely lunch, Lise. Thank you." She started for the gate.

"Sage!" Elise put her head through the car window, managed a smile. "It's none of my business, but that man who didn't come back for his dance—who was he?"

But Sage was already in the garden looking up at the piazza and seeing it crowded with New York bankers, local politicians, and Arab sheiks.

She went directly to the library to find a book she'd promised to bring to the Readers and Writers meeting. Paneled in cypress, with a large fireplace and Georgian-style overmantel, the room housed the books of generations of Benfords. Shelf upon shelf of dusty volumes rose to within inches of the fifteen-foot ceiling. It was when Sage noticed a loose panel on one side of the fireplace that she thought of Clay's offer. More deterioration, more repairs needed. Lise was right. Damn Lise anyway.

She couldn't find the book she wanted, *The Carolina Low Country,* published in 1931. It was not in its place among the Caroliniana. She'd put the library in order herself, years before, cataloguing every volume. Looking closer, she saw that whole shelves were mixed up, as if books had been removed then replaced in reverse order, not all of them but enough to make it noticeable. She stared at them, trying hard not to overreact. It must have been Leola who came to clean once a week, she insisted to herself. She'd told the girl to skip dusting the books but Leola liked to surprise her. She finally found the book Beatrice Bonham had asked her to bring, reminding herself to reclaim from Bea the original of Auralee Benford's journal. Driving to her Aunt Octo's, she thought about Auralee and Charlotte. She imagined them riding in carriages along these same streets, going in and out of the same houses, dreaming their dreams and at last settling for what life offered them.

Each generation of the family tree seemed to produce its obligatory spinster, girls with no negotiable charms who realized, by age sixteen, that marriage was not in their future. This often meant teaching music or looking after elderly parents or both. Gran's sister-in-law, Sage's Aunt Octo, didn't fall neatly into this category. She was a spinster by choice. She'd been a beauty from birth, made a spectacular debut, and broke countless hearts. For some undisclosed reason she chose to remain single. One family story had it that her true love had been killed in the Battle of the Marne, another that he was a married man, obliged to remain with a demented wife. Sage's grandmother scorned these tales. "Octo was just plain stubborn," she'd said, "always setting impossible standards. She read too much. She wanted a hero from one of her books. He didn't appear. And that's about the size of it."

It took Sage less than five minutes to drive to her aunt's, but she sat for a moment trying to catch her breath, to forget about Clay's offer and the disordered library shelves. Octo lived on a street of late-eighteenth-century houses, none of them quite as grand as Elise's. Built two rooms deep and three or four stories high, most of the old dwellings had been enlarged over the years with additions that reached beyond their double piazzas. To the south of Octo's was the house David Raeburn rented from a doctor who was spending two years abroad. Its rose exterior, clean white woodwork, new guttering and drainpipes attested to the owner's care and affluence. North of Octo's was the house rented by Bea Bonham. Though its pale green walls showed no cracks, an open gate revealed a poorly tended garden. Sage looked at her aunt's home. She couldn't remember the last time Octo's house had been painted. The ocher had faded to a washed-out tan. Patches of brick showed through holes in the stucco. A second-floor shutter hung at a tipsy angle.

She heard voices before she went through the enclosed door that led from street to piazza. She paused at an open window, glanced into Octo's drawing room, and reflected that it had the same down-at-the-heels look as her own; all the handsome furniture sold to pay for upkeep or taxes, nothing left but ponderous Victorian pieces. She remembered that a print of Audubon's curlew against a background of Charleston harbor had been sold years ago, when the pipes burst.

As usual, there was a preponderance of female Readers and Writers. The early birds had taken possession of sofa and armchairs, the less fortunate perched on folding chairs. All faced the fireplace and Viola Spinner. An aging wraith who bore a striking resemblance to the late Edith Sitwell, Viola was reading her work with considerable eye-rolling. Octo, slim as a teenager, her hair a mist of white curls, leaned forward in a trance of encouragement. All present held copies of the poems to be read, including Viola's. The expressions on their faces ranged from trepidation to torpor. Sage slipped into the house and stood quietly in the hall, not wanting to disrupt Viola's performance.

She heard a snuffling sound behind her and turned to find Bea Bonham in the doorway of the dining room, inhaling nose spray. "In here," she whispered, motioning Sage to join her. They tiptoed to where the table was extended to accommodate a punch bowl and the culinary contributions of the members.

"Did you bring it, Sage? The Low Country book?" Bea asked, groping in a macramé bag for her handkerchief. Sage gave her the book. "Bless you," said Bea and sneezed. "Damned allergy!" She blew her nose. "And damn Octo's miserable folding chairs. They give me a royal pain in the—"

"Arse," suggested Sage with a grin.

"Can you believe Viola?" Bea chortled. "If I put her in one of my books I'd be accused of lapsing into allegorical satire. But I love them, all of them! Where else could you find such delicious, nineteenth-century goings on?"

Sage enjoyed Octo's friends. Most of their poems were awful and the criticisms crazy. They were far from brilliant, and at times absurd, but the group shared a common passion—they cared. Still, she was glad that Alfred Freeman wasn't on hand to review the proceedings.

"Listen!" said Bea.

From across the hall, they could hear Eldredge Pratt-Baines giving his critique of Viola's poem. Retired from a small college in Ohio where he had taught English for many years, Eldredge was a big badger-like man in a hairy suit that he frequently and proudly announced had been bought during his sabbatical in Scotland in 1951. He spoke with oracular authority. "Granted alliteration is a useful poetic device, I'm afraid I find 'slothful, slumberous, and slugabed' redundant."

Viola's eyes flashed. "There is value," she retorted sharply, "in sheer extravagance."

"I think it's a splendid poem," piped Aunt Octo quickly. "The language, the imagery—"

Bea choked on a giggle and moved farther into the dining room. "Listen, Sage, I appreciate your bringing the book. I've got lots of material on the Revolution and Civil War eras, but next to nothing on the early nineteenth century." She groped again in her purse. "Incidentally, I'm sorry I didn't return this sooner." She pulled out Auralee's journal and handed it to Sage. "Oh, and I almost forgot, I brought something for your hound. A great, delicious bone!" Delving in her bag, she produced a package wrapped in foil. She sneezed again, blew her nose. "God, but I'm starved. Had no lunch." She moved around the table, inspecting the collation with a skeptical eye.

Sage wondered how Elise would have reacted to Bea's costume of the day, a voluminous batik dress cinched at the waist with a wide belt of beaten silver, lacy gray stockings, flat patent leather pumps with gray silk pompoms. Over the titian waves of her hair, Bea had arranged a lavender chiffon scarf. "Try one of these." Sage pointed to a tray of sandwiches cut in half moons. "Juanita Whipple's Waccamaw crab delights."

Bea popped one of Juanita's crab delights into her pouting mouth, chewed for a few seconds, and then swallowed with a gagging sound. "Crab, indeed. Soy beans, cat food, and bug spray!" She patted her lips with a paper napkin marked Season's Greetings, then turned to Sage. "How are you coming with Charlotte's diary? How far have you gotten in your typing?"

"I've reached August of 1863," said Sage, "the bombardment of the town. Charlotte and her family are getting ready to evacuate."

"I loved reading it, Sage. It's quite a document. I hope you don't mind but I let David have a peek at it. He saw it on my desk one day, and he sat down and read for a couple of hours. He was fascinated. So I let him have a look at Auralee's diary as well."

"You did?" As she spoke, Sage glanced into the drawing room and saw David Raeburn sitting in a far corner. She hoped Bea didn't notice her sharp intake of breath.

But Bea noticed, looked over her shoulder. Her eyes narrowed. "I'd really like to know his story." Her voice was cold, almost calculating.

"What do you mean?" asked Sage. "I thought you liked him."

"Oh, I do," said Bea quickly. "We're good neighbors. Just yesterday he lent me a tube of Elmer's glue and a bottle of vodka. And he's a dazzling specimen. I'd cast him as the hero in any of my books. 'His face,'" quoted Bea, "'was chiseled in lines of breeding and melancholy. The hooded black eyes held a look both penitential and yearning. Absently, he pushed the dark curls from his brow with a hand fashioned for command.'"

Sage, entertained by Bea's on-the-spot fictionalizing, decided that David's hand probably wanted to command Viola Spinner to take her paw from his knee. "What on earth's he doing here, Bea?"

"He and Octo have become great friends. Besides, I told him that if he really wants to put down roots in Charleston, understand what the town is all about, he ought to bag the chic cocktail parties and cultivate the old guard, people like Octo."

"I wouldn't say Aunt Octo is typical."

"She's a character, Sage, in a town of characters. No identity crisis. Individuality runs rampant. You don't notice it because you grew up here."

"Hasn't David told you anything about himself?"

"With that splendid, aristocratic reserve? I know he's supposed to have taught in a boy's school somewhere, history I think. Then there was a car accident, spending a year in the hospital. As I said, he's pretty reticent. Of course, who would blame him, with every hostess in town hot on his trail?"

"What about Peter?"

They both stared at the exotic young man sitting next to David. He might have been a Comanche Indian except for the green eyes, the white blond hair. A well-tailored suit did little to disguise a body designed to ride bareback over the plains. "What's his connection with David? Is he a friend, or—" Sage stopped herself, not wanting to appear inquisitive.

"As far as I can see, he's a combination companion and servant. He cooks the meals, drives the car, tends the garden and, when questioned, answers in monosyllables. They might be gay, but I'm inclined to think not." Bea sneezed, groped again for her handkerchief.

"I just wondered," said Sage idly, "how David happened to choose Charleston."

"How does anyone end up here? He came, he saw, he was conquered. I think there's a good bit of money there. And my God, he's attractive!"

This Sage couldn't deny, especially when he looked across the room, caught her eye, and winked solemnly.

"I feel I must point out," spoke Deirdre Fletcher, biology teacher, "the anatomical unlikelihood of Viola's 'rebellious, rosy breasts.'"

"Time for refreshments!" cried Octo, rising swiftly. "Deirdre, we'll get back to you but I think we can all do with a short break."

Leaving behind their papers, purses, briefcases, and umbrellas, the group swarmed into the dining room, greeting Sage, acclaiming the beauty of the daffodil centerpiece, and reaching for the hodgepodge of canapés. Gently David disengaged Viola's hand from his arm and made his way toward Sage. His smile was eager. There was an unconscious grace in the way he moved. Even his clothes, gray flannels, tan sweater, open-necked white shirt, had a casual elegance.

"Sage!" He took her hand. "I was afraid you weren't coming. Bea conned me into this, assured me you'd be here and then—"

"I was held up."

His hand felt warm and smooth. "Sage, I called you last night but there was no answer. That's why I'm glad you're here."

She didn't want to mention Elise's party where she'd faded into obscurity. "I'm sorry I missed your call."

"There's a concert at the auditorium on Thursday night," he said. "I hope you'll go with me. Maybe we could have an early supper at my place. Peter's a great cook."

In the months since he'd arrived, he'd never asked her for a date. He'd been friendly, even sent her a book of poems. She remembered the day she'd met him by chance on the steps of the Library Society, and he'd told her about reading Anthony Hecht, how much he'd liked the poems, and had promised to get her a copy. The encounter had been warm but formal. Now the very intentness of his look told her that he was seeing something in her that he'd missed before. She hoped she wasn't blushing. "Thank you, David," she said calmly. "I'd like that."

The hand that Bea had described as "fashioned to command" reached up and brushed the dark hair from his forehead. "Wonderful," he answered. There was nothing more to add but it seemed quite natural that they should stand in the noisy, crowded room simply looking at each other.

Then Octo was at Sage's elbow. "Sage, might I speak to you for a minute, dear? David, do excuse us. Have you had some punch? It's Deirdre's family receipt. I'll bring Sage right back. There's some wine in it but of course she didn't make it full strength for an afternoon meeting. Right back—a family matter."

Sage found herself being led through the Readers and Writers into the kitchen, which was in great disarray. Octo closed the door. The seventy-eight-year-old face was still pansy pretty, eyes brimming with life. "Sage, is it true you're going to sell the house?" Octo didn't wait for a reply. "Because I think David Raeburn is interested. He mentioned it several weeks ago, said he'd talk to you. He wants to start a boys' school, something small and select with high standards, special emphasis on the humanities. The thing is, I don't think you should commit yourself without professional advice—"

"Aunt Octo, I'm not going to—"

"That house should fetch a good price on today's market and David has plenty of money, not that you'd want to take advantage, but you're no businesswoman, dear."

"Octo!" Martha Bench Pooser lurched into the kitchen. A little tub of a woman, she managed to look like a messenger in a Greek tragedy. "The ceiling. The commode! Clytie went upstairs to use the—it's on the blink. An absolute flood! Straight through the floor onto the drawing room sofa."

"Great stars and crumbs!" cried Octo. She wheeled and headed for the passageway leading to the back steps. Martha followed, fussing and clucking as they clattered to the second floor.

Sage leaned against the sink, took a few deep breaths, then straightened. Quietly, she slipped through the back door. She made her way down the brick path of Octo's tangled garden to the street. She wasn't about to face David again. Lord, what an ass she'd made of herself, lighting up like neon when he'd asked for a date. She should have known that a man like David Raeburn didn't hold hands with a plain woman in a cheap raincoat without an ulterior motive. Face it, she told herself firmly. He's not enchanted by your peerless beauty. He's not beguiled by your wit and charm. He's not even after your spotless virtue. It's your real estate, lady.

FOUR

SHE DROVE HOME along narrow streets swimming in the gray rose of sunset, paused at a corner where three old buildings were being torn down to make way for a parking garage. She remarked to herself that the town at twilight often had an underwater look. Then she realized that her eyes were wet. Fool, she thought, are you going to cry at the loss of every old house?

Once she'd pulled into her driveway, she made no effort to get out of the car. The evening ahead offered bleak prospects. She could shuffle desperately through the stack of bills on her desk. She could watch an anesthetizing television show. She could work on Charlotte's diary. Even the latter was unappealing. Something about the diaries was beginning to disturb her. She felt as if she were only a step away from seeing ghosts and hearing voices.

Getting out of the car, she was further disconcerted to see Roper Chalfont standing in the doorway of the carriage house, Major at his side. The dog ran to greet her, licking her ankles and pawing her skirt.

"You hungry?" Roper called. Then he was striding across the small patio, looking considerably cleaner in a white shirt and neatly pressed khakis. Drops of water glistened on the reddish brown hair. "I was out on Edisto today and caught a big mess of shrimp." He loomed over her.

"Thank you. That's very kind of you, but—"

"I hate eating by myself. And I've heard that lone ladies live on lettuce leaves."

She thought of how much Elise would disapprove of her socializing with Roper Chalfont. She was tempted.

"Isn't that," she asked in tones of Eldredge Pratt-Baines, "a redundance of alliteration?"

"I have a redundance of shrimp. And I hope you don't mind my feeding your dog." He started back toward his house, assuming she'd follow. She did, but she stopped at his door, waited until he'd turned.

"Two questions," she said.

"Yes?" His face looked less the barbarian's in the fading light.

"Are you going to offer to buy my house?"

One shaggy eyebrow lifted in surprise. "Why would I do that?" He put his hands in his pockets, leaned in the doorway. "Question one is so damn crazy, I can't wait for question two."

"Do you have ulterior motives?" His mouth opened in astonishment but before he could answer she went on. "The last time I was invited to dinner, a date with a young doctor arranged by my sister, I was accused of being out of touch with my own sexuality because I wouldn't bestow my favors out of sheer gratitude for a lobster dinner." He did take her arm then, exploding with laughter, drawing her into the house. Still laughing, he went to his kitchen.

They ate supper sitting on the floor in front of the hearth, the dog asleep beside them. Roper had lit a fire. "The last fire of spring," he prophesied. Along with the boiled shrimp he produced hominy, salad with fresh herbs, tall glasses of beer, and then coffee. Sage expected him to turn on some music. From what she'd read in Elise's magazines and seen on television, this seemed de rigueur. But they ate in silence. Apparently, he felt no pressure to initiate conversation and Sage was damned if she was going to do it.

She looked curiously at Roper Chalfont's possessions. He was not yet settled but he'd hung a big watercolor of a marsh scene over the fireplace. An oriental bronze head sat in one corner. In another lay a jumble of ropes, fishing rods, skis, backpacks. There was an abstract sculpture in pale wood on a table by the window. A leather sofa, two matching armchairs, and a round coffee table were carelessly arranged. Looking at the half-opened cartons of books and tapes, she wondered if he was going to have enough shelves. She also wondered if he saw the potential attractiveness of the place. The carriage house was divided into a large, raftered living room, bedroom, kitchen, and bath. Remodeled years before, and once used as a guest house, the whole place was paneled in cypress, with wide floorboards of heart pine.

"Why should I want to buy your house?" asked Roper suddenly. He finished his beer, put down the glass.

"A lot of people seem to want it." Sage stared at the last remaining shrimp on her plate.

"Do you want to sell it?"

"No. I don't know. I—" she paused, finding it hard to hedge with this man. "I can't afford to keep it," she admitted.

"Even with the rentals?"

"Even with the rentals."

"But you'd like to hold onto it?"

"Elise says that living alone in that big place is going to turn me into another Charleston crackpot."

Roper's smile was distracting. "Charleston has always celebrated its crackpots."

"Maybe Elise is right." She hadn't meant to go on but there was a comforting neutrality in his attitude. "When you're alone at night, in an old house, you begin to hear things."

"Does it bother you being alone?"

"I'm just not used to it yet." She took a big swallow of beer. "But I'll be all right. I haven't seen the ghost of Dabney Benford yet."

"An inherited apparition?"

"My great-great-grandfather's rakehell brother, killed in a duel over a woman. He tends to appear in a bloody waistcoat as an omen of death and disaster." She felt she'd said too much about herself. "Aren't there any skeletons in the Chalfont closet?"

"I'm the only possibility, and I don't yet qualify."

"Rumor has it that you're an outstanding candidate."

"Rumor is the bread of life in this town." He rose, stretched, towering above her. "Are you prying, Mary Sage Eliot?"

"I have a right to be curious. Elise says I'm not too careful about choosing my tenants."

"Ah yes, the lovely Elise." Roper threw a small log on the fire, watched it spark. "Well, I guess I've got to level with you. I'll try to make it bad enough to be believable." He kicked at the log to settle it in place. "How about I'm a reclaimed drunk, just released from Bellevue, and I'm down here making a pitiful effort to get my act together."

Sage managed to laugh. Then he was squatting beside her, one big hand encircling her wrist. "You have a helluva nice laugh," he said. He was so close she saw again that his eyes were almost gold. She looked at his hand on her wrist. She felt oddly dizzy. The relaxed interlude was at an end.

His voice dropped. "Why the game, Sage? You must know the truth."

"Yes, I know the truth."

"Then why did you take me on as a tenant?"

"I didn't know the truth then."

"And now?"

She looked at him, so sure of himself, so quick to find humor in everything. So damned superior. "I signed a lease," she said flatly.

He nodded. "A woman of her word. Of course." He stretched out his legs. "Well, I'll put your mind at rest, Mary Sage. I won't be here long. I'm going to move to a bigger place as soon as I can find what I want. In the meantime—" his expression was part mischievous, part inscrutable "—it might liven things up to have an old reprobate on the premises."

"I wasn't aware that things needed to be livened up."

"From what I hear, the last few years haven't been too exciting for you, or too easy. Looking after your grandmother, stuck in that house. And I gather you've had financial troubles as well. Not much of a life for someone your age."

What she saw in his face could only be pity. She thought of his hilarity at finding the nightgown in the yard. She saw him embracing the dark-haired woman, a femme fatale who would never need to be pitied. Her blood boiled. What right had this convicted criminal to pity her?

She controlled herself. "Things are not always what they seem," she said smoothly. She inspected the picture over the mantel with narrowed eyes.

Slowly Roper leaned forward. She'd really gotten his attention. "Don't tell me you've been leading a double life, Sage."

Her glance moved from the picture to his face. She searched for some sign of disbelief, saw none. "Don't waste your pity on me," she said airily. "Of course, if you prefer to think of me as what you described as a leftover from the nineteenth century—"

"That bothered you! Good Lord, I was joking."

"I wouldn't say that it bothered me, simply that it was—inaccurate."

"Well." He leaned back, regarded her, clasped his hands behind his head. "I'm not really surprised. You're a damned attractive woman. There must be some men in your life."

Sage had an instant vision of squads of lovers lined up at her door. She didn't want to push things too far. "Not all at the same time." She smiled.

"Yet you've not married?"

She paused. "Actually, I'm not interested in marriage." She was pleased to see his eyebrows lift. He was looking at her quite differently. "Oh," he said simply.

She recalled her conversation with Barbara Jane Thorpe, Barbara telling her she still sang on the beat, saying she hoped Sage wasn't still a virgin. "After all," her voice held a hint of Long Island, "the world is changing."

Roper pondered this, his brows still raised. "Then there's no one in particular?"

Sage was about to tell him it was none of his damned business, but she was having too good a time. "There has been."

"But nothing permanent. Just casual encounters?"

"Not casual at all," snapped Sage, insulted. "More what you might call meaningful relationships." At that moment she felt a little drunk with power. She had the upper hand. "Of course there was one... one—"

"One what?"

"One what you might call commitment."

"Commitment?" He looked somewhat dazed, then his face cleared. "Oh. Of course, commitment." He leaned in again, fascinated. "You said 'was.' It's over? Finished?"

Sage lowered her eyes, aimed for a flat world-weary air. "I had to end it."

"He's a two-timing bastard?" suggested Roper hopefully.

"He's married," said Sage, her voice edged with tragedy.

"No!"

"Yes."

This really set him back on his heels. Mechanically he picked up his cup, drank some coffee, replaced the cup. "It's just as well, Sage," he said quietly. "That's no life for you."

She watched him shake his head, rub his chin reflectively. "Meeting at out-of-the-way cheap motels," he said, "always dealing with guilt, spending Christmas alone while he's with his wife and kids." He pulled a handkerchief from his pants pocket, blew his nose. "His wife refusing a divorce, threatening a scandal that would ruin his career."

She scanned his face. At first she saw only utter seriousness. She felt a little ashamed. She was about to say something, when she spotted it, the wicked telltale glint of deviltry in his eyes, the twitch of a smile. She was enraged. She wanted to hit him with his baseball bat, demean him, diminish him, throw him and his belongings out in the street.

She rose, contriving a smile of malicious if counterfeit triumph. "You can see," she observed ironically, "that I'm no more dedicated to the truth than you. I must say, you're quite gullible. It's rather charming." She picked up her purse and books, moved to the door, turned. "The actual truth, as they say, is far stranger than fiction. Thank you for the shrimp."

He was on his feet, returning her smile. What's more, he was looking at her with open admiration. "Your inning, Mary Sage." He followed her through the door. "As a matter of fact, I might ask to buy your house, after all. It would suit my purpose. You see, I plan to really settle down. But, first I have to find some love-starved spinster who will have me. On the other hand, you might be interested yourself, Mary Sage. I'm wide open for a meaningful relationship. I'm a sitting duck for a commitment. I'd even go so far as an old-time bona fide proposal. Granted, you could do better, but you also could do a helluva lot worse."

She pushed past him, almost tripping over the dog, then tried to walk regally across the patio. Roper followed with long, easy strides. "Give it some thought, Sage. We could found a dynasty." He stopped at her steps, watching her climb stiff-backed to the piazza. "All I need," he called after her, "is a little mercy and the love of a good woman."

In her haste she almost missed seeing the tall figure with a limp, hurrying through the gate to the street. Clay must have come by to see her, for some reason. She wondered if he'd heard Roper's remarks. No, he would have stopped to discuss it. She wondered fleetingly what had brought him to her house at that hour. She started to call him back, then stopped. She was in no state to converse with Clay.

Before she went to bed, she found a bottle of her grandmother's sherry, poured herself a glass, and drank it straight down.

She had the old dream for the first time in years. It had started after her parents were drowned in the boating accident at the Rockville races. But in the dream she was the one in the overturned boat, gulping for breath, her lungs filling with water. She woke as if wrenched from sleep by some giant hand, every muscle contracted. Gradually, she recognized her room and discovered with gratitude that she was still breathing. When she switched on the lamp, she saw the bedclothes in a heap on the floor, Major looking up at her in confusion, wagging his tail as if to reassure them both. She leaned over to touch him and his head lifted, turned toward the door.

The night sounds had never disturbed the dog before. He'd either found them identifiable or they'd been too subtle for his old ears. Now he stood stiff, listening. They both listened. Then they heard it, a soft, swishing sound from overhead, as if something were being moved, dragged. What filtered through the floorboards was as muted as the scurrying of tiny feet, the soft beating of wings.

Distrustful of her own senses, finding no shred of courage, Sage tried to distract herself. She clutched at her disappointment over David Raeburn, fastened on the idiocy of her having thought he found her attractive. She was determined not to think about Roper Chalfont.

Something fell. Something fell with a muffled thud. Major moved to the bedroom door, sniffed, whined. Sage pressed her back against the headboard, drew up her knees, and like a child squeezed her eyes shut. It was half a minute before she dared let out her breath. It was a full minute before she realized what she was doing, saw as if from a distance the pitiful creature she was, cringing on the bed, eyes closed, petrified. First came shame, then a great tide of fury at herself, at whatever was happening in her house. She swung her legs over the side of the bed, crossed the room, and pushing past the dog, opened the door.

The hall was lit only by a small lamp on the telephone table. As in the flight below, the stairs to the top floor divided at a landing, then rose on both sides. There was a window high above the landing, accessible by way of a narrow balcony from an opening in the northeast room. Sage reached out to turn on the overhead light, then remembered she'd not replaced the burnt-out bulb. But the one on the top floor was new.

I'm going up there, she announced to herself, to settle this, prove it's nothing but imagination. Major brushed against her leg. Except for the dog, she thought uneasily—he'd heard something, too. He's not imagining things. Or is he? Is he getting old and erratic?

She started up the steps, prodded by shame, determined to ignore the welter of childhood fears that rushed to meet her. They seemed to hover just above, gargoyle heads, scaly bodies crawling out of the sea or from yawning caves, bird beasts flying at her on giant verminous wings. She reached down and touched the dog, chilled by the fact that he didn't rush on ahead as usual but stayed close by her side.

She stopped on the landing, stared up into a darkness barely weakened by the reflection of a street light coming through the window above. Suddenly she remembered the bat in the folds of her nightgown, another bat that had flown about her room one summer night when she was a child. She remembered her screams, the terror. She pushed herself up the last flight of steps, her hand moving along the wall, already reached for the light switch. As she put her foot on the top step, she saw it, a darker mass than the darkness around it. Shapeless, hovering. For seconds she stood paralyzed. When she finally groped for the switch her hand felt boneless, sapped of strength. Frantically, she pushed the switch, pressing it back and forth but there was no light. Nothing. Then, swiftly, without a sound, the shape swept down on her. Great silent wings attacked, beat about her, covered her. She smelled the rankness, felt the oily softness, heard her own strangled cry. Flailing, she staggered, her foot touching the step then losing it; she fell backward into the black pit of the stairs. She fought with one hand, the other clutching the banister. She caught a stair rail, then lost it as her body plunged down to hit the landing.

FIVE

"YOU'RE SURE YOU'RE OK?" There was a sly, derogatory note in Duncan's voice. "When you called—I mean, at this hour—I thought at least the house was on fire."

Sage picked up her coffee cup, found that her hand was still shaking, and put the cup back on the kitchen counter. She wished she'd called someone else, anyone else. But here she was, sitting in her kitchen at two o'clock in the morning with her tenant, Duncan McFee. "I'm all right," she said. "Just a few bruises."

"That fur coat helped break your fall. It's lucky you grabbed it."

"I didn't grab it," her voice sounded pinched. "It was thrown over me."

"Sure." He wore his usual irrelevant smile. His doughy face, under wisps of uncombed hair, had a dull pallor. His glance slid away from her. He pulled at his T-shirt, then looked at the fingerprints left on the yellow cotton. He crossed his arms over his chest. "You want me to look around up there again?"

"I don't think you'll find anything," said Sage wearily, "and with the hall light not working—"

"It works fine!" He seemed delighted to tell her this. "All the lights up there are OK."

It was hard to see him as a third-year medical student, worse to envision him as a doctor. His intelligence seemed minimal. His manner bordered on being offensive. But maybe she was being unfair. He could have hidden talents, latent charms that would flower as soon as he got his diploma. At the moment, she wished to heaven she'd never called him. She wished she'd called the police. No, she didn't. She knew exactly what would have happened. A tired patrolman would have arrived, checked the house, found nothing, taken a few notes, and promised to keep an eye on the place. He'd have sized her up as another hysterical female.

"I'd say you got a bad case of nerves," Duncan said softly. "It figures, a girl living all alone in this big old place."

"Look, I won't keep you any longer—"

"That's OK. What do you say I stay up here tonight? And maybe I better check you over. Make sure nothing's wrong. A fall like that—" His stumpy hand was on her arm.

She recoiled with distaste. "Nothing's wrong. I'm sorry I bothered you."

"Then what do you say I just stretch out on that divan in the living room there? No sweat."

"No. Please, I'm all right."

"I'll stay anyway, just to make sure you feel safe."

"There's no need. Really." She wished fervently that she'd never called him. "I appreciate your help, but I'll be fine." Desperate to have him gone, she rose, winced at the soreness of her body. She started through the dining room, then waited for him. He trailed reluctantly. When they reached the front door, he stopped, held onto the door as if to keep her from shutting him out.

"You know," he observed, "it might be a good idea if you spent a few nights with relatives, get away from here for a while. Till you don't feel so jumpy, if you know what I mean."

"I know what you mean."

She all but pushed him through the door. Obviously unwilling, he went down a few steps, then turned, peering up at her. "I think I'd better stay." With surprising agility he was back up the steps, hulking within a few feet of her. He was breathing heavily and even in the cool night air he was sweating.

"I'll just stick around to ease your mind." He had a firm grip on her arm, almost lifting her off her feet as he propelled her back toward the door. "And I'll check you over to make sure nothing's wrong. Like I said, no sweat—"

"No!" She wrenched away from him. "I told you I—"

"Admit it, you're scared. Well, with me here—"

"The lady can take care of herself," a voice spoke firmly from the shadows.

Sage and Duncan wheeled. A commanding figure stepped from behind a pillar. Then Roper's hand was on Duncan's shoulder, not shoving but ushering him resolutely toward the steps. "I'm sure Miss Eliot is grateful for your help and concern." Duncan shook off his hand, gave Sage a quick look that she couldn't decipher. "She apologizes for the inconvenience," said Roper, "and extends her heartfelt thanks." Duncan started to speak, stopped, glowered. Shoulders hunched, he lumbered down the stairs.

Sage felt limp with relief. She took a gulp of air, tried to look coolly at Roper. She wished that she'd been rescued by anyone but this barefoot man in a brown toweling bathrobe. "I noticed your lights were on," he said. "That seemed odd in the middle of the night. I thought something must be wrong. I'd just come up here on the piazza when the two of you walked out of the house."

Sage knew she must make some explanation. "I called him," she tried to control the quaver in her voice, "because I thought I heard something—someone on the top floor." She refused to elaborate. She was grateful that he'd gotten rid of Duncan but she wasn't going to be further humiliated by another skeptical response to her story. Hands clenched, she met his gaze defiantly.

"Did he search the house, Sage?"

"Yes."

"And he found nothing?" He continued to look at her closely. "Why didn't you call me?" he asked quietly. "I've been home all night."

Was there a thread of disappointment in his voice? She searched his face. She'd been braced for a mocking remark about the nightgown in the yard and now Duncan in her house in the middle of the night. But Roper's thick brows were drawn together in concentration. There was no mockery in his eyes. What she saw could only be described as a look of real concern.

All at once the fears of the last months seemed to crash in on her. Worst of all was the recurring suspicion that she had imagined it all, attached a sinister significance to ordinary things, night sounds, books out of order, the bat trapped in the house. Maybe Duncan was right. No one had thrown the coat over her. She'd seen a shadow, stumbled against the coat, grabbed it. In the darkness she'd fallen against the banister, lost her balance. She was beginning to doubt her own senses, her own judgment. Her eyes filled with tears of frustration.

She couldn't look at Roper. His very presence, a few feet from her, was another threat. Her traitorous body responded to him in a way she could neither understand nor control. She must move, go back in the house. She must end this. But it was too late. Gently he was reaching out, pulling her into his arms. She found herself utterly enfolded, her body held close to his. There was no fight left in her. She sank against him, beyond thought. As if crossing some new border, she abandoned herself to feeling. First, a sense of total safety, reaching home before dark. Then an odd but wonderful languor, an acute awareness of herself and of him. She could feel the hardness of his muscles, the quickness of his breathing, the unfamiliar yet tantalizing scent of him.

She was unaware of how long they stood there in a tight embrace. But gradually, like a snake sliding through grass, thought returned, a sly, insinuating thought that brought back Elise's bitter words. "Roper cut quite a swath," her sister had said. "Half the women in town were in love with him." She had a flashing memory of him standing in the carriage house, holding the dark-haired woman as he held her now. Mortified by her own weakness, she willed herself to pull away. Her body refused, nestling against him, head burrowed on his chest.

It was Roper who finally drew back. His hands on her shoulders, he looked down at her. "Get some sleep, Sage." The deep voice was not quite steady. "Don't worry. I'll keep an eye on things. And if you're frightened by anything else, no matter what, call me. Right away." Before she could answer, he was gone.

She knew that she'd sleep no more that night. She knew also that she must put Roper Chalfont out of her mind. She took Auralee's journal upstairs with her, then went to her workroom and got Charlotte's diary. Followed by the dog, she returned to her bedroom and locked the door. Major dropped to the floor and was asleep in seconds. She sat in the big fourposter with the journal and diary before her. She'd been wrong to doubt herself, to agree with Duncan. Someone had been in the house just a few hours ago. Someone was systematically searching, room by room. When they'd heard her coming up the steps, they'd grabbed the old sealskin coat, thrown it over her to give them time to get away. She tried to remember where she'd left the coat. In the southeast storeroom by the trunk where she'd found it? In the upper hall? Most important, how had the intruder gotten out of the house? Duncan had found both the front door and the door to the laundry locked. The dead bolts had to be unlocked on leaving, then locked again from the outside. Whoever had been in the house must have a key. But no one had keys except Elise and herself.

She wondered who Roper's dark-haired lady was.

She didn't dare tell Elise what really had happened. Her sister wouldn't believe it, but she'd use it as another reason to get Sage out of the house. This would make Clay happy. And David Raeburn, who needed a place to open a school. Aunt Octo would want her to stay at her house. Bea Bonham would offer her a room.

Sage thought of someone, nameless and faceless, sneaking about her house in the dead of night. She saw them in the library, removing shelves of books, looking for a wall safe, prying loose the fireplace paneling. She saw them on the top floor, quietly rooting through trunks and boxes. She shivered. There had been no sounds, no sign of the invader on the second floor where she slept. They were waiting until she was safely out of the house, either pressured into selling the place or too frightened to stay on alone.

What were they after? What, in God's name, did they hope to find? There was nothing of value hidden in the house. Each old trunk had a handwritten inventory, dated and pasted on its top by Gran. There was no record of family jewels or silver being hidden to escape the eye of marauding Union soldiers. During the Revolution, the family treasures had been successfully cached in the cistern of the house on Church Street. In 1863, the valuables had been safely taken to Camden. In all the Benford papers, there was only one reference to anything being secretly stored away.

She wondered if Roper and the woman were having an affair or a fling.

Sitting on her bed, Sage searched through the pages of Charlotte's diary until she found the entry for August 22, 1863. The refugees were fleeing. Charlotte and her mother were packing what they were going to need and planned to join the refugees. Charlotte's father, who was to die in a last battle in the Shenandoah, had made arrangements for his family to move to a small town upstate where he felt they would be safe. Charlotte spoke of a letter from her father:

"Papa has found us temporary lodgings in Camden, with Mrs. Ainsley, a widow and distant cousin of Rosa Bridges. He warns us that the arrangements will be far from commodious and asks that we bring only what is most valuable or most necessary. He asks, too, that I hide the contents of his desk and library chest in a place he showed me before he left, telling me in his teasing way to remember the Madeira. I am sure he asks me to cache these things less to protect them from the enemy than from Mama, who is a great one for getting rid of what she feels to be of no worth, calling Papa 'an inveterate hoarder of dust-catchers.' I'm inclined to agree with Mama. When I emptied the drawers, I found nothing but old deeds, letters dating back as far as the Revolution, and great volumes of Auralee's pictures, which are far too bold and unlovely to hang.''

What on earth could have prompted Roper to shame his family, deny an honorable heritage?

She must keep her mind on Charlotte, on the family spinsters, who so often were the most interesting women of their generation. Like Octo. While her peers, now mostly widows, were playing bridge, gossiping on the phone, and assessing their worth by the number of entries in their social calendars, Octo was collecting ''oddities'' to confront subjects like the concept of the perfectibility of man in modern literature. Charlotte, a hundred and thirty years earlier, was keeping a diary of detailed and fascinating observations. Back beyond Charlotte, in the 1830s, Auralee Benford was painting faithfully if not brilliantly all that dazzled her in the world of nature. As a writer, Auralee couldn't hold a candle to Charlotte. Her scribblings were mere notations, reminders of her sightings of flora and fauna in places like Chisholm's Pond, Coles Island, and I'on Swamp. Only one of her notebooks had survived. The others, if they existed, must have been lost or destroyed. Sage wished she knew more about Auralee's friend and mentor, M, and about the visiting artist called Jostle, whose work was so much admired by both Auralee and M. A friend of M's clergyman husband, he took a passionate interest in the wildlife of the low country, going on frequent expeditions to shore, deep woods, and swamps.

Octo had been no help in identifying these people. At the time Sage asked her she'd been deep in a squabble about which poems should be included in the Readers and Writers annual mimeographed yearbook. "The only clergyman I can think of who lived on Rutledge Avenue at the time was Dr. Bachman," she'd said, "but his wife's name was Harriet." I will ask Clay, thought Sage.

She'd come to a dead end. The things Charlotte had hidden for her father must have been retrieved long ago, after the family returned to Charleston at the end of the war. Even if they were still in the house and someone knew of them, who would be tempted by defunct deeds, old letters, and Auralee's watercolors?

Sage leaned back on her pillow and looked around the room, reassured by familiar objects—the silver dresser set that Gran had given to her on her sixteenth birthday, an aquatint of Roman ruins, the tall pier glass before which four generations of women had stood to arrange their bridal veils. She hoped they had married men they loved. She had a quick unbidden memory of the way she'd felt in Roper's arms.

Briskly gathering up diary and journal, she put them on the table by the bed, then stretched out. She fought to direct her mind, deal with the new distrust of her own body. At last a calm descended, partly from exhaustion, partly from thinking of Auralee and Charlotte, as if hands had reached out from the past to comfort her.

When her aunt Octo telephoned the next morning Sage was sitting in a tub of hot water, trying to soak some of the stiffness out of her body. After the eighth ring she ran into the hall, clutching a towel around her.

"Mary Sage! Where were you?"

"In the bathtub, Aunt." She observed herself in the big hall mirror: too tall, too lean.

"Oh. I hope you're not dripping onto the rug. At any rate, I'll be brief. I just wondered what happened to you yesterday. After Eldredge had fixed the commode I came back downstairs and found you gone. Everyone was so disappointed. I didn't know what to say so I told them you'd had a sinking spell."

"You were right, Aunt."

"Mary Sage, you sound so odd. Is anything wrong?"

Sage watched the water drip off her legs onto the floor, shivered. She felt a sudden, sharp need for sympathy; the old voice on the phone sounded like Gran's. "Not really. I mean—it's just that I had a fall last night."

"A fall, child! Whatever happened?"

"Down the stairs. From the top floor." Too late she realized that she shouldn't have mentioned it. "But I'm perfectly all right, Octo. Just sore."

"A fall down those stairs! Child, you could have killed yourself! I remember when Mama lost her footing and fell down those steps. It was on Labor Day. I know because your grandmother was packing a picnic lunch for an outing on Edisto Island. Mama insisted she was right as rain, that we go as planned. It wasn't until later that we discovered she had a fractured ankle. As Papa always said, Mama had spunk."

"I didn't get hurt, Aunt. I tell you, I'm fine." Sage clutched the towel around her, standing patiently in a small puddle.

"You should see a doctor, make sure there are no broken bones."

"Aunt Octo—"

"I'll be right over." Before Sage could get in another word her aunt had hung up.

Sage didn't dress in her customary work clothes, jeans and sweater. She put on a skirt and blouse, tied back her hair with a scarf, and prepared herself to Octo's ritual family crisis visit. Sitting in the drawing room, she wondered if it was only in Charleston that the custom persisted. Any out-of-the-ordinary occurrence, from storm damage to death, brought forth kinfolk bearing food. It was unthinkable not to call, express sympathy, and offer consolation in the form of some culinary delight.

When Octo arrived it was evident she had not ridden her bicycle, but been brought by car. She swept into the house bearing a large tray of canapés left over from the Readers and Writers meeting and accompanied by Bea Bonham. Obviously Octo had dressed in haste. The jacket of her bouclé suit was unevenly buttoned, her pince-nez entangled in a long string of amber beads. Bea, in a hopsacking dress girded with a leather thong, looked as if she might have come straight from tending sheep in the Andes.

"Child!" Octo thrust the platter onto the coffee table, then took Sage's arms. "Let me look at you." The beautiful, dark-fringed eyes, unfaded by age, moved over Sage like a scanner. "The bruise on your forehead! See it, Bea? We should apply ice!"

"It's nothing, Aunt. Sit down and I'll fix you some coffee."

"You're sure, dear?" Octo peered at her for a moment longer, then dropped onto the sofa and whisked the wrapping from the platter. "Well, maybe some food will help. I'll wager you've had no breakfast."

"I'll fix the coffee." Bea Bonham put a bottle of bourbon adorned with a blue ribbon on one of the end tables. "I know where things are." Winking at Sage, she went off through the dining room.

"I had a presentiment," said Octo sharply. She looked up at Sage. "For days I've had a feeling of imminent danger to someone close. Don't laugh, dear. I had the same feeling days before Hurricane Gracie hit in nineteen-fifty-whatever-it-was. I also had it that Sunday afternoon when your parents were—" The sound of the door knocker made them both start. Octo looked toward the hall. "That must be Clay."

"Clay? Aunt Octo, surely you didn't call Clay! I mean, all I did was take a little fall."

"He's worried about you. We all are. Get the door, dear. Clay's the only man left in the family, and though he's not blood kin—don't make him wait, child."

Clay's entrance made the house look even shabbier. As always, his skin glowed as if he'd just come from a sauna bath. Like David Raeburn, his lean body had an elegance that went beyond the whiteness of his shirt, the perfect tailoring, the expensive glow of his shoes.

"Sage, are you all right?" He put a hand on her shoulder. "Elise would have come but she had a dentist appointment."

"I'm fine," Sage said brightly. "Look, not even a Band-Aid." She wondered if he'd bought his suit in London. It didn't look like something he'd picked up in the Ashley Shopping Mall.

"Octo said—"

"Clay, you know how Octo loves a crisis. Come on in. Bea's fixing coffee."

She watched him greeting her aunt, realizing that every time she saw him she was reminded of the fact that the Hillmans had never suffered the poverty of other old families, weathering the Civil War, Reconstruction, and even the depression without visibly lowering their standard of living.

"Clay, you're too thin," Octo accused. "I hope you don't jog. Birnham Webster jogged himself right into a heart attack."

"No, Octo, I don't jog." Clay leaned over and kissed the old lady. "It's just that I haven't had any of your Huguenot torte lately."

"I'll make you some tomorrow, dear. Where's Bea? Oh. She's fixing the coffee. Sit down, Clay. Here by me." As soon as he was seated Octo rose, as if to propose a motion. "You know, I think I'd really prefer a nice cup of tea. No, Mary Sage, you talk to Clay. I'll get it myself. Bea makes wretched tea. Do you have some loose, dear? I detest bags." Not waiting for an answer, Octo sailed off to the kitchen, conferring with herself. "Mama never would allow a tea bag in the house, said the collapse of civilization would one day be traced to the invention of the tea bag."

At Octo's exit, Sage and Clay exchanged a smile. She sat down opposite him and watched him glance around the room, look up at the dusty chandelier.

"Good Lord," he said softly, "I forget how big this place is. These rooms are—"

"Twenty-two by twenty-two, with fifteen-foot ceilings. The hall is fourteen by forty."

She regarded her brother-in-law, wishing she had a closer relationship with him. Her aching body reminded her of what had taken place the night before and she shivered. If only she could trust him. But of course she trusted him, she corrected herself. He was Elise's husband. So why couldn't she tell him the truth, say, "Clay, help me! Something really frightening happened last night."

"Elise spoke to you about my offer?" His voice was quiet, neutral.

Sage pulled herself together, managed a cool smile. "Yes. I'm already seeing Arabs on the piazza, realtors in the closet, lawyers in the library—"

"Sage, listen—"

"Brokers in the bathtub. Clay," she leaned forward, clasping her hands on her knees, "this is a home. It was built to be a home.'

"I know how you feel, Sage. Believe me, I know. But before you jump to conclusions, let me say this, what I propose wouldn't be irrevocable. If anything, it's a way of keeping the house intact."

"But a club!"

"For the time being. Surely you realize that if you ever wanted the house, sometime in the future—say, you got married—" Clay let the thought complete itself. At least he had the tact to fix his gaze elsewhere. She was sure he thought that her chances of marrying were dim. Her chances of marrying someone with the money to repair and maintain the house bordered on the impossible. She didn't want to pursue the subject. She was talking to a stranger.

With his native courtliness, he always treated her kindly, advised her on all legal matters, as he had with Gran, but she couldn't help feeling his services were rendered more from a sense of obligation than personal concern. Clay's taste ran to beautiful, malleable women. Even if she were a knockout, she'd have trouble faking the malleable part. Elise managed, but Elise was in love with him.

"Clay, remember Auralee and Charlotte Benford's diaries? You read them, didn't you?"

Clay seemed disconcerted by this shift of subjects. "Yes, but I don't see what that's—Lise and I read the diaries. You know the Hillmans are related to Auralee through the Delacours." He ran a finger under the knot of his tie. "Why do you ask?"

"Do you remember reading about anything being hidden away in this house?"

Clay did glance at her now. "Hidden? Good lord, Sage," he teased, "are you hoping to find some family treasure?" When she didn't respond he went on, "There was that reference to Charlotte's storing her father's papers, but—"

"Just before they left for Camden."

"But none of that was of value except to the family. Anyway, it would have been retrieved when they came back from Camden at the end of the war."

"Not if they didn't know where it was."

"But they must have known." Clay stared at her. "Charlotte—"

"Charlotte wrote in the diary that her father showed her where to put his things before they left town."

"Exactly. So, when she came back—"

"She never came back. She died of the fever in Camden before the end of the war."

Clay's glance hadn't left her face. "You don't really think that somewhere in this house—" He shook his head, sat back, and crossed his long legs. "Sage, Octo said you took a fall on the top floor steps. What were you doing up there? Rooting for old valuables?"

"The dog heard something," she said. "I went up to look around." She couldn't bring herself to tell him about the coat being thrown at her, the escape of whoever was searching the house. Already he was regarding her with amused indulgence.

"Here we are." Octo was back, followed by Bea, bearing a tray of cups. "Put it there by the canapés, Bea. Bea, you know Clay. Now let's all sit down and have what Mama used to call elevenses." Once she and Bea were seated, Octo turned to Sage. "Was that Roper Chalfont I just saw by the carriage house? I was glancing out your kitchen window—"

"Yes, Aunt. He's a new tenant."

"And a damned attractive one," observed Bea.

Octo ignored this. "Mary Sage, I wish you'd spoken to me or to Clay before you took this step. The man is a—"

"Jailbird!" Bea announced with relish.

"I felt so sorry for the family," Octo sighed. "Poor Louis Chalfont. Losing his wife just the year before, and then that scandal with Roper. Of course, Roper always was the scamp, forever in trouble. Those two boys were like night and day. Young Louis was the apple of his father's eye. Graduated with honors from Groton and Yale—"

"Choate and Harvard," amended Clay.

"Went on to law school," said Octo, ignoring him, "and married a nice girl from Maryland."

"Virginia," Clay corrected gently. "An old Tide-water family. I believe there was a child."

"Roper," said Bea, "sounds a helluva lot more interesting. I hope he was thrown out of Princeton in utter disgrace."

Clay looked at her as if he'd just noticed she was there. "As a matter of fact, he graduated from Berkeley a few years before the drug charge. He'd been working with some environmental agency in Washington, but he came back here pretty regularly."

"Berkeley," muttered Octo. "I've never heard of a college in Berkeley County."

"It's a well-known university," said Clay, "in California."

Octo turned to him with a smile of great sweetness. "Clay, I bless the day when Elise made us kin. How often the incisiveness of your literal mind has saved us from the pitfalls of inaccuracy, to say nothing of an untidy dependence on allegory and metaphor."

"California," mused Bea.

"Buddhist monks," said Octo darkly, "and moral gypsies."

"Thank you, Octo." Clay accepted her spurious compliment with a smile.

Octo threw him an affectionate glance, popped three lumps of sugar into her tea. "It's a mercy," she said, "that old Louis didn't live to know what happened to young Louis. It would have killed him. Such a tragedy!"

"What tragedy?" Bea's eyes gleamed with shameless interest.

Octo sighed. "Both Louis and his young wife were killed last year. A skiing accident." She looked at Clay with defiant assurance. "In the Laurentian mountains."

"That's right," said Clay, with obvious relief.

Octo sipped her tea, dropped in another lump of sugar. "Mary Sage," she lowered her pitch, increased her volume for emphasis, "I have always championed the independence of women, but in this case I feel you should have consulted Clay or me. Renting to strangers is one thing, renting to local people who once left town under a cloud is another."

Suddenly Sage was sick to death of being prodded and censured. "Octo, Clay," she addressed them in firm terms, sitting straighter in her chair. "I've been running this house for quite a while, taking care of Gran, managing on my own. There's no reason to treat me like an incompetent child. I appreciate your concern and I'd like to feel I can call on you for help, but right now I want to make my own decisions."

Bea Bonham beamed at her. Octo sniffed. Clay bestowed a look of saintly patience. "Sage, we don't mean to interfere," he said, "but some of these decisions you speak of might require professional advice. I've no idea of the state of your finances—"

"Clay," Sage said, "you do look a little skinny. I don't think Elise feeds you enough. Here—" she picked up a canapé, long past its prime, and thrust it into his hand. "Try one of these."

"Waccamaw crab delights!" crowed Octo happily. "Only Juanita Whipple knows the receipt. Down the hatch, Clay."

Sage watched as Clay absently put the little sandwich into his mouth and chewed. With malicious pleasure, she saw his expression change from surprise to consternation. "Here," she said graciously, "have another. They're small."

When the three of them finally had gone, Sage was enormously relieved. The feeling lasted until, standing at the kitchen sink washing the cups, she looked out the window and saw Roper unloading boxes from his station wagon. She was finally over the shock of hearing about his going to jail. She told herself that his having a criminal record really wasn't surprising. He struck her as a man with little respect for law or custom. She put him out of her mind, wondering what to do with three dozen crab delights. Major, however, had solved the problem. When she returned to the drawing room she found the platter licked clean. Major waited by the front door, looking queasy. She let him out with a few sharp words about greed and his jaded palate. Before she had closed the door the phone rang. It was Elise.

"Sage, are you all right? I would have come over but you have to wait so long to get an appointment with Dick Harvey and I didn't dare break mine. Clay said he would stop by... Sage, what on earth happened? Octo said—"

"Nothing happened, Lise. I got out of bed to go to the john and fell over the dog."

"Oh. But Octo said—"

"Aunt Octo was having a dull morning."

"Is Clay there? I'd like to speak to him."

"He just left."

"Oh, damn!"

"I'll talk to you later, Lise."

"No, wait. There was something I wanted to ask you—now what was it? Oh, I remember! It was about the keys. Did Clay ask you about the keys? Having them duplicated?''

"Keys?"

"I lost my keys to your house. In fact, I lost all my keys. I think it was the day we had that big crowd at Octo's house to celebrate her birthday. I used Clay's to have mine duplicated, but I still haven't replaced the ones to your house.''

Sage found that she had been holding her breath. "No," she said, "Clay didn't mention keys."

"After I specifically asked him! Well, anyway, would you mind getting me a set?''

"You say you lost them at Octo's birthday party?"

"I don't know. I think so. All that confusion, all those Readers and Writers. Of course I could have dropped them anywhere but it's not like me. I never lose keys. Umbrellas maybe, but not—"

"I'll have a set made, Lise. Look, I've got to hang up now. I have an appointment.''

"Where are you going?"

Sage chose the destination most likely to shock her sister into silence. "To the beauty parlor," she said, and hung up.

For several seconds she sat staring at the phone. She thought of all the people who had been at Octo's birthday party. In her mind's eye, she saw a hand slipping into Elise's purse, finding the keys, taking them. But who could have known that the key to her house was included?

SIX

TEN MINUTES LATER Sage still was sitting by the phone. She'd made a list of the people who had attended Octo's birthday party and was rechecking it to see if she'd forgotten anyone. There had been the usual gathering of family members, with Aunt Meta arriving in a wheelchair, her least favorite cousin Corinne hauling along two obnoxious children, most of the Readers and Writers, Bea Bonham, David Raeburn, and Peter Larson. Sage added Clay's name, remembering that he'd come late.

Octo's party had been two weeks before Gran died. It was shortly before her grandmother's death that Sage began to hear the night sounds. At first she'd thought it her imagination, the stress of those last days. Later she decided it was a neurotic reaction to being alone, the sudden emptiness of the house after the bustle of nurses arriving and departing, going down to the kitchen at all hours.

It was not possible that anyone at Octo's party could be a thief. She wished she could remember more of what happened that day. She'd stayed less than an hour, anxious to get back to Gran, lingering just long enough to have a fragmented conversation with David while Peter Larson watched from a few feet away. No. It was unthinkable that anyone at the party would have taken Elise's keys. Sage tore the list from the tablet, crumbled it, and threw it in the wastebasket by the table. When the phone rang she grabbed it with a sense of reprieve.

"Sage? It's David. I just wanted to remind you about the concert tomorrow night. May I pick you up around seven?"

"That would be fine, David."

"I was thinking it might be fun to go out for dinner. A new place just opened down on the waterfront. It's supposed to be quite good."

"I'd enjoy that."

"Around six-thirty, then?"

"Fine."

"Sage, I've really been looking forward to this."

"So have I."

After the call, she sat staring at the watercolor over the telephone table. Auralee Benford had painted a wren perched on a mimosa branch. Sage wondered who had had it framed. Over a hundred years ago, Charlotte had written that Auralee's paintings were "too bold and unlovely to hang." The colors might have faded but the composition was, if anything, downright timid.

If this were a week ago, she thought, I'd be thrilled at the prospect of an honest-to-God date with David Raeburn. I'd have had no idea that it was leading up to a real estate offer. I'd have been a damn fool. She still ached from her fall, but before she went upstairs for another hot bath she called the beauty parlor to make an appointment with Elise's favorite operator, Billy. She was in luck. Billy had a cancellation and could fit her in between two and four o'clock.

A few minutes later, standing naked in front of the pier glass, she decided it was a good idea. She studied her reflection objectively. Her waist was still narrow, her bosom still small but adequate, her legs still fashionably long, but her body no longer seemed to be her own. She knew it was capable of traitorous feelings for the wrong man. Forget it, she told herself. Think of David and tomorrow night. She marveled at herself. Just an hour ago she had learned that quite possibly someone had a set of keys to her house and could come and go as they pleased. Yet here she was checking her physical assets. Someone was making a nightly search of her rooms looking for God knows what. If they were determined enough to steal a set of keys there was no reason to think they would stop short of violence. She could have been killed or badly hurt in that fall downstairs. And what was she doing about it? Knowing that no one would believe her and beginning to doubt herself, she was going to the beauty parlor. The victim, she reflected grimly, gave herself every advantage.

At two o'clock Sage meekly presented herself at La Salle Bleue, a noisy, blue and white beehive of cubicles reeking of mixed perfumes and evil-smelling lotions. The receptionist, whom Sage perceived as regarding her with pity and disbelief, told her that Billy was finishing a comb-out. Sage scanned the pages of three women's magazines, carefully reading an article that announced that "Image Is Everything." She realized that she must select a persona with speed and skill. At any moment Billy might appear and beckon her to a booth of transformation. She hoped Billy was not one of the young men in tight pants who darted about crying, "Sweetie, trust me!"

In opting for an image Sage was torn. She was drawn to a fashion shot of Brigitta Bligh, a snarling actress wearing nothing but British rugby shorts and a necklace of ocelot teeth, poised with one foot on the tattooed chest of a linebacker for the Rams. On the other hand she knew that Oyster Bay socialite Amanda de Vries would be a more realistic choice. Amanda's polished arrogance had it all over Brigitta's bravado. The sweep of her tawny hair, the distance between eye and brow proclaimed that all her clothes had French seams, that men like David Raeburn fell daily at her feet, and that Dracula could live in her attic without so much as a ho-hum from Amanda.

Once Sage had made her decision she relaxed, read a recipe for "An Aphrodisiacal Ragout for Two," then moved on to an article entitled "And So to Bed," which promised to revive flagging love affairs with arcane sexual gymnastics documented by the author during a two-year stay with a remote tribe on the Sepik River in New Guinea.

"Sage Eliot!" She looked up to see the face of her cousin Corinne, prettily pink from the dryer. "What on earth are you doing here?"

Sage was groping for a put-down when a heavyset woman motioned from an empty booth. "You Eliot? You're next." Shrugging with the bored air of Amanda de Vries, she swept past Corinne and disappeared behind the bulk of the waiting Billy.

A far cry from the average beauty operator, Billy revealed that she had been a makeup artist in the golden days of Hollywood. As she unpinned Sage's braids she spoke knowingly of problems involving Joan Crawford's hairline, Debbie Reynolds's neck, Audrey Hepburn's nose. A swart, Mediterranean type, lightly mustached, she obviously had little inclination to practice what she preached, but she surveyed Sage with a professional eye. "Great figure," she proclaimed. "Swell bones. Long neck. Small head. Thick hair. The camera will love you."

Sage held out the magazine, pointed to Amanda de Vries. "What do you think?" she asked.

"Duck soup," croaked Billy.

As the transformation got underway Sage realized that no one had touched her hair since the long-past mornings when Gran would braid it before sending her off to school. The experience was pleasantly lulling, soporific. She dozed as Billy, a cigarette hanging from her lips, measured, clipped, razored, tipped, washed, rinsed. She nodded off under the dryer, half wakened during the comb-out, was dimly aware of Billy applying makeup. Then she heard an explosion of astonishment and pride. "Well, I'll be damned!" Billy said.

Sage looked into the mirror and met the gaze of another Amanda. The wide-set green eyes had a cool emerald glint. The sensual mouth was faintly scornful. A tawny mane of hair swept back from her brow, then fell in glossy wings to her shoulders. The woman in the mirror had never worn ill-fitting clothes or spent a teenage Saturday night alone. On weekends at Sweetbriar she would have been the first to pack her suitcase and take off for houseparties at the University of Virginia. Surely she never had been known to read four books a week.

Sage left the beauty parlor wearing a scarf over her head and clutching a blue and white tote of costly cosmetics. She drove in a trance to Woolworth's, parked her car, and then with a giddy laugh of self-recrimination pulled off the scarf, shook out her tawny hair, and strode into the store to have her keys duplicated for Elise. While she was there, two older women whom she'd known all her life walked by her with no sign of recognition.

She carried her euphoria home with her, but hurried into the house lest she encounter Roper Chalfont. She moved from room to room, mirror to mirror until satisfied that she wouldn't look suddenly into the glass and see her old face. She could hardly wait for her sister to come by that evening and pick up the keys.

She was not disappointed. For once in her life Elise was speechless. "Good lord, what have you done?" she whispered at last.

Sage was enjoying herself immensely. "La Salle Bleue. Billy, the magician. Don't you approve? Lise, come on in. You look like you've just seen a UFO." Sage dropped the keys into her sister's purse. "How about some supper? I'll fix a salad."

"I'd love to but I can't." Elise still stared at her. "Clay and I are going to a dinner party. Sage, you look—fantastic! I should have dragged you to Billy ages ago."

"The time wasn't right. Lise, come on in for a minute."

"I really can't. It's late. I've got to dress." Suddenly Elise stepped forward, put her arms about Sage, held her close. "Darling, whoever he is, I hope he's wonderful."

"Lise—"

"I've got to run. Clay hates to wait." Elise kissed her, turned to start down the steps, then glanced at the carriage house. "Sage, don't tell me it's—"

"Look," Sage laughed, "I may have gone to the beauty parlor, but I haven't lost my wits."

"Thank God for that!" Elise took another long look at her sister, shook her head in amazement, then, grinning, hurried down to her car.

After she'd finished her supper Sage was too keyed up to read or watch TV so she straightened the kitchen cupboards, then cleaned all the small objects in the drawing room, including the miniature from which Clay had blown dust that morning. It was almost eight o'clock when she carried a basket of sheets and towels down to the laundry room on the ground floor. Franny Barth was already there, turning on the washing machine.

"Oh, Miss Eliot, I'm sorry! You must need the washer. Look, I can turn it off, do my things later." Franny was wearing the red robe, and her jet black hair, hanging loose, made her seem years younger. She stared at Sage.

"No," Sage assured her, "I'll just leave my basket here and put these things through tomorrow. I usually do laundry during the day, anyway. It's just that—"

"You cut your hair!" Franny couldn't contain herself. "It's sure becoming."

"Thanks."

"I hope you don't mind my saying so, but it suits you much better than the braids."

"I don't mind."

Franny's wide smile unwittingly revealed the wholesome upcountry girl who hid herself so well in tailored suits or sexy negligees. It belied the brows, plucked to a thin arch, eyelids tinted a smoky gray. The dark eyes, usually guarded, looked at Sage with a sudden kinship as if she completely understood the trip to the beauty parlor. "A change sure helps, sometimes,'' she said. "Gives us a new picture of ourselves.''

"That's true.'' Sage listened to the hum of the washing machine, beginning to feel self-conscious under Franny's admiring scrutiny. "I'd better put out my trash,'' she said. "Tomorrow's Thursday, collection day.'' But Franny followed her from the laundry room through the small entry hall. They both went outside to where the garbage and trash cans were lined against the wall under the piazza. The night air was almost warm, heavy with the scent of the tea olive shrubs that grew along the driveway.

"Might as well put mine out, too,'' said Franny. "Last time, I forgot.'' Together, they carried the containers out to the street, then walked back to the house. Franny stopped before they reached the door, looked at the dark garden. The glow from the street lamp was kind to the unweeded lawn, the unpruned shrubs.

"I still can't believe I'm here,'' Franny spoke softly, "in Charleston, living in this beautiful home.'' She turned to Sage. "I'm the first one in my family to move from Holly Hill in thirty years. Except for Uncle Harlow. He was in the merchant marine.'' She looked again at the garden and the carriage house. "It took me a long time but it was worth it.''

"How did you happen to come here?'' Sage asked politely.

"Happen to come?'' Franny laughed. "Honey, it didn't just happen. I saved for four years, clerking in a convenience store. When I'd set by enough, I came to Charleston and lived with friends of my cousin. I went to Rice Business College and took the medical secretary courses. Then I got my job with Dr.

Hooper." Franny drew in a deep breath. "This sure is a pretty town."

Sage looked at the red robe, thought of Franny's darkened windows the other night, the sound of music. Without a doubt there was a man in Franny's life. She hoped to heaven that he wasn't married or an out-and-out bastard. "Yes," she said, "it's a pretty town."

"Just smell that tea olive!" Franny drew in another long breath, hugged her arms. "You know what I like about spring? No matter how down you feel during the winter, when spring comes it's like the whole world's going to change. All kinds of good things can happen. You know what I mean?"

They said good night, but before Sage started up the steps, Franny stopped her, speaking shyly, a little anxiously. "Miss Eliot—"

"Please call me Sage."

"Sage. I just thought that some night—I mean, both of us being alone—you might like to come down to supper. I'm a pretty good cook and my daddy keeps me supplied with quail and venison—"

"Thanks, Franny. And maybe you can come up and have supper with me."

"I'd like that. I've often wondered what it looks like up there. I mean, I've never seen the inside of one of these houses."

Sage thought of the antiques she'd had to sell, of her relief that Elise hadn't yet noticed that they were gone. "I'll be glad to show you," she promised.

It wasn't until a few hours later, after she'd climbed the stairs to go to bed, that she faced the prospect of another night alone in the house. When she reached the second floor she saw the sealskin coat, still lying on the landing above her like a dead animal. She waited for some tremor of fear, and felt nothing. Followed by the dog, she went into her room and closed the door. As she was finally hanging up Elise's glamorous hand-me-downs she realized she wasn't afraid. She felt certain that the person she'd encountered the night before had thrown the coat to stop her, distract her while making an escape. She'd not been stabbed, shot, or raped, as often happened during robberies. No, whoever it was hadn't intended to harm her. The fall had been her fault. She lost her balance when she stepped backward. She wasn't dealing with a hardened criminal; a thief, perhaps, but not a murderer. She also had the feeling that last night's encounter might have discouraged the invader. She held up a brown chiffon dress, looked at herself in the mirror. Touched again by the chilling hand of doubt, she thrust it away, regarded the young woman in the mirror. "Yes?" she addressed the stranger. "Can I help you?"

Tired as she was, she couldn't sleep. She lay in bed, trying to remember some mention of family valuables, some hidden cache. She recalled Gran's remark that the Benford women didn't seem to inspire gifts of important jewels. The money went into land and more land, all gone now. What jewels existed had been sold during the war, in the 1860s, or later during Reconstruction. Gran had always marveled that her engagement ring and pearls had made it through the depression.

It wasn't until she was half asleep that she remembered the picture in Octo's attic. Elizabeth Benford, an eighteenth-century belle, had been painted in gray satin, wearing diamond and sapphire earrings and a matching necklace. Octo had refused to hang it. "A lady of dubious discretion,'' she'd proclaimed, "rendered by a man of questionable talent.'' I must ask her about it, thought Sage. I must ask her tomorrow.

She wakened the next morning to the happy fact that she'd heard no night sounds. She remembered her date that night with David. Her first impulse was to jump out of bed, run to the mirror, and check on her new image. I have a date with a very attractive man, she thought. It's going to be special. Belatedly she reminded herself of David's ulterior motive. She wondered whether he'd spring his offer for the house over soup or dessert. When she stood before the pier glass she saw that her face without makeup showed more of its old candor, but her hair had held its shape, as Billy promised. "You won't have to mess with rollers,'' she said, "I cut it the way it grows.''

After breakfast Sage thought of the bag of makeup she'd bought, and wondered if she should get to work on Amanda's face. She decided that, even unskilled as she was, it wasn't likely to take ten hours. She made a list of household chores: marketing, vacuuming, cleaning bathrooms, getting rid of old clothing on the top floor. She left the list in the kitchen and decided to type some more of Charlotte's diary. But once in her workroom, she found she couldn't face the typewriter. Instead, she went onto the upstairs piazza and stretched out on an old wicker chaise longue, abandoning herself to the morning sun. She saw a lone egret heading inland toward the swamps, listened to a jay making an announcement from the rooftop next door, heard Franny's car backing out of the driveway, the squeak of the iron gate as Duncan left for school. She wondered what Roper Chalfont was doing, what he had been doing since he got out of jail.

She tried to imagine him in a cell, the big, lean body slumped in despair, the face with its look of arrogant amusement no longer amused. It was hard to believe he was bred to gentility. It was easier to think of him smuggling diamonds out of South Africa or leaning from the window of a stolen jeep to throw an IRA bomb. David Raeburn, on the other hand, could easily sit for the portrait of a Charleston gentleman. Put him in a satin waistcoat...

"Hey! Is that you, Mary Sage?"

Sage scrambled out of the chaise and went to the railing. Roper stood by his doorway, peering up at her. He wore a business suit and his hair was combed. He looked as if he were in costume.

"That guttering under your slate roof is all rusted out," he called, looking toward the top of her house. "If the piazza roof below it isn't leaking yet, it's damn well going to. I can pick up some guttering and do it myself, save you from—"

"Don't bother!" Her voice sounded both thin and shrill. "I've called the roofers," she improvised.

"There's no point in paying roofers when I can do it in a morning."

"It's been taken care of," shouted Sage.

He kept staring up at her, then he was moving across the patio. "What have you done to yourself?" he yelled.

"Thank you for your offer," she called and stepped back from the rail.

"You've cut your hair!"

"I appreciate your—"

"Why in hell did you do that?"

A window flew up next door and a head appeared. Sage fled into the house. It wasn't until she heard the station wagon back out of the driveway and start down the street that she began to breathe normally. She wondered if she could break his lease.

SEVEN

WHEN SAGE CALLED Octo that afternoon and questioned her about the portrait of Elizabeth Benford, the old lady laughed. "There's not much known, Mary Sage. By the by, I made a big pot of okra gumbo this morning and I thought you might like some. If you'll stop by—"

"Aunt Octo, don't stall. After all I'm old enough to know the worst."

"Did I ever tell you about Fanchion Benford Leize? A woman of incredible courage, a real heroine of the American Revolution."

"Aunt!"

Octo sighed. "She eloped. Bolted."

"Fanchion?"

"Elizabeth."

"What's so bad about that?"

"She was a married woman!" said Octo tartly.

"Oh ho!"

"It's not funny, Mary Sage. It's a chapter the family would as soon forget."

"Even after two hundred years?" Sage tried not to giggle. "Who carried her off?"

"A person from Atlanta. He was of a good family, which makes it worse—a gambler and a womanizer."

"Elizabeth left husband and kiddies for this rotter?"

"Twin girls and a boy. It's said she came to a degrading end," added Octo darkly. "But we don't know the particulars."

"What about the diamond necklace and the earrings?"

Octo chuckled. "The parure! How we used to laugh about that! Whenever the family was in dire financial straits, someone would say, 'Maybe we'll find Elizabeth's parure.' Surely you remember Charlotte mentioning it in her diary. It was while she and her mother were at Camden near the end of the war."

Sage did remember. But Charlotte's entry had made no sense, simply saying that when confronted with the fact of their badly dwindling funds, her mother had made her laugh by speaking of "the parure." Sage had made a mental note, subsequently forgotten, to look up the word *parure*.

"Personally, I think Elizabeth took it with her," Octo went on. "And if she didn't it would have been sold, sooner or later."

"But you're not sure?"

"The lady, mercifully, kept no diary. And her name was seldom mentioned in family circles. Mary Sage, that bruise on your head—I've been worried about you—"

"Aunt, I'm fine. As a matter of fact I did something exciting, yesterday."

"You didn't sell the house?"

"I went to the beauty parlor."

Octo gave herself a few seconds to digest this news. "Your sister means well," she said at last, "but you mustn't let Lise run your life."

"Elise had nothing to do with it. Octo, I got my hair cut!"

"Your hair? But you've always—since you were a child—those braids! I can't imagine what you look like."

"Aunt, you wouldn't believe it but for some reason I'm the spitting image of—"

"Your mother! I've always said you favor your mother—"

"Elizabeth Benford," laughed Sage.

Octo gave a cluck of disgust. "I'll put your soup in some mason jars," she said briskly, "and you can stop by for it later." She hung up.

Sage spent the day inventing ways to avoid thinking of the evening ahead. When she did dwell on it she noticed a feeling of weakness, as if she were coming down with a mysterious ailment. Despite her resolve she kept returning to the upper piazza, leaning against a pillar, and looking down into the garden. The Charleston spring was about to make an entrance. Even the old trees, the big pecan, the sweet gum, the narrow poplars against the house next door, looked young in their budding green. In a matter of days the jessamine would erupt in a shower of gold, the wisteria by the piazza steps would send a lavender froth over the wrought iron. She stared at the carriage house. An elusive fragrance, mixed with the scent of the sea, was like a drug, draining her of everything but a yearning she couldn't name.

She went back in the house and shut the French doors against the perfumed air. To distract herself she went through every room, trying to spot a possible hiding place, a suspect floorboard, something odd about a wall panel. She stood again in the library, staring at the books that someone had removed, then put back in haste. She made herself go to the top floor,

picking up the fur coat and putting it back on the pile
of clothes she'd been sorting. She kept staring at the
old trunks, the cardboard cartons. She went to the
playroom, looked at the big rocking horse, the old
wicker baby carriage, the jumble of toys. She paused
in each of the other two storerooms, one crammed
with worthless pieces of furniture, the other with piles
of books and pictures, wondering if behind the
patched walls someone might have hidden a diamond
necklace and earrings. She crawled through the
midget-sized door in the northeast storeroom, which
led to the narrow balcony built for access to the window above the second floor landing. Behind the wall
it extended half the length of the room, under the pitch
of the roof, dark and quite empty. Groping on the
floor, she found a candy wrapper and a dusty copy of
Wind in the Willows. In the northwest storeroom, she
climbed on a stepladder to the attic, pushed open the
trap door, and, standing in that vast, vacant space,
looked into every corner.

Back in her work room she leafed through Auralee's journal, hoping to find some mention of Elizabeth Benford's parure. There was none. She read the
final entry. Auralee, by then a woman in her thirties,
was engaged to a widower with a large family. The
prospective bride mentioned receiving a number of
wedding gifts but none of them was jewelry. Her
present from her father seemed to give her great
pleasure but was never described. If the parure was
still in the family it might have been an appropriate
gift from father to daughter, but that wasn't the case.
Auralee wrote: "My gift from Pappa was the biggest
surprise of all. To think that he remembered, after all
these years. Mamma says he happened to hear of it,

when a friend mentioned a private sale of items belonging to a Dr. Geddings..."

Here the notebook ended. The marriage never took
place. Auralee's intended was thrown from his horse
and died two days before the wedding date.

Discouraged, Sage abandoned her search. She
ironed three blouses, made a grocery list. She opened
the needlepoint kit given to her by Elise for Christmas, and for half an hour stared at the instructions.
By a quarter to seven a creditable replica of Amanda
de Vries stood in the drawing room, sipping some of
the bourbon that Bea Bonham had left. She was more
pleased with herself than she dared admit. The pier
glass had already told her that her skin reflected the
glow of the apricot organdy blouse, that what Elise
described as "a café au lait tissue wool cocktail suit"
fit to perfection, that the stiletto-heeled sandals did
astonishing things for her legs. As she straightened a
somber portrait of her great-great-grandfather, she
composed a caption for herself: "Socialite Sage Eliot
in the drawing room of her antebellum house, where
a clever use of worn fabrics and Victorian whatnots,
enhanced by a daring aura of disrepair, reflect the
owner's unfaltering sense of seedy grandeur."

By seven-thirty she was sitting on the sofa trying to
dispel the same hollow sensation she'd felt at her debut party. He'd forgotten. It was the wrong night.
He'd call in a minute and make a lame excuse. Twice
she got up to go to the bathroom. She ran upstairs and
brushed her hair again. She called herself an idiot, a
mush-minded adolescent. Then with an echoing announcement that all life is change, all things are possible, the sound of the door knocker shook the house.

He didn't appear at all late. He wasn't breathless or perspiring or full of apologies. He stood there in his beautifully tailored gray suit, quite at ease. Nor did he comment on her changed appearance. The dark eyes searched hers as if to make certain that what he'd once found was still there. "Sage," he said quietly and took her arm. As they went down the piazza steps she glanced toward the carriage house. She was disappointed that Roper Chalfont wasn't on hand to see her depart. She would have enjoyed acknowledging him with a nod and an icy smile. Peter Larson sat behind the wheel of the dark blue Mercedes. As David helped her inside Peter inclined his head and with no expression muttered a flat "good evening."

Sitting beside David, her hand close to his on the velvety gray seat, she felt like a figment of her own imagination. They drove down familiar streets, past houses she'd known all her life yet she was filled with a sense of strangeness, newness. It was high time there was some romance in her life. She was sitting beside a man who, by any woman's standards, filled the bill. She tried to scold herself. Remember what this is all about, she warned herself. But some reckless part of her ignored it.

When she got out of the car and walked with David into the restaurant she took small, careful steps as if any jarring movement might shatter the mood. Only vaguely did she wonder about Peter, whether he would wait in the car or have dinner at a table by himself. Sitting by an arching window overlooking the harbor, she was half aware of other people, voices, the profusion of tropical plants, someone playing the piano, old songs by Cole Porter and Jerome Kern. At one point, turning to meet David's glance, she marveled at the fact that they felt enough at ease to be silent. Everyone talks too much, she thought. We have plenty of time. Still, there were things about him she longed to know.

He must have read her thoughts because he put down his glass and rested his arm on the table. "You know," he said, "we've only seen each other five or six times but I feel we've been friends for years."

"I'm glad, David."

"You're so different from the women I've known. There's a calmness about you even when you're in a crowd." He smiled. "Talking to you is like coming in out of a storm." The smile turned into a grin. "If I didn't know better I'd be tempted to think you were a daydream, a lady from another century."

So much for Amanda de Vries, thought Sage. But she was pleased. "We know so little about each other," she ventured, "I mean, you probably know a good bit about me, living next door to Octo, but—" she smiled back at him. "As Bea says, you have an aura of mystery."

He turned to look out at the harbor. "There's no mystery. I'm an ordinary person really. What do you want to know?"

Sage sensed his withdrawal but couldn't stop herself. "Oh, the usual things I guess. Where you're from, what you've been doing with your life. I don't even know if you have a family."

"Just my mother," he said. "My father died when I was a child. No brothers or sisters." He took a deep breath, as if he found her questions painful. "I grew up in Boston, went to Exeter and then Princeton, got my graduate degree at Stanford, took a teaching job at a boys' school in Delaware."

"But you had to stop," she said gently.

"Yes. The accident." One narrow hand, touching the edge of the table, tightened, then relaxed. He dragged his gaze from the window to glance at her, turning back almost at once to watch a lighted cargo ship moving up the river. "The doctors insisted that I stop working for a while. There were a couple of operations. It's been a long haul."

Sage noted the controlled features. Only his eyes betrayed him. "Oh, David, I'm so sorry. You've had a rough time."

"I've had my blessings." Suddenly he was looking at her again, his face cleared. "I rediscovered Charleston. I was here years ago, but I really didn't get to know the town."

She studied him as if he was a piece of sculpture, the fine detail of the deep-set eyes, the straight nose, the curve of his lips, all painstakingly modeled. Oddly, she thought of Roper's face with it broad brow, square chin, jutting cheekbones. By contrast it might have been chipped from stone with primitive tools. "I'm glad you like the town," she murmured. Then he was leaning back in his chair, away from her, as if all questions had been answered. "Peter," she found herself blurting out the name. "Have you been together for a long time?"

"He was a physical therapist at the hospital. He worked with me after the last operation. I talked him into giving up his job for a while. I wanted to travel and there were things I couldn't do for myself in the beginning, like driving. I think he liked the idea of a change." David took a big drink of his martini.

"Your mother—"

"At the moment she's at the family house in Boston." He laughed. "A great echoing vault. She was here a few months ago I think at Mille Fleurs, the plantation."

"I knew Mille Fleurs had been sold, back in the seventies, but I didn't know who'd bought it."

"I've always loved it. I spent a couple of Christmas vacations there several years ago. As a matter of fact I went to some of the debut parties here in town. It's even possible that we met then."

"Yes," she said.

He paused as the waiter served bowls of cold cherry soup, then he leaned toward her. "You can still see the pattern of the old rice fields and there's an honest-to-God gazebo down by the water. Of course Mother's made some unfortunate changes but—"

"I've been there, David. Oh, not since I was a child but it used to belong to friends of the family, the Darcys. I remember the camellia garden and playing croquet on that side lawn—"

"Sage, let's go out there, tomorrow! Would you like that? It only takes about an hour to get there."

"I'll fix a picnic lunch!"

"Great. We'll make a day of it."

They ate their soup in companionable silence. Over the crabmeat *ravigote* and *blanquette de veau* they talked about memorable picnics. David described clambakes on Cape Cod, and Sage told him about the oyster roasts on Wadmalaw Island. It wasn't until they'd finished their chocolate mousse that David began to ask questions of his own.

"Tell me about your family," he said. "I was fascinated with the diaries, the ones you loaned Bea. I hope you don't mind that I read them. History's my passion, you know, and nothing gives the feeling of an era like diaries."

Sage told him about the Huguenot Delacours who came to America to escape religious persecution, about Louis Benford, the Hampshire shopkeeper who'd cleared the land, made a fortune in indigo and then rice.

"The house where you live now—" David's eyes shone with interest. "It must have been built about 1840 or a little later. Where did the Benfords live before that?"

"On the plantation. Of course they had a place in town, much smaller, but that was sold when my great-great-grandfather built the new one. When Union soldiers burned the plantation the family moved into town permanently."

"And you grew up there?"

"Yes. My parents died when I was child. Gran raised Elise and me."

"I can't imagine living so long in one house. My mother has a mania for buying and selling houses. We've always had the echoing vault in Boston, but when I'd leave school for holidays or the summer I'd have to check and see if I was going to Palm Beach, Charleston, Bar Harbor, or Antibes. One summer, it was a crumbling castle in southern Ireland."

"What fun!" said Sage, suddenly envisioning him on a white stallion riding through an Irish mist. The pianist was playing "Night and Day." She hummed a little under her breath, wondering why she liked the music of her mother's day so much more than the current songs.

"I know it will be hard for you to give it up," he said softly.

"Give it up?" echoed Sage. Here it comes, she thought. He's going to make an offer. She felt as if she'd fallen from a great height.

"Bea said you'd probably have to sell it."

Sage looked down at Gran's wide gold bracelet on her wrist. She thought of the beauty parlor, the cosmetics, her waiting for the knocker to sound, running upstairs to comb her hair again. She couldn't speak.

There was no need. Peter Larson was beside the table, with his blank face. His eyes looked opaque. "It's almost nine." He addressed David as if she wasn't there. David ignored him. Whatever Sage was feeling must have been written on her face. David was staring at her in bewilderment.

"I said you're late." Peter's voice was harsh. Then his hand was on David's arm as if he were apprehending him. "It's time to go."

David shook him off, pushed back his chair, and stood. "We're not going," he said thickly, his eyes still on Sage.

Peter moved in a step, hands clenched at his side. "You promised—"

"I've changed my mind." David pulled out his wallet, threw some bills on the table. "Take care of it," he snapped at Peter. Then he was helping Sage out of her chair, leading her between the tables.

When they reached the street she realized that they'd passed the parking lot. She stopped. "David, where are we going?"

"Let's walk." His voice was strained. "I hope you don't mind missing the concert."

"David, I—"

"Just a few blocks. Please."

They went more than a few blocks and finally reached the Battery. In silence they moved along the wide sidewalk above the sea wall. Across the street stretched a line of nineteenth-century mansions. On the other side, the dark waters of the harbor broke against the rocks below. At last David stopped, looking across at a house of particular grandeur with long piazzas, French doors leading onto wrought-iron balconies. "In 1860," he said, "there were howitzers mounted right here by the wall. Later, that house over there was almost hit, when the town was bombarded from across the harbor. A shell burst in the yard."

She saw nothing. She was aware of the water moving over the rocks, the sound of passing cars. David continued to stare at the house as if trying to solve some puzzle. "If I believed in reincarnation," he said, "I'd be certain I lived in this town in another life. When I first came here, walked down these streets, I couldn't get over the beauty of it. Still I wasn't surprised. It all seemed so familiar. Sage—" he took her unresponsive hand in his "—you'll never guess what I've done. I'm buying that house. I sign the papers next week. I'm going to open a school for gifted children, just eight grades." He squeezed her hand. "It's a dream I've had for a long time."

At first she was too stunned to answer, too mired in the certainty that the evening had been designed with ulterior motives. She'd been wrong. He didn't want her house. That wasn't why he asked her out. Her hand quickened in his. "I'm so happy for you," she choked. "David, that's wonderful!"

"Sage, don't mention it to anyone yet."

"I promise. Yes," she said.

"We'd better go back. Peter will be looking for us. Poor old Peter tends to be too protective of me. You mustn't mind him, Sage."

Hand in hand they returned to the parking lot but Peter was nowhere to be seen. "I don't know where he could be," said David. "He always waits."

All at once the voice came from behind him. "Are you ready to go?"

The street lamp eerily highlighted Peter's face, turning it into a tribal mask.

In silence they drove back to her house, Peter at the wheel. Still silent, David walked her to the door, took the keys from her hand and unlocked it. He looked into her eyes, touched her hand to his lips and smiled. Then he was gone.

Followed by Major, she went dreamily up the steps to the second floor. She noticed with some surprise that there was a light on in her work room. That was odd. When she'd left the house it was not yet dark. She went in, paused by her desk, looked around with some trepidation. Nothing seemed disturbed. Then she saw the book lying face down on her typewriter. She had no memory of leaving it there. Picking it up, she saw that it was a book of nineteenth-century poems. It had been left open with one verse marked by a blue line. She frowned. Could her mind have been such a jumble that she'd forgotten handling the book? Could she have taken it from the shelf, started to read it, then been interrupted, maybe by a phone call?

The poem, by Edward Rowland Sill, was called "A Morning Thought." She read the verse marked in blue. She read it again.

And what if then, while the still
Morning brightened,
And freshened in the elm the
Summer's breath,
Should gravely smile on me
The gentle angel
And take my hand and say,
My name is Death.

EIGHT

IN THE cold light of day she decided that the book on the typewriter was her own doing. Certainly she'd been distracted the day before, getting ready for her date with David. The verse could have been marked years before, by someone of Gran's generation. But it had unnerved her. She moved in a trance of inefficiency, forgetting to plug in the coffee pot and neglecting to let out the dog until he barked with indignation. She went out with Major and was standing on the steps looking into the garden when Roper appeared on his patio. Dressed in his usual work clothes, he carried what looked to be a large bag of groceries as well as a fishing rod and a cooler. "Good morning!" he shouted.

Before she could turn to go back in the house he'd stashed his things in the station wagon and was striding toward her. "How about a day in the country, Sage? I'm heading for my aunt and uncle's place on Edisto."

Sage glanced down at him as if he were selling vacuum cleaners. Despite the fact that she was wearing an old cotton wrapper that Amanda de Vries wouldn't be caught dead in, she moved in an aura of superb aplomb.

"Go throw on some clothes. I'll wait for you." Roper took the steps two at a time and was suddenly beside her, his big, muscular body exuding vitality.

She avoided his eyes, fixed her gaze on the cleft of his chin. "Thanks," she said with the trace of a Long Island drawl, "but I'm tied up today." Languidly she brushed back her hair. "Another time, maybe."

His eyebrows rose. With annoyance she saw him suppress a smile. "There's nothing like country air to clear the mind," he said.

"I assure you, my mind is clear as a bell."

"By the way, who's the guy in the eight-hundred-dollar suit? The tall, dark stranger?"

So he had seen her leave with David the night before. The thought gave her keen pleasure. "A friend," she said casually.

Roper leaned against the iron railing, hands in his pockets. He shook his head in mock concern. "You've got to be wary of strangers, Mary Sage. Didn't your granny tell you? Especially now, with the town under siege. All these Yankees coming in to steal our way of life. All these carpetbaggers insisting our local girls learn to read and write and cook French."

Sage aimed at a brittle laugh. "I'm sure we'll survive."

"So am I, but we've got to close ranks. Look at it this way, the town's been three times occupied by enemy forces. First by the British during the Revolution, then by the Union army in the 1860s, and now by all these greedy developers and romantic strangers in big, shiny cars—"

"And sexy ladies in yellow Corvettes?" She looked at him squarely, quite pleased with herself.

For an instant he was puzzled, then his face cleared. He threw back his head and laughed. "Why, Mary Sage Eliot! Shame on you! Spying on your tenants.

Tell me, did you use binoculars or crouch in the bushes?'' He laughed again with pure delight.

"If you'll excuse me, I have things to do.'' Sage turned away, but Roper grabbed her arm. "Was it jealousy, Sage? Do tell me it was jealousy.''

"Will you please—''

"The sexy lady in the yellow Corvette, I'm sorry to say, is my first cousin, Serena. Surely you remember Serena. No, maybe you don't. She's a good bit older, married and left town years ago. She just came back. She's in the throes of a divorce and having a pretty bad time.''

"It's no concern of—''

Without warning he moved in, his face very close. She could see a film of perspiration on the deeply tanned skin. "Never mind Serena. What's going on, Sage? Aside from the dark stranger? More sounds on the top floor? What is it?''

She couldn't meet the scrutiny of those searching topaz eyes but she lifted her chin. "Nothing,'' she mumbled.

"Dammit!'' He released her but before she could move away his hands were cupping her head. For a wild moment she thought he was going to kiss her. He did, a quick kiss on the end of her nose. Before she had time to retaliate he was down the steps and headed for his car.

David was to meet her at Mille Fleurs at twelve o'clock. She knew he was disappointed that she was taking her own car, but he'd accepted her phony excuse that she would be stopping on the way to visit an aunt in Georgetown. She had no intention of riding to and from the plantation with Peter Larson seething behind the wheel.

She went upstairs to survey her new wardrobe. Walking around a plantation called for plain, country clothes, comfortable shoes, but she looked longingly at a flowered dress that evoked visions of a fête champêtre. She thought of the old leghorn hat she'd found in one of the storerooms, and imagined the blue velvet ribbons trailing down her back.

The sound of the phone shattered this reverie; Bea Bonham's voice brought her back to earth. "Sage, Octo left some jars of murky-looking soup for you. Asked me to drop it off. She's gone to a meeting of the Friends of Old Charleston. Are you going to be home?"

"Bea, I'm going out. I'll stop by your place and pick it up." She didn't want to entertain Bea or anyone else that morning.

"If you can't find a place to park," said Bea, "just honk, and I'll dart out with the soup."

Sage settled on a gauzy Indian cotton dress, full-skirted and the color of periwinkles. She could imagine the remarks that Roper would make if he spotted her in yards of flowered batiste and a leghorn hat. She decided it was warm enough to go without a coat and instead wrapped a creamy cashmere shawl around her shoulders.

She drove to the supermarket where, in the gourmet boutique, she spent far too much money on fresh crabmeat salad packed in ice, a whole Brie, French bread, grapes, and a bottle of wine. When she parked in front of Bea's house she noticed that David's car was not in the driveway. She decided that he must have gone to the plantation earlier to prepare for her visit. She sat for several seconds, enjoying the thought.

Opening the door, Bea didn't speak at once, giving herself time to adjust to Sage's new look. "The butterfly has emerged at last," she said with finality, as if no further comment was needed. "Come on in, sweetie." She wore a black and white Japanese kimono; an orange towel was wrapped turbanlike around her head. "I'll get you a cup of coffee." She led Sage into the house. "I'm glad you came by. I'm bushed. Been writing like a mad woman. Just finished the chapter where my heroine almost gets raped by a Yankee deserter but is saved in the nick by a carpetbagger, who's really the hero and a Confederate spy. He—"

"Bea, I can't stay. I've got an appointment." Sage was struck anew by the way Bea had made an eighteenth-century house look like a camper trailer. When she'd first met her, she'd sensed something off-key, fraudulent. Bea's ready smiles never seemed to reach her eyes, as coolly appraising as an insurance adjustor's. Now, like the rest of the town, except for Elise, Sage was disarmed by Bea's quick intelligence and amusingly bizarre ways.

"Sit for a minute." Bea moved into the drawing room, gathered a bunch of old newspapers from a lounger and deposited them on a black plastic coffee table. Sage sat reluctantly, imagining what Elise would say about the overflowing ashtrays, the dust balls in the corners. An acid green shag rug looked like the bottom of a fish bowl.

"Something important?" Bea's eyes glinted with interest.

Sage decided not to be coy. "I'm meeting David Raeburn out at Mille Fleurs Plantation."

"The dashing David. A tryst! Splendid!" Bea dropped into an overstuffed sofa, pulled a withered apple core from between the cushions, and tossed it into the fireplace. "I heard his mother has a place down here. Apparently the lady's really loaded. Paying off two former husbands didn't even make a dent in the Raeburn pile. David's daddy made the fortune, you know, died when David was a tyke." She put her slippered feet on the coffee table, knocking over an empty glass. "How nice to be able to afford one's lapses of judgment."

"Did David tell you about his mother?" Sage felt a pang of disappointment that David should confide in Bea.

"Lord, no. He's not about to give out information. I have my own sources."

"Sources?"

Bea laughed. "Sweetie, I'm a novelist, remember? I'm a hound for research. There's a graduate student up in Richmond who does a little work for me on the side." Bea lit a cigarette, threw the lighter on the coffee table, and ignored the fact that it bounced onto the floor. "She's working on a degree in library science and can use a little extra cash. Also, one of her ex-lovers used to work for the FBI. He still has friends—"

"You had her investigate David?"

"She's just getting a little background material for me." Bea blew out a long stream of smoke. "I admit to an insatiable curiosity about people. Part of being a writer, I guess." The fleshy face under the turban looked old and secretive. "The unexplained, the mysterious, the inscrutable drives me up the wall."

Sage felt that she was no better than Bea but she couldn't help herself. "What else did she learn about him?"

"So far Barbara's only come up with *Who's Who* type of info but she's still digging." Bea squinted reflectively at a wall empty of pictures. "I have a gut feeling that there's something fascinating about Mr. David Raeburn. To say nothing of that son of a Nazi, Peter Larson."

Watching Bea, Sage thought of a great spider waiting in its web. She looked away. Bea must have noticed her gazing at a battered wicker chair on one side of the Adam fireplace. She snorted. "Not exactly *House and Garden,* is it, sweetie? But I'm a gypsy not a nester. Though Charleston tempts me. Who knows, I may pitch my tent for keeps, mend my ways, and become president of the DAR."

Sage stood. "Bea, I really have to go."

"OK." Bea got to her feet with an ease that denied her weight and her years. "It's a perfect day for the country. Heaven smiles and the whole world bursts into bloom." When they reached the hall she picked up the mason jars of soup from a table piled with books, papers, and manila envelopes, and handed them to Sage. "Is everything OK with you, Sage?"

"I'm fine, Bea."

"I think you should have a change of scenery. You need to get out of that house. It's been a kind of prison for you these last years. I have a reasonably comfortable guest room—"

"I think I'd rather stay put right now, Bea. But thanks."

"The offer stands." Bea patted her arm. "As soon as I get the dope on our man of mystery, I'll call you."

Sage drove uptown, crossed the Cooper River bridge, and was several miles beyond Mount Pleasant before she was able to relax. She'd been shocked to learn that Bea was investigating David and ashamed of her own curiosity. Of course the last few days had brought a number of shocks. A week ago the most exciting thing in her life would have been an Ashley Hall alumnae tea. She realized that her recent encounters with men had been limited to Elise's agonizing dinner parties and streetcorner meetings with doddering friends of Gran. She had given up hoping for a David Raeburn, finally accepting the fact that life, far from being true to fiction, often was a parody of it. She wished she could find this amusing. To the very end, Gran had been able to laugh at herself. "I expected more structure," the old lady had said, "a third act that provided some great revelation, resolving the plot and completing the theme." Staring at the road ahead, Sage worked at a wry smile, wishing she didn't feel sixteen again.

The air coming in the car window smelled of the sea, the marshes, new growth. She took a deep breath. The day stretched ahead of her, golden and promising.

Still she felt a stab of self-doubt. What if she was wrong about David? What if he assumed that her coming to Mille Fleurs meant a sexual fling? Worse, what if he expected her, at twenty-six, to have some experience. Worse still was the fact that she found it hard to think of David in this way. She recalled the talk she'd had with Elise the same year that Gran had tried to teach her how to flirt. Elise was not much better equipped than Gran to explain sexuality. "The new feelings you begin to have about men? There's nothing wrong with them. They're normal." Turning from the searchlight of Sage's gaze, she'd lit a cigarette, caught a glimpse of herself in the pier glass, and smoothed her hair. "You've had these feelings, haven't you?" she'd asked. "I mean, when you look at men?"

"I've had them," said Sage, "but mostly when, well, when I listen to music. Like the 'Liebestod.' Or read certain poems, like—" she'd stopped at Elise's look of bafflement. "Or sometimes when I walk alone on the beach," she'd finished lamely.

Over the years she'd admired certain actors, but never yearned for them. None of the males she'd grown up with had sent her blood racing. A handsome face, an imposing set of muscles viewed out of context failed to arouse her. But one worn fantasy still left her weak with longing. She'd kept it for years like a spray of flowers pressed between the pages of a book. She saw a family sitting before an open fire, one child reading, the other two playing checkers. She saw herself sitting on the floor, leaning back against a still faceless man, feeling his arms encircling her, knowing that later in the night they would lie together in an ecstasy that shut out loneliness, fear, confusion, that was both an avowal and a benediction.

She wondered about Elise and Clay. It was obvious that Elise adored him, ran herself ragged trying to keep a flawless house, look like a vision, and make up for the fact that she hadn't produced an heir. Everything revolved around Clay. Once Sage had seen her sister drag herself from her bed and, flushed with a high fever, preside at a seated dinner for eighteen. "It's important!" Elise had insisted, as Sage helped her dress. "Two of these men are bankers from New York and—my God, I look a fright!" Elise worried constantly about falling short of perfection. Sage wondered if she ever was happy and relaxed, if there were nights when she and Clay lay in each other's arms and he reassured her, praised her, loved her. Then, in one of those moments relevant to nothing, she thought of Roper, an unwelcome thought that she quickly thrust from her mind.

The road to Mille Fleurs turned inland from the coast. Sage left behind the stretches of salt marsh and drove west. Here there were still tracts of pine forest opening on savannas deep in rushes and small cane, fields of broomgrass. Within my lifetime, she thought, all this could disappear, be lost to housing developments, factories, highways. We pretend we can save it but we can't. Let it go, she told herself. You can't keep the Charleston, the Low Country of your childhood, forever. Each generation must accept change, have faith. She wondered if all the changes in her life and the town could be making her paranoid, prompting her to invent noises in the night, convincing her that she'd seen a dark figure when she'd crept to the top floor. She could have left the fur coat on a chair by the steps days before, picked it up that night without realizing it. The maid could have moved the books.

She turned into a dirt road, passed an unused field, and began to drive through the woods, pines and scrub trees rising from a tangle of underbrush. She passed the small sign that said Mille Fleurs, drove another half mile, and then saw the caretaker's house, a one-story frame cottage with a vegetable patch. It looked uninhabited but she noticed a red pickup truck parked near the mailbox.

It was as if she were ten years old again, eager to reach the house and see Anne and Thomas Darcy running out to meet her. They would all get in an old rowboat and paddle around the river. Thomas, as usual, would win at croquet. After an enormous family dinner and with dusk falling, they would chase fireflies, running along the brick paths of the garden from which the plantation took its name. For generations, Mille Fleurs had been celebrated for its extravagance of camellias. Sage remembered her feeling of awe when she first saw the garden in full bloom, walked through the profusion of velvety flowers, white, pale pink, burning red. She had asked her grandmother why they had no fragrance. "That much beauty," Gran had told her, "feels no need to announce itself."

The road curved and formed a circle in front of the house, which faced the river and the remains of the rice fields. Plain in comparison to the neoclassical mansions built later, it made no apologies, standing in the grace of fine proportions and practicality, the great garden of camellias spread out below.

Sage stepped on the brake and caught her breath. The camellias, the brick path, the fountain with its dancing faun had disappeared. In their place was a huge, free-form swimming pool, paved round with flagstones set in cement. There were a number of potted plants, lounges, wrought-iron chairs and tables with furled umbrellas.

NINE

WHEN SHE PARKED near the pool she noticed that David's car was nowhere to be seen. He hadn't come early after all. She sat on one of the wrought-iron chairs, looked at her watch. If anything, she was a bit late. Feet primly together, hands folded over the purse in her lap, she stared at the bottom of the emptied pool where a dead raccoon lay, crawling with insects. She closed her eyes, trying to unscramble her thoughts. Forget about the camellia garden, she commanded. It's gone forever. Anyway, all the old Darcys have died. Anne and Thomas have moved away. David may not come. He could have changed his mind. Face that possibility. This isn't the end of the world. The worst that could happen is a canceled picnic, not a shattered romance. There are far more important things to think about. There are decision to be made. Like selling the house, paying for graduate school. When I open my eyes, she thought, I'm going to take control, make a new start. When she opened her eyes she saw him.

Framed in the arching branch of a huge oak, the distant figure sat at the river's edge. She could make out the graceful lines of his body. He held a drawing pad and his hand moved over it with small, swift strokes. The dark clouds banking in the north sharpened the blueness of the sky, the shadow of the great oak, the light on the river. She walked almost in slow motion as her feet sank into the soft grass.

She was certain he was unaware of her. His hand now lay still on the drawing pad. Dark head raised, he looked out beyond the river toward the marsh, the ruined ditches and canals. Then when she was within a few feet of him, he spoke without turning. "They really shaped the land," he said, "turning marshes into rice fields, swamps into lagoons, built gardens in the wilderness. I wish I'd been here." He stared down at his drawing, then started to erase something. Abruptly he threw the pad to one side. Still facing the river, he lifted his arm. "Give me your hand."

She was surprised to find that his fingers were chilled. He pulled her down beside him. When he finally turned, his eyes reflected none of the sadness in his voice. After briefly searching hers they shone with pleasure. "This makes up for my failed effort," he said with a smile.

"May I see it?"

"No. It's not good. I have what my mother calls 'a small but charming talent.'" He looked back across the river. "I come out here often just to watch the light change, particularly in the late afternoon."

"I'm glad you love it here." Sage wanted to rub his hands, warm them.

"She's going to leave the place to me." David glanced back toward the house. "Someday I'll restore it, tear up that pool and bring back the garden." Sage thought of the generations who had worked to create the garden, the years it had taken; but she smiled in agreement.

"Of course I'll have to have the house in town," he said, "if I open a school, but I'll come here every weekend and for holidays. Can you imagine celebrating Christmas here?"

"I've been here at Christmas, David. It was wonderful! A big tree from the woods, smilax over all the doorways, a Yule log. I remember we had roast wild turkey and venison, syllabub and three kinds of pie. All six Darcy children were home. We sang carols and popped corn and Mr. Darcy and old Grandpa Darcy took turns telling stories in Gullah."

"I'd like to have children," he said, holding her hand in a firm grip. When he turned to her there was more color in his face. "We're very much alike, you and I. I felt it the first time I saw you. It was months ago, at that gathering for some concert pianist. I had a halting conversation with a Wall Street broker and lost a battle of wits with a local music critic. Then I saw you standing in a corner. You looked like a young queen waiting to be executed."

Sage grinned. "My sister is determined to sweep me into her social whirl. I keep telling her it's hopeless." She looked out across the broken dikes, the greening marsh. "As you said, I was born in the wrong era. I'm not sure where I belong."

"The age of chivalry." He looked down at her hand in his. "You remind me of words no one uses anymore, words I'd want to teach my children. Honor, fidelity, grace." He released her hand, picked up the drawing pad, flipped over his sketch, and looked at a blank page. For what seemed minutes, he studied the empty paper, as if expecting some vision to emerge.

"May I see your drawing?" she asked softly.

"No!" He spoke sharply, then turned back to her apologetically. "As I said, it's a failed effort. But I did catch this once." His look traced the curve of the river, the fields fading into the dark line of trees at the horizon. "A watercolor, painted on a wet page. Later than this, though, almost at dusk. For some reason it worked.''

''I'd love to see it.''

''It's back at the house somewhere. In my room, I guess. I'll have to look.'' He pulled himself to his feet. ''I was going to find us a bottle of wine anyway.'' He stood motionless above her. ''You'll wait?'' It was a light question. She was astonished to see concern in his face. He covered it with a smile. ''You won't vanish?''

''I won't vanish, David.''

''I was afraid you wouldn't come today.''

''And I had no idea you were already here. I didn't see your car.''

He hesitated. ''I parked behind the caretaker's cottage.''

''Peter—''

''Peter couldn't make it,'' he said shortly.

She didn't watch him head for the house. She watched the tarnished clouds moving south, the weakening light on the river. In the water below her a blue teal glided by, followed by six ducklings. She sat quietly, reflecting on what he'd said about her.

She thought of going to the car to get the picnic lunch, but didn't want him to come back and find her gone. A thin rain began to fall. Spots widened on the drawing pad, then she felt it on her head and shoulders. She rose without haste, glanced at her watch, and realized that David had been gone for almost half an hour. Gathering up her purse, the drawing pad, and his box of paints, she began to run toward the house. When she reached the pool, she looked up at the blank windows, then made her way through the tables and chairs, climbed the steps to the back entrance. The door was half open. Inside the air was ten degrees cooler.

It bore no resemblance to the room she remembered, the Darcy living room that had seemed always filled with children and dogs, open books, bowls of fruit, half-finished crossword puzzles, Mr. Darcy's collection of pipes. Fragile curtains of patterned silk hung at the windows. A huge sofa covered with ivory velvet faced the fireplace, dominating a careful arrangement of modern and period furniture. One end of a grand piano and several tables were crowded with silver-framed photographs.

"David?" she called. She called him again as she walked to the front entry hall. The dining room was also unrecognizable. One wall had been completely mirrored, the pine floor covered with black and white tiles. The table was made of chrome and glass.

She was aware of the stillness of the house, a bated feeling, the darkening world beyond the windows. She called again, then went back to the living room, unsure of whether she should wait there or go in search of him. She stared at the profusion of photographs, trying to find one of David. Again and again she saw a particular face, an exquisite blond woman meeting the camera with a defiant smile. She was never alone. A polo player posed with his arm around her waist. She leaned against a bare-chested young man on the deck of a sailboat. She and an escort of piratical good looks were caught, in full evening dress, entering what looked to be a Moorish palace. David's mother. In group pictures taken on terraces, on beaches, in nightclubs, that beautiful face trapped the eye. A few pictures seemed to be of David. One showed a boy of about five waiting in front of a doorway, his face in a rigid frown. A few years later he sat stiffly on a pony. A young man of twenty wore a cap and gown and a smile that didn't reach his eyes. As she picked up the picture, a sudden sound from overhead almost made her drop it. She replaced it quickly, looking up at the chandelier of painted metal flowers. He must be in the room above.

The stairway, thickly carpeted in pale green, rose at the end of the hall. Each step greeted her with a faint creak. "David?" she called again. The house swallowed her voice. Four doors faced her on the second floor. She tapped on the first one, waited, then opened it. Even in the failing light the room had an eerie glow. At first she thought it was the pervasive whiteness of walls, carpet, and tangle of pale sheets below the carved, gold headboard. Then she realized it was light caught and held in the fragments of glass strewn on the floor by the dressing table. There was a great jagged hole in the mirror. Shattered bits of it lay amid the litter of perfume bottles, empty pill containers, silver combs and brushes.

She took a compulsive backward step, expecting the owner to appear from inside a closet, return from another room in rage or tears. Her eyes moved to the open door of a bathroom. Inside a blue basin with gold dolphin faucets lay a crumbled towel, darkly stained. The room seemed charged with violence, as if something unspeakable had happened there minutes before. Yet, she saw dust, like a film of snow over everything, even the two glasses on the bedside table, the empty champagne bottle.

At first she wasn't sure she'd heard the sound. Then it came again, lost in a clap of thunder, sharp as gunshot. A flash of lightning fired the windows, turned the trees beyond an iridescent green. When it was over the sky was even darker. Sage went into the hall. She looked uncertainly at the other three doors. The nearest one was not quite closed. She looked inside. It was a decorator's idea of a man's room, in tones of beige and brown with a handsome sleigh bed. Above the mantel was an antique sword hanging below a fox-hunting print. A high-backed armchair faced the window. The room was so dim she almost missed the hand on the arm of the chair. Then she moved into the room and saw him. His face was bloodless. For the first time she realized that he hadn't changed clothes since the night before. His tie was undone, and in his wilted shirt, wrinkled suit, he had an almost vagrant look. His eyes were closed.

"David?" she whispered. She moved to the window, faced him. "David?"

When he opened his eyes she saw no recognition, then slowly the color returned to his face. "Sage."

She thought of the pictures downstairs of the boy, the young man, and of the woman with her succession of men. She thought of encounters ending in broken mirrors and blood in the basin. "I found you," she said gently. He reached out, groped for her hand. She knelt down next to the chair. On the floor beside her lay a crumpled drawing. He said nothing, clung to her hand and closed his eyes again.

She was confused. Why had he left her for so long? Why was he sitting here, looking like a stricken child? "The rain doesn't matter," she said. "We'll have our picnic indoors."

"It was a mistake." His words were almost inaudible. She knew at once what he meant. Anything reminding him of his mother, his childhood, was painful.

"Then we'll go," she reassured him. He opened his eyes and stared out at the driveway, the river. She spoke tentatively, her hand warm in his. "David?" She held his hand tighter, as if this might force him into some contact with her. "It's good to be back at Mille Fleurs," she said. "I have wonderful memories of this place. You know, when I turned in the drive I felt ten years old again. I found myself looking for Thomas and Anne. Sometimes they used to hide in that big oak by the back entrance. They'd jump down and surprise me." She paused, hoping for some response, then hurried on. "I expected to see all the other Darcys on the piazza, Sam playing chess with his grandfather, Grandma Darcy with a lapful of embroidery, Mr. and Mrs. Darcy sitting on the swing with palmetto fans, 'talking lazy,' as Gran used to say, Aunt Belle bringing out a tray of iced tea. When Gran and Lise and I got out of the car, we always heard them laughing. One Sunday—" she stopped. He'd turned to her and she realized he hadn't heard a word she'd said. "David?"

"Why haven't you married?" he asked suddenly.

She caught her breath. It was so unexpected, so absurd, she burst out laughing. "There must have been someone," he cut off her laugh, waited for an answer.

"Why, I—David, I—" The fierceness of his gaze shook her. She groped for a response. She didn't want to announce that there had been a dearth of proposals. She was suddenly reminded of a similar conversation with Roper. She tried an Amanda de Vries insouciance. "I'm a free agent," she teased airily. "No

long-term commitments for me. Haven't you heard of
women's lib or, as we say in Charleston, ladies' lib?
Meaningful relationships with an open door pol-
icy—'' The look of shock on his face astounded her.
He was taking her seriously. He actually believed that
she...she couldn't stop herself. She was laughing
again, mostly from nervousness, laughter that rose in
pitch and volume until she was shaking with it. "Oh,
David," she choked, "if you could see your face." She
was laughing beyond control, tears streaming down
her cheeks.

He slapped her. He slapped her so hard she felt her
neck snap, found herself knocked back on her heels.
He leaned toward her, eyes black with rage. She jerked
away, so appalled she could barely speak. "David,"
she whispered, "I was joking. You must have known."
He grabbed her arm and she braced herself for another blow. Roughly he drew her to her knees and then
his arms were around her, holding her against him.
She could feel his heart beating, feel his breath against
her brow. Abruptly he grabbed her by the hair, pulled
back her head. His lips were on hers, hard, desperate.
He does care about me, she told herself. He only
slapped me because I'd become hysterical. She
clutched his arms, trying to respond, already seeing
what was going to happen, she and David lying naked
on the bed, transformed by passion. His grinding kiss
was painful. She ignored this, intent on experiencing
whatever was to come. She was no longer singing on
the beat, no longer a leftover from the nineteenth
century. It didn't matter that she felt no unbridled lust.
That would come in a minute. What she did feel was
a determined recklessness.

All at once he stiffened. He lurched away from her, thrusting her backward. She stared up at him, saw that he was looking at something beyond the window. Scrambling to her knees she looked out and saw for herself. She watched Peter Larson walk away from a small, gray car and head for the house. He passed through the rain as if unaware of it.

In an instant David was on his feet, fists clenched, his whole body braced. He turned from the window, his eyes searching the room. "David." Her hand reached for him.

He struck at her hand, gave her a vicious glance. "Stay here!" It was a command. Then he was tearing the old sword from above the mantel, wrenching it from the hooks. He threw down the sheath and with the blade in his hand rushed to the door and grabbed the key. She heard him lock the door on the other side.

She didn't move, stunned by the wild improbability of what had happened. Then she remembered Peter Larson's cold fury when he'd forced David to leave Elise's party, remembered him following her and David the night before with the stealth of a jungle cat.

The shout of rage rang through the house, rising from below, echoing in the upstairs hall, a tearing cry. Sage ran to the door and pressed against it, trying to identify the voice, but the voices ran together, shrill with anger. She heard them on the steps, heard the thud of blows, grunts of pain, a loud, metallic clang. Then silence.

For what seemed an eternity there was no sound at all. Then she was aware of creakings, soft, measured, as someone cautiously climbed the stairs. She knew who was coming. Within seconds the key would turn the lock, the door would open. She'd see that mask of

a face under the silvery hair, look into those colorless
eyes. She stumbled across the room, pulled up a window. The wind-driven rain beat against her face and
arms as she crawled out to the upstairs piazza. Not
daring to pause, trying to remember which room was
closest to the back stairs, she ran to the far end of the
house. She reached what she was sure was the old
nursery above the curve of the driveway, tried to push
up the window. Again and again she tried to raise it.
In desperation she pulled off her shoe and struck at the
pane over the lock. The glass fell around her, biting
her legs. She put her hand through the broken pane,
turned the lock. Once inside she stopped in panic, sure
it was the wrong room, then realized it was no longer
a nursery. It had been turned into another bedroom
with pale blue furniture, blue flowered curtains and
spread. She crept to the door, opened it and gasped
with relief to find that she was in the back corridor.
She remembered the narrow steps leading to the pantry, with another flight down to the ground floor under the main piazza. She paused, listening. There was
no sound but the rain. She stopped again when she
reached the ground floor, standing among garden
tools, a rusting bicycle, coquet mallets. She moved
under the steps leading up to the front door, put on her
shoes. She made a run for it. Praying for invisibility,
she tore past the side of the house, the swimming pool
and hurled herself into her car.

The rain was slashing through the windows on the
far side. She twisted around, closed them quickly, then
slid back under the steering wheel. At first, in her
haste to roll up the window beside her, she thought it
was stuck. Then she saw the broad fingers holding
down the glass. She glanced up. He looked as though

he'd crawled out of the sea. Rain flattened the white blond hair, streamed down the crevices of his face, a blank mask.

With a strangled cry she pulled away, tried to turn the key in the ignition, but one of the hands shot through the window and gripped her arm. The other hand grasped her face, turned it toward him.

"Leave him alone." His voice was guttural, without expression, frighteningly at odds with the violence in his hands. "Leave him alone," he repeated, his eyes cold, awash with rain, the color of rain.

With a great wrench she freed herself, turned the key, stepped on the gas. The car hurtled forward. Heedlessly she made a turn on the lawn, got back on the drive, and headed for the road. The ruts were filling with water and the branch of an old oak had fallen near the bathhouse. The small car kept skidding. Leaves and twigs fell on the hood, blew against the windshield, but she dared not go slower. As she reached the caretaker's house, she looked in the car mirror and saw him still standing there as if he were not only unaware of the storm, but a part of it.

The slow drive home on the flooded highway through a clawing wind forced her to concentrate on handling the car. Her clothes clung wetly to her body. Her hands and feet felt frozen. She couldn't stop shaking. She was profoundly shocked by what had happened, the frightening behavior of the two men. David, so endearing one moment, had turned on her like a maniac. Questions crowded her mind. By the time she reached the rise of the Cooper River bridge the rain had slackened. She was half surprised to see that the town was still there.

When she pulled into her driveway, she noticed with relief that the carriage house looked closed. The station wagon was gone. She went in the ground floor entrance by the laundry room and was starting up the dimly lit steps when the door to the apartment opened.

Franny Barth was wearing her red robe. Her face was lustrous with fresh makeup, her long hair pulled back and tied with a silver ribbon. "Miss—Sage—I've been waiting for you to come. I— Can you hold on a minute? I've got something for you." She smiled with the anticipation of a child. Her eyes glowed. Then she looked at Sage's soaked dress, muddy shoes, wet hair hanging in rat tails. "Say, you really got caught in it!"

Sage managed a smile. "I was out in the country. It took me by surprise." She edged toward the stairs, longing to be alone, exhausted by terror and confusion.

"Well, I know you want to go upstairs and get out of those wet clothes, so I'll just be a minute." Within seconds, Franny was back, holding a market basket. Inside was a white kitten about three months old, looking up at Sage with keen interest. Franny chattered nervously, as if she feared the offering might seem presumptuous. "I just thought—I mean, you being alone and all—this girl in the office is moving, had to give it away. I'd take it, but being gone all day—"

Sage could have cried with exasperation. She didn't want a kitten, had never cared for cats, but the fact that Franny was concerned touched her. "Franny, how nice of you! It's a beautiful kitten. I've never had a cat."

Franny giggled. "Well, you sure got one now."

"I'll have to find the right name," said Sage, taking the basket.

"I hope you don't mind, but I put some Kitty Litter in a box in the hall by your kitchen door."

"You've thought of everything. Thank you again." Despite the fact that she was wet, miserable, and longed to be alone, Sage found herself saying, "Franny, would you like to come up and have some supper with me? I could fix us a couple of omelets."

Franny looked stricken. "Oh, I wish I could! I'd sure like to, but—" Her eyes softened. "I'm expecting someone. Will you ask me again?"

"You can count on it."

Sage was aware of Franny watching her climb the stairs, sensing that the girl wanted somehow to cement this new friendship. A few minutes later when she stood outside her front door waiting for Major to come up from the garden she saw Franny's caller. She caught only a blurred glimpse of him, a tall figure dashing in the gate as if the rain had not stopped.

After she'd showered and dried her hair she went downstairs to feed the animals. The kitten had leapt onto the kitchen counter. Major sat close below, regarding it with a fond and proprietary air, paying no attention to the hisses of protest. Sage hadn't eaten since breakfast and was feeling a little dizzy, but once she'd fixed a plate of scrambled eggs she couldn't bring herself to eat. Guilt hit her like a falling building. Not only had she abandoned David but she'd fled like an animal in a mindless scurry for survival. She forced herself to eat two bites, swallowing with difficulty, reaching for some acceptable explanation for her cowardice. The best she could find was Gran's rule that one doesn't intrude on the private matters of others. How often when confronted with raised voices, arguments too heated to be considered civilized, Gran had managed to change the subject or gracefully excuse herself.

Sage realized that all along she'd been backing away from the idea of a homosexual relationship. She faced it now, admitting it was a logical explanation for Peter's jealous vigilance, David's moments of distracted torment. She remembered the way David had looked at her, searching her eyes for what he seemed to need most, her eloquent vision of him. She grasped at another explanation: Peter was blackmailing David. She could imagine David convalescing in the hospital, weak and dependent, confiding to his therapist, telling him things he'd never told anyone. About his mother? She'd been repelled by Peter Larson from the beginning. There was something unsavory, no, frightening about him, an aura of repressed violence. Poor David. Her concern was no longer for the romantic hero she'd fashioned in her mind but for someone far from heroic. She worried now for the man who seemed still half a boy and, in some strange way, a victim.

Bea sounded only half awake when she answered the phone. "Oh, Sage, it's you. I was watching this Hungarian make goulash on ETV and I fell asleep. How was the country? Did it rain on your parade?"

"Bea, I was just wondering—I mean, I was worried about David driving back in the storm. Did he get home all right?"

"No idea. Hang on a minute and I'll go take a look." Sage found herself holding her breath until she heard Bea's voice again. "There are lights on," Bea said, "and his car's in the drive. All safe and sound."

Sage fell asleep early that night, with Major snoring nearby and the kitten curled under her chin. She dreamed of gliding, soaring above the town at sunset, finding the two rivers, the steeples of St. Michael's and St. Philip's, looking into the flowering gardens behind familiar houses, seeing the world in beautiful and reassuring wholeness. Then the light shifted. The rivers were still there but what lay between was a foreign city, soaring pinnacles of concrete and steel.

TEN

WHEN THE PHONE RANG early the next morning, she thought with dread that it might be David and didn't answer at once. She was enormously relieved to hear Bea's voice.

"Sage, I don't want to upset you but I think you'd better come over and look in on Octo."

"What's wrong? Bea, she isn't—"

"No, no, she's all right. I mean, physically she's OK. It's just that—well, while she was at a Preservation Society meeting last night someone broke in, stole things, bits of jewelry, some silver, her TV. She's pretty upset. The place was really a mess."

"Bea, you're sure she's all right?"

"I swear it. I wouldn't have known what happened but she phoned late last night and asked if I'd seen anyone prowling around. She refused to call the police, swore me to secrecy. But I think someone in the family should know."

Twenty minutes later when she parked by Octo's house Sage noticed that the downstairs shutters were closed. For the first time she was struck by the coincidence that someone could be searching her house and that Octo should be robbed. She found the door leading from the street to the piazza locked. She entered by way of the garden, unlocked the front door, and let herself in. She called several times from the hallway but got no answer. The shuttered rooms had a funereal look. The daffodils on the dining room table drooped despondently. She called again. Glancing in the drawing room she saw with some bafflement small bits of paper propped on the furniture, pinned to the curtains. Going from one to another she found that each was a calling card, engraved with the name Octavia Lamar Benford. Above the name, in each instance, was a handwritten word. Spunky, proclaimed the card on the mantel; Level-headed said the one pinned to the curtains. On the sofa she found Lively, on the coffee table Cheerful. Starting up the stairs, she discovered Adventurous on the newel post. The card on the landing said Thrifty. The one on the top step showed the word Reverent crossed out and Optimistic written below it.

Her aunt was fast asleep, fully clothed and propped in a sitting position on her bed. The room could only be Octo's, sparsely furnished with bed, bureau, easy chair, a few small tables. What looked to be hundreds of books crowded the shelves, covering every flat surface. On the walls were cheaply framed prints of Octo's favorite paintings, a Giotto, an El Greco, Vermeer, Monet, Hopper. Swallowed by the huge four-poster Octo looked like a doll. In one hand she clasped an old dueling pistol. Its mate lay in an open velvet-lined box on the bedside table where a lamp still burned.

To Sage, Octo never had fit into the generation to which she undeniably belonged. Even Gran had seemed years older. There was a spark in Octo's eye that kept her spine straight, gave a sprightliness to her step. Each day presented her with some energizing revelation. But today Sage saw a very old lady, skin like wrinkled tissue paper, mouth agape, chin sagging. Patches of pink scalp showed through the thinning white curls.

"Aunt Octo," she whispered.

Octo's eyes flew open with a look of pure terror. It was seconds before they focused on Sage. The fear ebbed, replaced after a few uncertain blinks by a glance of contrived composure. "Why, Mary Sage," she said smoothly, "you surprised me."

"Are you all right, Aunt?"

"Of course I'm all right," said Octo briskly. She swung her short legs over the side of the bed, placed the pistol in the box. "I was up early and decided to clean great-grandfather's pistols. One must take care of old firearms or they rust. I declare, I seem to have nodded off." Ruffling her short curls, she stood, straightened her skirt. "Would you like some coffee, dear?" Without waiting for an answer, she trotted into the hall.

"Aunt Octo, all those cards downstairs," said Sage following. "Is it some new game?"

"I suppose you might call it that." Octo started down the steps, choosing not to touch the banister. Her back was straight as a drill sergeant's. "There was an article in the newspaper not long ago by a psychiatrist, a lady doctor, mind you, who advocated certain methods of dealing with—well, problems of uncertainty, self-esteem—"

"Stress?"

"Yes. She suggested that one make a list of one's positive character traits, write them out on small cards, and leave them about the house. In that way—" Octo stopped near the bottom step, turned to Sage. "One might be a bit depressed about putting the phone book in the refrigerator but instantly reassured to find a card that says Dependable on the kitchen sink." Her eyes held some of their old mischief.

While Octo made instant coffee, Sage went to the refrigerator for milk. She was shocked by its emptiness, finding, besides the pint of milk, two jars of okra gumbo, a package of carrots, and an apple. Fetching the sugar from the cupboard she found little more, a few cans of tuna fish, one of baked beans, and a jar of bouillon cubes.

Sage would have preferred sitting cozily at the kitchen table but Octo sailed into the drawing room where, perched on the stiff horsehair sofa, they sipped their coffee. Octo was determined to draw Sage into a conversation of some intellectual substance. Sage found herself at nine o'clock in the morning listening to a sharp critique of contemporary female writers—"I prefer to be a reader, my dear, not a priest on the other side of the confessional. Where are the Jane Austens? The Charlotte Bröntes?" She had veered into the shortcomings of modern poetry "—blatant elitism, sophomoric obfuscation—" when Sage decided they must put their cards on the table.

"Aunt Octo," she said abruptly, "Bea told me what happened last night."

Octo didn't speak at once. Her lips tightened. The hand putting the cup on the coffee table trembled. She snatched it back, buried it in her lap. "Bea promised," she said accusingly. "She said—"

"Bea was worried about you. She did what she thought best."

"If you tell Elise and Clay—"

"I won't tell anyone."

But her aunt seemed not to hear her. The small figure went rigid. "This is my home, Sage. And as long as I can do for myself it's going to remain my home."

"Of course it will. It's just that we have to—"

"I am not a doddering, incompetent old—"

"I know you're not. Octo, listen—"

"Anymore than Maybelle Jay. You know what happened to Maybelle."

Sage remembered clearly. Two months ago the old lady had been found half conscious in her house on Beaufain Street. Not only had she been beaten and robbed but it was discovered that it had happened twice before. She'd said nothing to her children, knowing that they'd hasten to put her in a nursing home.

"Maybelle's at the New Hope Home on Mount Pleasant," said Octo coldly. "She has a clean, sunny room, nourishing meals, medical supervision, instruction in arts and crafts, and the fellowship of her peers. She can't wait to die."

"Octo—"

"They sold off her furniture and gassed poor old William. Said he was incontinent. Called it a mercy killing."

"William?"

"Her cat. Someone from upstate bought the house and dug up all the oleanders."

"Aunt," Sage took one of the tiny hands in hers, held it firmly, "I'm not going to say anything to Elise or Clay. Trust me. We'll figure out some way to—"

"I've solved the problem." Gently Octo withdrew her hand, picked up her cup, took a sip, then put it down again. "I'm going to ask Eldredge Pratt-Baines to come live with me. He can have two rooms and a bath on the top floor."

"You're taking in a roomer?" Sage remembered the old badgerlike man in the hairy suit, who'd been a college professor.

"It's been done before, Mary Sage, in troubled times."

Sage took a deep breath. "I think it's a great idea." She considered Eldredge a pompous old windbag but it occurred to her that he must have a pension. At least there would be more food in the house. "Doesn't he already have a place?" she asked.

"A cramped little room above a dry cleaning establishment."

"Let's give him a call right now," said Sage.

While Octo was in the hall phoning her friend, Sage noticed the broken pane in one of the windows facing the piazza. Apparently the thief had used the same method as she when she escaped from Mille Fleurs. She wondered what was going on next door with David and Peter Larson, if David would ever call her again. She doubted it. She felt empty and foolish thinking of David and her own concerns after what had happened to Octo. The old French clock was missing from the mantel. She wondered if it had been stolen, or sold to pay bills.

When Octo returned to the room she was beaming. "He'll move in tomorrow," she announced. "He couldn't be more pleased." She cocked her head, giving Sage a keen look. "I know what you're thinking. He's an old bore. But we've been friends for many years. Since he first came."

"How did he happen to end up in Charleston?"

"It was fate, Sage. He was driving from Ohio to St. Petersburg where he planned to share an apartment with a distant cousin. His car broke down. While it was being repaired, he walked around town. After only a few hours he realized he couldn't leave."

"But do you know anything about him, about his—"

"He never discusses his past. This usually indicates either something shady or humble beginnings. I'm fairly certain it's humble beginnings." Octo shook her head, smiled. "Perhaps one day he'll trust me enough to confide."

"I hope so," said Sage.

"He's good company, my dear. He's an avid reader, someone who cares about the written word. Oh, now and then he holds forth, but he was a teacher, Sage, and a good one. Besides," she added with a hint of coquetry, "he thinks I hung the moon."

They talked all morning. Octo seemed to forget her problems, engrossed in a discussion of the religious symbolism in the works of Flannery O'Connor. After a good bit of persuasion she finally agreed that Sage should go home, pick up a few things, and come back to spend the night. Sage was about to get into her car when Octo ran after her, called from the street door. "Sage, I quite forgot. The artist you asked me about some weeks ago—I was so involved with the yearbook, all that dissension about Viola's poem—the name Jostle, remember?"

"Aunt, we'll talk about it when I get back."

"No. I'll forget. If it hadn't been for Viola—she has an unusual talent but can be so dreadfully stubborn, and a few of the words she used were, well—"

"Aunt, I'll be back in an hour."

"Audubon! Jostle was the nickname given to him by Dr. Bachman. As to M, Auralee must have been referring to Maria Martin, Dr. Bachman's sister-in-law. She ran the household, you know, the wife being an invalid." Across the street a woman leading a small child stopped to listen, but Octo paid no attention. "Maria Martin," she called, "was quite extraordinary, a naturalist like Bachman and an artist to boot; she painted the backgrounds of some of Audubon's pictures."

Sage noticed that they'd caught the attention of a few more neighbors as well as a yardman who'd paused to lean on his rake. She left the car and went back to her aunt. "Thank you for solving the mystery," she said, "I'll add a footnote to the diary. Look, Octo, I'll be back—"

She noticed Bea, leaning out of an upstairs window, listening to this exchange with amusement and interest. Bea waved to her.

"Wait." Octo was clutching her arm. She gave Sage a look of uneasy concern, then dropped her eyes. "About Eldredge moving in—you know how people are here in town. Do you suppose they'll talk?"

Sage put her arms around the old lady, hugged her close. Stepping back, she managed to keep a straight face. "Oh, Aunt Octo," she said fervently, "I do hope so!" For the first time that day, Octo laughed.

Driving home Sage realized that Lise and Clay would be furious if they knew she'd covered up for Octo. Would her aunt be safe? What if the thief came back? It was hard to envision Eldredge in the role of knight-protector. If she sold the big silver tea tray she might have enough money to put iron grills on Octo's windows. She wished Octo would have a brainstorm revealing the whereabouts of the infamous parure, some shred of information that would lead to a walled-up door, a mysteriously marked floorboard. When she got out of her car, she remembered that the picnic lunch was still in the trunk. She took it in with her, feeling again a profound confusion, unable to make any sense of what had happened at Mille Fleurs.

As she let herself in the ground floor entrance she heard the door to the dryer slam shut. "Franny?" she called. When there was no answer she went to the laundry to see for herself. Duncan managed to look both apologetic and defiant. "Oh," was all he said.

"I thought you were Franny."

He shifted his bundle of laundry. "I was in a bind. Timewise. She offered to—" He got a firmer grip on his bundle. "Hope you don't mind."

She did mind. She thought of her last encounter with him. She wanted to turn and run up the steps. Her voice didn't show it. "No, it's all right." She knew she should say, don't make a practice of it; the use of the laundry isn't included in the rent. "I'll wait and lock the door," she said firmly, "after you go."

"I asked her out on a date, as a kind of return for the favor, but she turned me down. I guess I'm not in her league." His grin was not engaging. "You know something? You look different. In fact, if I hadn't known it was you—"

"I said I'll—"

"No sweat. I can cut back through her apartment." Surprisingly he was not putting up an argument. He brushed past Sage, left the laundry room, and stopped at Franny's door, deciding an explanation was in order. "We got keys to each other's places. You know, in case of emergency." Sage's consternation must have shown. He went on. "Like when she went over to Holly Hill for the weekend and remembered she'd left the heater on. Say," he rubbed one dirty sneaker against the other, "how's that ghost up on your top floor? Still throwing around fur coats?"

Sage didn't answer. She walked past him and hurried up the steps. She found the kitten on the dining room table. Major looked up at it fondly, trying to communicate his good intentions. After she'd fed them both she went to the library to get a book on Audubon that had belonged to her father, then went up to her workroom to add the footnote to Auralee's diary. She realized that a trip to the Historical Society could have quickly established the identity of the mysterious Jostle. In fact, she should have figured it out for herself. It was a matter of common pride that the great Audubon had spent time in Charleston, befriended and housed by the naturalist-clergyman, Dr. Bachman. Audubon's rendering of a curlew, with Charleston harbor and the old city in the background, hung in prints of varying quality over many a local mantel, as it had at Octo's.

Sure enough the book described the white mansion on Rutledge Avenue, the garden with its profusion of verbena, sweet alyssum, mignonette, camellias, trumpet vine. Here she found Maria Martin, a gifted artist, helping the Frenchman with backgrounds for his paintings of birds, going on field trips with Bachman, Audubon, and the artist's two assistants. It was on one of these outings that Bachman nicknamed the artist Jostle, both amused and shocked by Audubon's profane response to being bounced along deeply rutted roads. Fascinated, Sage read about the print-by-print publishing of *The Birds of America,* of Dr. Bachman's efforts to interest local people in buying the series, of Audubon's attempts to get subscribers in both Europe and America. It seemed such a waste that this talented man should be forced to spend time marketing his work. It also seemed a great irony that, ever plagued by financial problems, Audubon had no idea that his folios of birds would one day be considered world treasures.

She packed an overnight case, went back downstairs, and opened the picnic hamper she'd taken to Mille Fleurs the day before. Not only had the crabmeat salad begun to spoil but her once high hopes seemed to lie like moldy leftovers between the wine and the cheese. She threw out the crabmeat and decided to take the rest of the picnic with her to Octo's.

She'd gathered her things from the kitchen and was about to leave when the sound of the knocker echoed through the house. Major barked only once, then ran ahead of her into the hall and waited expectantly at the door. She couldn't imagine who it would be. Judging from the dog, she thought it must be a relative or someone she knew. She had few callers and she didn't want one now. She was anxious to get to Octo's.

She opened the door and gaped at Peter Larson. Her heart seemed to stop. She almost slammed the door in his face, but something about him made her hesitate. One part of her was remembering his iron grip on her arm, as she tried to start her car, escape from Mille Fleurs. Another part of her was struck by the fact that he looked so ordinary, harmless. He looked like any young man in jeans, T-shirt, and running shoes. He appeared less massive. There was nothing mysterious about him. Most distracting, his usually expressionless face actually showed emotion, an embarrassment that bordered on contrition. He looked at her directly. "Can I talk to you a minute?"

Normally she would have stepped back so he could enter. She didn't. Despite his new manner, she still felt a thread of distrust. "Of course." She noticed that though his upper body seemed relaxed, his hands hanging at his side were clenched.

"About yesterday—" he began, "out at the plantation...maybe I was out of line. I didn't meant to—" The words dwindled away. He bit his lip, glanced at her almost shyly. She didn't help him. She waited.

"I don't know what you thought." His voice was deep, rough. "I'm sorry if I...if I upset you."

She was amazed that this big, once menacing man was no longer menacing at all. He looked like a schoolboy. For some reason, she knew then that the homosexual relationship she'd tried to deny was a reality. Peter had seen her as a threat. He was making amends. And David. David's agony came from a desperate attempt to find another way of life, a life with a woman. Depressed, somehow ashamed, she looked at Peter for the first time without resentment. She could only feel pity for them both. "It's all right," she said, wanting to end this.

He had more to say but it was hard for him. "David...he mustn't be hurt...or hurt himself." Then his mouth moved in a facsimile of a smile. He regarded her for a few more seconds, decided he had no more to say. She acknowledged his abrupt nod, stood looking after him until she heard the gate swing shut.

She returned to Octo's and vacuumed her aunt's top floor, scrubbed the new tenant's bathroom. Octo made up a bed for Eldredge and put out fresh towels. Together they did some weeding in the garden and dusted the rockers on the piazza. That night they dined in some splendor. Bea Bonham joined them, bringing two roast chickens from a delicatessen. They sat at the candlelit table like uneasy celebrants. When they'd finished Sage's wine, Octo produced a dusty bottle. "I have a few of these left," she said. "Papa used to store them between the attic and the eaves, just as in the days of Horace and Maecenas."

No mention was made of the break-in or any other unpleasant subject. Knowing full well that they must deal with the outrage of the recent past and the uncertainty of the immediate future, they ate, drank, and managed to laugh. Bea outlined the plot of her new historical novel, describing how her heroine was almost but not quite ravished on four continents, preserving her virtue until page 376. "It's a living," she apologized to Octo. "It's in my poetry that I make no compromise." Sage promised to be the first at Bea's autograph party. Octo planned an additional festivity for Bea, already making notes as to which of the Readers and Writers could be counted on to bring hors d'oeuvres. As they finished the last of the wine Sage thought of Charlotte's diary, the account of the party held in the face of the news from Shiloh.

Elise telephoned just after Bea left; Sage and Octo were about to go to bed. "I was driving Etta home earlier," she said when Sage answered, "and I saw your car at Octo's. I wanted to tell you that I found my keys. They were lying right under the front seat of the car! When I think of how Clay and I both searched that car—"

"Your voice sounds funny," said Sage.

Elise ignored this. "I just thought that if you aren't doing anything tomorrow...I hate Sundays—and Clay flew to Atlanta this morning for a meeting. He won't be back until Monday, so—"

"We can drive out to the country, Lise, or maybe walk on the beach."

"There's a lecture on art deco at the Gibbes Art Gallery tomorrow afternoon. I think it's at three."

"Great. We'll go. Why don't you pick me up at a quarter of?"

"Fine."

"See you tomorrow, then."

"Sage—" For a moment she thought Elise had left the phone, then her sister's voice came through, distantly. "Nothing. It's nothing. Good night, Sage."

Lying in a narrow brass bed in Octo's spare room, Sage reviewed Elise's account of finding her keys. She'd not only been frightened but repelled at the idea that someone she knew might have stolen them. She was greatly relieved. But relief didn't help her to sleep. The thought of David and Peter filled her with sadness and self-disgust. She'd been an utter fool. She'd closed her eyes to everything but her own little dream of romance. She'd cast David as the perfect hero. She'd cast Peter as some kind of monster. She'd cast herself as the heroine moving unerringly toward a happy ending.

She was not given to structured prayers, but she prayed now. She prayed for her sister. She had the feeling that all was not right in Elise's life. She prayed for David, for Octo's safety, and, with some ambivalence, for Roper Chalfont's reformation. Last she prayed for herself, not knowing what to specify, asking finally, with a kind of desperation, for the ability to profit from experience. As she drifted toward sleep, a phrase of her grandmother's came to her, bringing cold comfort, "We learn only from adversity, my dear."

ELEVEN

SAGE AND OCTO went to early service at St. Michael's and then came home to a breakfast of grapes and French bread left over from the picnic. Octo was as vibrant as a young girl. She wore the new dress that Elise had given to her for her birthday. There were spots of pink in her cheeks. "Eldredge will be quite independent," she insisted. "We'll each lead our own life. I have no intention of fussing over him." Hot on the heels of this declaration, she went to her garden, picked an armful of azaleas, and carried them in a vase to the third floor.

A little before noon, as Sage was leaving, a maroon sedan coughed up the street and lurched to a halt two feet from the curb. Standing by her car she waved, watched Eldredge squeeze from under the steering wheel. Though the thermometer outside the house read seventy-five degrees, he still wore his hairy tweed. Anxious to avoid a lengthy conversation, Sage took off. In her rearview mirror she noted happily that after hoisting two worn suitcases and a bag of oranges from the back seat he didn't stop to catch his breath, but picked up his luggage and headed briskly for Octo's door.

With each block her spirits rose. She was surprised to find herself humming; she cast about for a reason and realized that her body already quickened to the news of the day, announced from the treetops, relayed from garden to garden. Spring had arrived.

Yesterday's buds on dogwood, wisteria, jessamine
were beginning to show streamers of color. Aged pe-
cans, oaks, chinaberries vied with saplings in the bril-
liance of their young green. People on the streets,
townsfolk and tourists, paused dreamily at garden
gates, took time to glance upward at the clear morning sky.

Sage marveled. In the last months she'd not only
lived through the grief of losing Gran but had had to
face the fact that she was almost penniless. She had no
job, no prospects. Added to this was her worry about
Octo, and the growing conviction that she could no
longer trust her own judgment. She still couldn't think
of what had happened with David at Mille Fleurs
without feeling appalled and stupid. Yet here she was,
driving along in a car that could fall apart at the next
corner, humming a chorus of "Oh, What a Beautiful
Morning."

Not even the sight of Roper Chalfont daunted her.
As she pulled into the driveway she saw him at once,
stretched out in the hammock that he'd hung between
two trees on the patio. He was drinking a can of beer
and reading the newspaper. Three pigeons darted
about, grabbing at crumbs. Music poured from the
open door of the carriage house: Bach's B-Minor
Mass.

Sage got out of her car, paused. He wore no shirt.
The muscular chest and shoulders, deeply tanned,
shone like metal. She wondered what Elise would say,
what Gran would have said, finding a half naked man
in the garden on Sunday morning. "You'd better
hurry," she called sweetly, "or you'll be late for
church." Without waiting for what was certain to be

an insulting reply she went quickly to the ground floor entrance, her nearest escape.

As soon as she opened the door to the laundry room, she smelled the fumes. Her heart sank. The water heater had betrayed her again. The last time she'd had it fixed the service man had noted its age and made dire predictions. What if Franny or Duncan should come in the room with a lighted cigarette? She envisioned a gigantic explosion, the whole house going up and then coming down in a pile of rubble. She wasn't sure what to do. Duncan? No. Definitely not.

With great reluctance she went back outside to the patio. Roper looked up from the newspaper and watched her approach, his heavy brows lifting expectantly.

"Look, I'm sorry to bother you, but—" she spoke haltingly, "well, my laundry room is full of fumes—"

"Gas fumes?"

"I'm sure it's the water heater. I wouldn't ask but it's Sunday and I doubt if the repair people—"

"I'll have a look." Big as he was he swept past her with the economy of a dancer. Before she reached the laundry room he was back in the doorway. "Do you have a key to that apartment?" He nodded at Franny's bedroom door.

"Sure, I have, but—"

"Give it to me!"

She groped in the bottom of her purse and finally pulled out the ring of keys to the apartments. "They don't open that door," she said. "We'll have to go to the entrance. Here. This one opens the door to the tenants' entrance hall and this one opens her apartment door. But—"

"Wait outside." It was a sharp, unequivocal order. He was running.

All at once she realized what he already knew. She stood frozen, staring at Franny's windows. The blinds were drawn. She could see nothing. Incoherently, she prayed.

In less than a minute, Roper reappeared, gulping for breath, his arms full. She recognized the red robe. She'd only seen death once before, but she felt she was seeing it again in Franny's vacant face, sagging against Roper's shoulder. Roper seemed not to accept it. "Call EMS! My place. Quick!" he yelled at her. As she stumbled away, he lowered Franny onto the ground, cupped her head, pulled it back and, almost breathless himself, tried to breathe life back into her.

Roper's living room rang with music: "...et in terra pax hominibus bonae voluntatis" sang the choir. Her hands were shaking so badly she had to dial twice to get the number. After she'd made the call, she sat without moving, Bach's mass reverberating in her bones. If I'm quiet and wait, she thought, I'll wake up. It will all be over. "Qui tolis peccata mundi..." The hospital was less than five minutes away. Maybe they'll get here in time. Maybe it isn't too late. She made herself move.

Roper still crouched over Franny, trying to revive her. But as Sage knelt down beside him, he sank back on his heels. She brushed dust from the sleeve of the red robe, stared at the high school ring on Franny's finger, gold with a small blue stone. The scent of tea olive made her stomach heave. She heard the siren, the ambulance pulling up at the curb, the gate opening then clanking shut, footsteps. Then Roper was holding her arms, lifting her. Two men in blue shirts and dark trousers knelt by Franny. "Rigor's set in," said one of the men, getting back on his feet. As Roper led her to the carriage house, she could hear someone in the ambulance talking to the dispatcher.

She was aware of pushing away the glass of brandy that Roper tried to force on her. "Crucifixus etiam pro nobis," proclaimed the choir. She wrapped her arms around herself, crouched forward in a fetal position, head pressed to her knees, eyes shut. He snapped off the music, then he was back, pulling up her head. The brandy stung her lips, her tongue, rolled down her throat like a ball of fire. She choked, shoved him away.

"I don't allow catatonic females on my sofa," he said. "Nor do I put up with southern lady type vapors and sinking spells. So you'd damn well better get it together, Sage!"

Energized by outrage, she half rose. "I'm going home," she snapped. She felt herself swaying.

"Sit!" With one finger he sent her back onto the sofa. "You're in no state to go home."

"Why?" she whispered. "Why did it happen?" Again she covered her face with her hands. "She was so happy, so full of life. Why—"

"In a few minutes the police will be here. They'll want to talk to you."

Sage lifted her head. "The police?"

"It's customary in cases like this."

"Don't call her a case! She was a person, a human being. She was—"

"She was a suicide," said Roper. "To all intents and purposes, she shut herself in that little windowless kitchen, pulled up a stool, and turned on the gas. You can't change that. You can't bring her back. If we're lucky, we may find out why. But some official types will be getting here pretty soon to ask a lot of questions. It's going to be a long day. I expect you to be cool-headed and cooperative. I expect—"

"*You* expect!"

"I expect you to show a little class." She glared at him. Bracing herself, she drew back her foot and kicked him as hard as she could. He didn't flinch or rub his leg. He smiled grimly down at her.

Finally she made a pot of coffee. Roper put on a shirt. At last, she dared look out the door toward her house and saw that Franny was gone. She was about to turn away when a young man in a police uniform and an older man in street clothes came through her gate. "They're here," she said to Roper. She watched him cross the garden to meet them.

It seemed hours before they came to the carriage house. Actually it was about twenty minutes. Sage had drunk a third cup of coffee and swept the kitchen floor with a broom that looked as though it had never been used.

She and Roper sat on the sofa and the two men balanced themselves on the edge of the big leather armchairs. The patrolman perched like a new-hatched owlet, never opening his mouth. The older man, who looked to be in his fifties and who introduced himself as Sergeant Meigs, spent a good bit of time cleaning his glasses, leafing through a notebook, and adjusting the length of lead in his Scripto pencil. Except for a Piedmont accent, he reminded Sage of her Uncle Henry Lamar, an ex-University of South Carolina football star, run to fat and given to emphasizing the obvious with considerable throat-clearing.

"Eliot," he mused. "Would you spell that, if you please." Sage obliged. "All this property in your name?" he asked. "Including the carriage house?"

The questioning went on for half an hour. To Sage most of it seemed totally irrelevant. Much of it regarding Franny's family and job she couldn't answer. Finally, Sergeant Meigs realized she'd run dry. "Thank you, little lady. You've been a real help. We won't keep you, just want to talk to Mr. Chalfont here and that young fellow in the other apartment. What's his name again?"

"Duncan McFee," said Sage. "He's home. I heard him drive in a few minutes ago."

"I see." The sergeant scribbled something, paused, then as if remembering his mother's instructions to be mannerly, hauled himself to his feet. "Thank you, ma'am. I guess that'll be all for now." He cleared his throat, took an envelope from his pocket. "Found this in the apartment. Letter from Holly Hill, same name as hers. Must be her folks. I'll have to notify them."

Sage allowed herself one look at Roper before she left the carriage house. He stood by the fireplace, hands in his pockets, staring at a charred log. His face was remote, guarded. She phoned her sister at once, bracing herself for a barrage of I-told-you-so's. But after she'd given a terse report of what had happened, Elise surprised her. "Oh, Sage, how terrible. My God, how awful for you!"

Encouraged by this compassion, Sage went on to tell her about Eldredge moving in with Octo, omitting the robbery. She was surprised again by her sister's response. "Well," said Elise calmly, "at least she won't be alone anymore. Look, Sage, I'll be right over. Suicide! In your own house. I just can't believe—"

Sage fed the dog and cat, then sat staring out of the kitchen window. She wished Elise wasn't coming so soon. More than anything she longed for some time to herself. She felt stunned, as if she'd wakened from a nightmare and found it was true. Why had it happened? Franny seemed so happy, so obviously in love. Why?

It was no time at all before the troops arrived. Obviously Elise had alerted Octo, who had passed the news to Bea. They sat like people at a wake, though none of them except Sage had known Franny at all. Eldredge stared at the portrait of Thomas Benford, Octo at Eldredge, and Elise at Bea's straw hat, which looked as though it might have been worn by a riverboat gambler in the 1800s. Bea took a piece of chocolate from her purse and gave it to Major, who swallowed it gratefully.

It was Octo who spoke first. "Such a tragedy," she murmured. "So young."

"It's hard to believe."

"Yet you hear about things like this every day."

"This certainly brings it close to home."

It was Bea who disrupted the litany, her voice crackling with impatience. "As some wag observed, life is a bowl of gray rats. Only the tough survive. I'll bet the poor kid fell in love with a prime rat, some sleazy bastard who left her in the lurch, probably pregnant."

Elise looked at Bea with unconcealed distaste. Eldredge hastened to restore a formal tone. "You know, I can't help but be grateful that I enjoyed my youth in a gentler world." He paused, intoned:

*"Oh born in days when wits were fresh and clear,
And life ran gaily as the sparkling Thames—"*

"Eldredge, how beautiful," Octo broke in. "And how apt!" She regarded him with a mixture of pride and amusement.

Elise shifted uncomfortably in her chair. "I tried to reach Clay at the hotel in Atlanta," she said, "but there was no answer. Some lunch meeting, I guess. But he'll be home this evening."

Mercifully, they didn't stay long. Octo promised a pecan pie. Eldredge patted Sage's hand. "Take heart, my dear, and if you need us, call at once," he said as if he and Octo had shared a lifetime of vicissitudes. Elise didn't insist when Sage refused to spend the night at her house. She made a halfhearted mention of the lecture they'd planned to attend that afternoon. When Sage said she thought she should be on hand in case Sergeant Meigs called again, Elise looked almost relieved. "Clay will be calling you as soon as he gets home," she said, giving Sage a brief, distracted kiss.

Bea was the last to leave. She waited until the others started down the piazza steps, then pulled Sage back from the door. "I wanted to tell you," she spoke in a half whisper, "that I finally got a line on our friend David."

"A line?"

"From my researcher in Richmond. The one with the ex-FBI lover. Remember?"

"Bea!" Octo called from the gate.

"Coming." Bea tucked a red curl under her riverboat gambler's hat, gave Sage a shrewd look. "I'll tell you later. You know," she said, "when you're my age you shouldn't be surprised by anything. After all, everyone's got something to hide." She grinned, headed for the steps. "Sweetie," she called over her shoulder, "we're all incognito."

Mechanically Sage locked the door, went into the living room, and sat down. She felt no inclination to think or move. It was as if she were waiting for a train, suspended between destinations. She was unaware of time passing until she heard the sound of a car in the drive. She saw then that the light had shifted, leaving the room dimmer, beginning to slant through the western windows of the room across the hall. It must be Clay, she thought. She dragged herself to the door.

From the piazza she saw a red pickup truck parked next to Roper's station wagon. Two people stood beside it, staring up at the house. The rawboned man was faded to the color of straw. He wore a dark suit, the collar of a flowered sports shirt lying open and flat against the lapels of the coat. The tiny woman beside him looked as though she were dressed for church, in a purple dress and a brown straw hat. She stood awkwardly, feet wide apart, in high-heeled patent leather shoes.

Sage went down to the driveway. With no change of expression the couple watched her approach. "Mr. and Mrs. Barth?" she asked. The man nodded. "I'm so sorry—I can't tell you—" Her voice trailed off. "I was very fond of Franny."

"The Charleston Police Department," the man read to her from a scrap of paper. He turned suddenly to the woman beside him. "You forgot to call 'Stell and have her phone Calder and them." The woman's small, pinched face showed nothing.

He glanced back at Sage. His eyes had a flat, dazed look, as if he'd been struck from behind. "One-eighty Lockwood Drive," he said. "Now where's that?"

"When you leave the driveway," said Sage, "turn left, go to the street by the river, turn right and keep on going, past the bridge. You'll see a sign."

The man carefully folded the paper and put it in his pocket. He smoothed his slicked-down gray blond hair, his gaze moving to Franny's car. The woman pulled a shred of Kleenex from her purse and held it to her lips.

"That's her car," said the man.

"The keys to the car," said Sage, "all her things— if you want to go in the apartment—"

"We'll be back." He walked over to the car, brows drawn fiercely, stared at it, kicked on of the back tires. He drew a long, shuddering breath. Then he turned and headed for the pickup. The woman walked stiffly after him. Sage ached with pity for them.

She watched the car leave, then went across to the carriage house. Roper sat sprawled in one of the armchairs. He had a screwdriver and seemed to be taking apart a small radio. Major lay beside the chair. Sage thought of Roper talking to Sergeant Meigs, answering questions, knowing the police could press a computer button and find out he'd been in prison. Not that there was any reason to check on him.

She went into the kitchen and opened the refrigerator. Fortunately, it was better stocked than Octo's. She found eggs, bacon, steaks, lettuce, tomatoes, beer, and milk. She took out a steak, turned on the boiler, and began making a salad. When she brought in the plates of food and put them on the coffee table Roper smiled but made no comment. He got up and slid a tape into the stereo. They ate as a Mozart piano concerto gracefully affirmed a world of order and harmony.

Even after she'd washed the dishes and returned to the living room Roper said nothing. He poured her a brandy and returned to his chair, where he began to work again on the radio. Sage curled up in the armchair opposite him. She studied the planes of his face, the wide brow above the jutting cheekbones, the line of his mouth. Fleetingly, she saw something of the boy in him. She wondered what had led that boy—no, he was a young man then—into the despicable business of drug dealing. Suddenly, she thought of David. She wondered what Bea had discovered.

She got up and poured herself more brandy, returned to her chair. She longed to get drunk, stagger home, and fall blindly into bed, outdistancing the conflict inside her. But the brandy didn't help. Phrases kept coming back to torment her—David sitting by the river with his failed drawing, talking about forgotten words, "words I'd want to teach my children: honor, fidelity, grace." Franny, standing in the fragrant night, saying, "No matter how down you feel during the winter, when spring comes, it's like the whole world's going to change."

She didn't know she was crying until she felt the hot tears on her cheeks. She squeezed shut her eyes, tried to stop, but the tears kept coming, rolling off her face, dropping onto her hands as if they'd been held back for a lifetime. She was seeing Franny's parents, standing by their truck, stunned, inarticulate. She saw them getting the call from Sergeant Meigs on an ordinary Sunday between church and dinner, dressing again in their good clothes, driving miles in frozen silence to find out what had happened to their daughter who had come to the city for a better life.

She was aware of arms around her, of being lifted like a child. He carried her to the sofa and sat down, holding her on his lap. With a sob she pressed her face into the curve of his neck. Suddenly she longed to let out all the grief and anger at what had happened to Franny, to admit to the plaguing fear that someone was secretly searching her house, to tell him about the strange episode with David. She didn't care if he'd been a criminal or if he still was. She didn't care if he made her feel like a fool. She could no longer bear her burden alone. "Roper—" she whispered.

"Hush," he said, his big hand smoothing her hair. "Hush."

TWELVE

SHE SENSED THAT IT was morning before she opened her eyes. She felt dizzy, heavy-headed. I have to get up, she thought, let the dog out. But she couldn't move. She was enclosed. Arms held her. With increasing amazement she became aware of the warmth of his body next to hers, his slow, even breathing. Then she was fully awake. She was still in Roper's arms. They were not on the sofa but lay in an enormous bed. The impact of this should have knocked the breath out of her. It didn't. What stunned her was the fact that lying in bed with him seemed the most natural thing in the world. She stared at his face, inches from hers on the pillow. He looked quite defenseless in sleep. His eyelashes were darker than she'd realized, almost black. She continued to stare, invaded by a feeling she couldn't identify, both excitement and languor, a sharp desire to fit her body to his. She moved closer, lifted her hand, touched the curve of one thick brow. "Roper?" The green gold eyes opened slowly. "What time is it?" she asked.

Raising his head, he squinted at his watch. "Almost six," he said. Braced on one elbow, he regarded her for several seconds, then leaned over and kissed her gently. "Good morning."

"How did I get here?"

"It's a long story, Sage."

"Tell me."

He looked at her, his glance lingering. "Well, to be brief, you finished the bottle of brandy, humming along with Mozart and Vivaldi. After that you recited several Shakespearean love sonnets and two rather questionable limericks, all in a thick Long Island accent—"

"I did not!"

"Finally you made a shocking attempt to seduce me. I fought pitifully to defend my virtue as you chased me round and round the room, your teeth bared, panting with passion." He rubbed his chin. "Once I had to hold you off with the fire tongs. At last, disarmed, flattened against the wall, I knew I was trapped. Then all at once—"

"What?"

"You passed out," said Roper, sinking back on the pillow with a grin.

Sage laughed, punched at his shoulder. But she had keen misgivings. She'd spent the night in the arms of this man, who obviously didn't live by the rules. Surely he was not one to suppress his appetites. Why was she still fully clothed except for her shoes? There was only one explanation. "Roper," she said in a small voice, "am I so unattractive?" The words were out before she knew it.

He observed her with great care. No one had ever studied her like that before. It was as if she were being seen for the first time in her life. "We didn't—we didn't—" she floundered.

"No. We didn't." His voice was husky. "But I was sure as hell tempted."

"You've had lots of women." She lay back on the pillow, her gaze intent.

"Legions." There was mischief in his eyes. "To be frank, I was just about to make my move when the wind changed. I could hear the bells of St. Michael's announcing the hour—"

"Roper—"

"Proclaiming, as it were, old values, ancient rites. All at once I saw Mary Sage Eliot, all in white, walking down the aisle, a celebration of innocence." He gazed down at her. "Amazing." He shook his head in wonder. "You still have no idea of how beautiful you are." Slowly, with infinite tenderness, he reached down and held her head between his hands. At first, his kiss was soft, his lips barely touching hers. Then gradually it changed, deepened. She could feel the fierce drive of his longing. Her own rose to meet it. They clung together in answer to all the hunger and loneliness of their separate lives. She was beyond thought, trembling, yearning only for the final, primitive intimacy that would make them one.

The chimes, carried on the wind, began to strike six. With great effort Roper pulled away. Their glances met, locked in longing. Then at the same moment, they laughed. Roper threw back his head and roared. Sage buried her face in the pillow and shook with mirth. Their laughter filled the room, a release, an acknowledgment that they had all the time in the world.

They ate breakfast at a card table on the patio, Major and the pigeons darting after scraps. She was touched, enchanted by the way Roper held her chair, buttered her toast, went to fetch his sweater to put around her shoulders.

Then in the midst of her happiness, she was remembering Franny; the horror returned.

"I'm glad I got drunk," she said, feeling tears in her eyes. "It kept me from thinking."

"It did that." Roper glanced toward her house, the blind windows of Franny's apartment. She followed his gaze, turned away quickly.

"Do you know what I'd like best in the world?" she blurted.

"A couple hundred feet of new guttering?"

"To get out of town. Go to one of the islands."

By nine o'clock they were headed south. Roper had called his aunt and uncle and told them to expect company. Sage had gone to her house only long enough to feed the animals, take a shower, and dress. Briefly, she had been tempted by the blue and white bag of cosmetics, an Amanda de Vries ensemble of Elise's pink linen pants with a matching silk blouse. Instead, she put on fresh jeans, a faded shirt, and old sneakers. She picked up a worn blue sweater. Reluctantly she phoned Duncan, who seemed disinclined to talk. "Her parents may come by," Sage told him, "and I want to be certain they can get in her apartment. Do you still have a key? If you could—"

"Yeah," said Duncan abruptly, "I still got a key. I'll be here all day." Before she could thank him, he'd hung up.

Of all the sea islands south of town, Edisto was her favorite. Unlike Kiawah and Seabrook, it hadn't yet been turned into a fashionable resort, though she'd heard that plans already were under way. Separated from the sea and the mainland by wide stretches of salt marsh, Edisto had once produced fortunes in sea island cotton. Now some cattle and truck farms still thrived on the fertile island. Unpaved roads still led to fine old houses. In spring, the woods were a glory of yellow jasmine and Cherokee rose.

Sage, however, was not engrossed in the landscape. She was marveling at her new emotions. The horror of what had happened to Franny was still there but transcending it was pure joy. She compared the girlish fantasy she'd contrived around David with this reality. She looked at Roper's strong, square hands on the steering wheel, aware of the relaxed power of the tall body. She'd fled from him from the beginning just as she'd fled from life itself. The crime he'd committed years ago now seemed less a crime than an act of youthful rashness. She gazed at the line of his profile, the way the tanned skin stretched across his cheekbones and jaw. She longed to touch him, study him inch by inch, as one might some unexpected and extraordinary gift. Perhaps sensing her need or answering his own, he reached over and pulled her close. Caught in a wave of dizzying wonder, she rested her head on his shoulder. She knew she was living entirely for the moment and she didn't care. He could be Jack the Ripper and she'd feel the same. But he wasn't Jack the Ripper and she knew that every day he regretted the terrible thing he'd done, and he was trying in his way to make amends, start a new life. It would take courage to live it down, but Roper Chalfont wasn't short on courage. What's more, she thought, looking at her hand resting on his arm, he won't be alone.

"I think you'll like my aunt and uncle," he said as they passed a shopping center and headed toward open land.

"Is your uncle retired?"

Roper laughed. "Gabe was pretty much born retired. He does a good bit of writing, articles for natural history magazines, pieces for the newspaper. He doesn't make a living at it but it's what interests him, that and the challenge of surviving off the land. Janet sells a painting now and then. She's damn good."

Sage found the idea of Roper's aunt and uncle living off the land appealing. She imagined Gabe astride a horse inspecting his acres while Janet sat in her morning room working on a small but beautifully detailed watercolor. She thought they probably were of Octo's vintage and wondered if they'd be on the piazza, he in white linen, she in flowered voile, awaiting the arrival of their guests.

They left the highway and drove by small and large farms, pine woods. When they turned onto a rutted dirt road Sage was wiped clean of everything but anticipation; going down an unpaved road in the low country was like opening a surprise package. Peace lay here, like a hand on one's shoulder. The woods on either side were thickly overgrown and it wasn't until they passed a tall stand of bamboo that she saw the neatly tended garden.

"They grow just about everything they need," said Roper, "beans, potatoes, okra, eggplant, tomatoes, squash, greens. The rest of their food comes out of the water. About all they buy are a few staples."

The house was a two-story cabin of weathered cypress with a screened porch; it faced a tidal creek. A clothesline with drying sheets hung between two trees near the back door. Giant oaks arched above the house on three sides. A rusting sedan was parked near the garden.

Three people came out of the house, a tall thin couple with a small boy standing between them. As soon as Roper got out of the car, the couple hurried toward him. The woman embraced him, then Roper came back and brought Sage forward. "This beautiful girl is my Aunt Janet," he told her, "and this homely old codger is her husband, Gabe." He put an arm around Sage. "I want you to meet Sage Eliot who is among other things my long-suffering landlady."

Sage shook hands a little shyly, as if they might suspect how wrong she'd been in her expectations. They certainly weren't of Octo's vintage. They could be anywhere from forty to sixty, she thought; their skin, hair, even their worn shirts, pants, and sandals had a seasoned look, like driftwood. Gabe wore a fishing cap that once might have been blue. His eyes, the same soft color, held the brightness of light on water. Shaking Janet's narrow, callused hand, Sage wondered how a woman in a work shirt and patched pants, hair knotted casually on top of her head, could project such an image of spare elegance.

"And this is Charlie." Roper went back to where the boy stood and led him to Sage. Small and sunburned with a mop of red curls, he looked like a miniature man. The child's face had already taken on rugged lines. His hands and feet looked too big for the rest of him. He shoved what Sage recognized as some fossilized shark's teeth into the pocket of his shorts and held out a grubby paw. They shook hands formally.

"Roper, I'm making some great soup," Janet spoke in a husky voice, "with the bones of that rib roast you brought us." She took Sage's arm. "Come help me, Sage." As they started toward the house she called back to the boy. "Charlie, how about getting some herbs?"

Roper and Gabe headed for the dock, where a rowboat was moored and shrimp nets hung drying on posts. In the far distance beyond the marsh lay a barrier island, Eddingsville, the summer retreat of planters over a century earlier, now turned by winds and water into a barren stretch of sand.

On the porch stood a long unvarnished table and six camp chairs. Along the horizontal beam supporting the screen lay a collection of conchs, starfish, channeled whelks, sea urchins, sand dollars. At the far end there was a cot covered with a patchwork quilt. "Charlie's choice," said Janet and opened the door to the house.

Sage walked into a room filled with light. It was some seconds before she realized that the room, shaded by the porch, was in fact dim. The light came from the big watercolors on the walls. Slowly she walked from one to another, her eye drawn to the violet fastness of the deep swamp, the bars of sunlight thrusting through pine woods, a beach where sea and sand came together in a wash of gold.

The furniture was sparse. There was a round table with tubes of paint, jars of brushes, a plastic egg carton used as a palette. Another table by the window held a typewriter, stacks of paper, books. Two daybeds had been turned into sofas and were flanked by shabby armchairs. Crates had been painted and turned into tables for old lamps. The brick floor was bare and there was a solid wall of books.

Behind her Janet laughed, pausing to look at the room herself. "We had some old family pieces," she said, "but we gave them to nieces and nephews. I don't plan to spend my best years waxing mahogany."

"You have no children?" Sage asked.

"No, but my sister shares hers with us, as well as her grandchildren."

Which explains Charlie, thought Sage.

While Janet stood at the stove dropping vegetables into an iron pot, Sage cut up greens on a slab of marble mounted on cinder blocks. She wanted to tell Janet how moved she was by the paintings, but couldn't find the words.

"Roper told me what happened," said Janet in her soft, low voice. "I know this isn't an easy day for you."

Sage thought again of Franny standing in the garden, saying that spring could change the world. She blinked back tears. "I can't tell you how glad I am to be—where I am, Janet."

"I hope that means you'll come often."

"I'd like that. Have you lived here a long time?"

"Thirty-five years. We lived in town when we were first married. Gabe had started working in his father's real estate business. I was teaching art classes." She paused as Charlie came in and went to the sink with a small basket of herbs, which he began to wash. "One April morning," she said, "a particularly glorious one, we decided to play hooky from our jobs. We drove out here. Gabe had inherited this place from his grandfather, who'd used it for fishing weekends. It must have been something about the day or the timing but the minute we drove past that stand of bamboo we knew we couldn't go back to town, not to live. Oh, our families raised a great hue and cry for about a month, and then left us to what Gabe's dad called 'the idiocy of our own choices.'"

"And you never regretted it?" asked Sage.

"Of course, I did!" Janet laughed. "I regretted it every day that Gabe floundered around putting in wiring and plumbing. I regretted it on freezing winter mornings and scalding summer nights. Spending every nickel from our small investments to pay property taxes and medical insurance. I certainly regretted it when Hurricane Gracie flooded the whole downstairs and we perched up in the bedroom for two days."

Sage watched Charlie drop the herbs into the iron pot. "But you stayed," she said.

Janet stirred in the herbs. "The alternatives were unthinkable." She took a sip of the soup, gave Charlie a taste.

"What was unthinkable?" inquired Gabe. He stood inside the back door and held out a bucket of crabs.

They ate lunch at the table on the porch. Sage wondered if the soup seemed the best she'd ever eaten because of those sharing it. They laughed a lot, particularly about Janet's upcoming exhibit at a museum in Richmond. "This fellow came to call," said Gabe, "to discuss arrangements for the opening, and he looked at my Raggedy Ann there, and he says kind of hesitatingly, 'We were planning a champagne reception.' I swear to God, he was wondering if she had a dress."

"Gabe, you'd better watch out," said Roper. "Put her in a dress and send her to Richmond and she'll be discovered. She'll end up on ETV, talking about hard-edge geometric abstractions and the use of discordant found objects." He popped a piece of crabmeat into Charlie's mouth, grinned at his aunt. "She'll sell a lot of paintings and buy a big fur coat. She'll come home and make you take a bath."

"A bath?" Janet mused, looking at her husband. "I had a dress. I'll have to find it."

"Do you believe in ghosts?" Charlie spoke suddenly to Sage, intending to introduce a more interesting subject.

Sage looked into the wide, gold-flecked eyes. "I'm not sure," she said. "Sometimes."

"Tell one." Charlie turned to Roper.

"Which one?"

"Fenwick Hall. No, Henry Laurens."

"Well," Roper pushed his chair back from the table and stretched his legs, "a long time ago, Henry Laurens lived up on Mepkin Plantation in Berkeley County. He had this daughter who took sick. Now in those days they thought fresh air was bad for sick people so they closed the windows. The girl went into a coma and everyone was sure she was dead. They raised the windows, and went to tell the bad news. When they got back they found the girl had come to life. The fresh air had done it. This really scared Henry. Shoot, he could have buried the girl alive. He told his servants that when he died he wanted to be cremated. And that's just what happened when he died a few years later. They wrapped him in white cloth and set his body on a stump atop a bluff, looking over the rice fields." Roper paused, stared at the ceiling.

"And then?" prompted Charlie.

"It's gone clean out of my mind."

"They lit a fire," said Charlie helpfully.

"Oh, yes." Roper gazed solemnly at the small boy. "They lit a fire at Henry's feet. It burned his legs, then his body and right on up to his arms and his neck and then—his head rolled off! It rolled right down the bluff into the rice fields like a rubber ball. The servants looked everywhere for it. They searched those fields for days. They never found it. Now, legend has it that—'' Roper paused, looked expectantly at Charlie.

"On rainy nights," continued Charlie in sepulchral tones, "you can see Henry Laurens riding his horse up and down the rice fields, looking for his head!"

Sage shivered. But Charlie was watching her hopefully. "Do you have a ghost in your house?" he asked. "Uncle Gabe says most Charleston houses got ghosts."

Sage thought of the Benford apparition in his blood-stained stock, supposedly haunting a house built years after his death. She wanted to tell Charlie about him but all she could think of was the muffled sounds that had wakened her night after night, the terror of seeing or imagining the dark figure, the coat thrown or picked up, the falling. "If there is a ghost," she said faintly, "I haven't seen it."

She realized Roper was giving her a narrow-eyed look. He rose abruptly. "Gabe, Charlie," he said, "how about resetting the crab traps?"

After they'd washed and dried the dishes Janet and Sage returned to the porch with cups of tea and sat again at the table. Sage couldn't remember when she'd felt so relaxed. Sleepily, she watched the two men and the boy on the dock. Janet was watching them, too. "I'm going to be sorry to lose Charlie," she said.

"Lose him?"

Janet paused, seemed surprised at Sage's question. "We've just been keeping him until Roper got settled." She turned her chair to get a better view of the dock. "His grandparents took him after what happened, but they just can't keep him any longer. Neither of them is strong and they've had to give up their home, move to a retirement condominium, you know, where they have medical supervision. It's no place for children.

"His grandparents?" said Sage blankly.

"His mother's people. They've been taking care of him. Frankly, I think Roper is ready to be a father. A few years ago, maybe not, but now—" Janet smiled. "I remember when he'd finished serving his sentence he came down here and I asked him where he was going to go. 'Not indoors,' he said, very firmly."

Sage kept hearing Janet's words: "His grandparents took him after what happened . . . I think Roper is ready to be a father." She couldn't take her eyes from Roper and Charlie. They knelt on the dock close together, Charlie holding the crab trap while Roper baited it. She was stunned by what she should have noticed the moment she arrived. With his red hair, blunt young features, and the promise of rangy height in his small body, Charlie was a duplicate of Roper.

"God knows he was true to his word," said Janet. "He spent as little time as possible indoors. First we got a letter from the oil fields of Oklahoma, then from a lumber camp in Oregon, and after that most of the ports in the Near and Far East. He worked on freighters. Between jobs he climbed mountains, to rest up, he said. Austria, Switzerland, even the Himalayas."

"He married?" Sage barely managed to keep her voice normal.

Janet gave her a curious glance. "Good heavens, no! Would you like some more tea, Sage?" Sage shook her head. "I hope he will marry," Janet remarked lightly. "It would be good for both him and Charlie. And, he's in excellent shape financially. I mean, he's never touched the money his father left him."

She couldn't believe it, refused to believe it. She couldn't be that wrong about him. She'd experienced his gentleness, kindness firsthand. Every instinct told her that this was a sensitive, loving man and even more, she thought stubbornly, remembering the night before in his arms, a man of honor.

"Now he's going to take Charlie?" Her words were flat.

"We'd be glad to keep him," said Janet, "but he needs a good school right now, other children. At first I think Roper was a bit daunted at the idea of raising a child, but he rallied pretty quickly. He's always been fond of the boy."

Fond? Sage felt as if the ground had opened up and swallowed her. She searched Janet's face, saw only utter candor. With pain like none she'd ever known, she let her perception of Roper begin to disintegrate, crumble. Unable to bear the pain, she grasped at rage. Accept it, she cried inwardly. He's not only a criminal, he's a monster, who fathered a child and didn't bother to give it a name. He abandoned his own son, then went off to indulge his fantasies all over the world. What about Charlie's mother? Discarded? Forgotten? A suicide, like Franny?

Janet laughed. "I can't say I've ever known anyone like Roper."

Sage didn't think she could get through the rest of the afternoon. She heard herself making easy conversation as Janet showed her more paintings, walked her through the garden, gathering vegetables for her to take home. They all stood on the dock and watched Gabe pull in three good-sized bream with an unbaited line. Sage couldn't take her eyes from Charlie, sitting on the edge of the dock by his father. When she saw him reach out and put a hand on Roper's knee she turned away, blinded by pain and anger.

As they drove back to town, Roper seemed unaware of her cold silence. When he referred to the boy it was without embarrassment. "I suppose Janet explained about Charlie," he said.

"Yes, she did."

"He's a good kid. I'm pretty damn lucky."

This blithe hypocrisy made her sick. She could forgive him, already had forgiven him for the mistake that sent him to prison. He'd been young then, behave rashly. Lying in his arms she'd known she could live with that. But his treatment of the child.

"Sage," he said, "I hope you won't mind renting to a man with a child. Charlie won't be any problem."

"I'm sure he won't," she said in a tight voice.

"I'm glad we went out there today. I wanted you to meet Janet and Gabe. They're very special to me."

I'll bet they are, thought Sage savagely. They overlook every rotten thing you've ever done. You're three of a kind, turning your backs on responsibility, demanding everything on your own terms. She was amazed that he could be driving along with a half smile on his face, oblivious to the fury beside him.

"Look, Sage, I was going to say this under more, shall we say, romantic circumstances, but it's been such a good day—" For the first time she saw him having trouble with words. "What I mean is—" He hesitated. "You know all about me. Janet said you talked about it."

"Yes."

"I'm going to be the town leper for a while. I know that. Maybe I've no damn right to ask, but do you think you could—I mean, it's important to me that you, of all people—"

"That I forgive you?"

"Yes." The word was almost inaudible.

She couldn't speak. She was too filled with outrage. She'd been able to forgive him for a wretched crime, but abandoning his own son... Not only was he an ex-drug dealer, he'd fathered an illegitimate child for whom he was only now taking any responsibility. As soon as he'd been released from prison he'd gone on a spree of self-indulgence, expecting others to care for the little boy while he worked in lumber camps, on freighters, climbed the Alps and Himalayas. What kind of husband would such a man make? What kind of father? The word *contemporary* sprang to mind. Roper was a product of his times, like the young men she'd read about who took pride in avoiding marriage, who prized their life-style above all else. Fleetingly, she wished she could be indifferent, accept the changing world. She knew she could never wrench him from her heart. Yet she must. When she finally spoke she was appalled at how self-righteous she sounded. "My grandmother always said we must forgive the person, if not the behavior."

"A good Christian precept, but it has a chilly ring to it." He gave her a quick look, his eyes baffled.

"It's the best I can do." She heard herself as if from a distance. "Chalk it up to my being reared with old values. I admit," she said coldly, "to seeming behind the times."

"But just a few hours ago—"

"Let's say I've had time to think." She wasn't about to discuss the child. She had to stay cool. "As you said, I'm a throwback. It may come as a shock but I still believe in words like honor and integrity." Oh, God, why couldn't she phrase it differently. She couldn't stop herself. "What's more, it's part of my heritage. Your heritage."

"But, last night...this morning." He shook his head. His voice was hollow. "I guess you've answered my question."

She had to turn to look at him, make certain she'd inflicted the maximum pain. She was not disappointed. His face was drawn and gray. They rode mile after mile through the spring twilight in silence. As soon as they pulled into the driveway Sage got out of the car and without a word walked to her house. She knew he was standing there, watching her. There were lights blazing in Franny's apartment. She hesitated, deciding that Franny's parents had come back and that she should go to them. Then she saw two men come out of the door to the tenants' entrance hall. One was carrying a black case, the other had a camera. Without noticing her, they headed for the gate to the street.

Duncan stood at the top of the piazza steps. He was carrying a slip of paper. "I was about to leave a message for you," he said. Sage looked at him blankly.

"You're to call a Lieutenant Carney, at this number." He handed her the paper.

"But I've already talked to the police," she said wearily. "There's nothing more I can—"

Abruptly he hurried down the steps, brushing past her. As he touched her, she pulled back. A coldness seemed to spread inside her. At the foot of the steps, he stopped and spoke without turning. "They've decided it wasn't suicide, after all," he said.

THIRTEEN

SAGE WATCHED Clay watching her. She sat stiffly on the drawing room sofa. She still was trying to deal with the fact that a murder had been committed in her house. She knew it was a reality, but she shrank from the thought that came with it, the chilling conviction that Franny's death was somehow connected with her illusory night prowler.

Her head throbbed. She knew that her eyes were swollen. The racking sobs of the night before had not only been for Franny, but had come from learning the truth about Roper and his child. She'd been savaged by a sense of loss, of being given what she wanted most in life only to lose it. After a sleepless night, she'd managed to pull herself together; she'd survive. She'd applied Amanda de Vries's face and was wearing Elise's yellow satin lounging robe. She was certain she looked like a woman in control of herself.

"Perhaps I should stay," Clay said, "to be with you when you talk to the lieutenant."

"Thank you, Clay. I'm sure I can handle it. I've been through it once with Sergeant Meigs."

"If you'll just remember, Sage, to be—"

"I know, cooperative but not expansive, involve myself no more than—"

"Exactly."

She was determined to set herself at a distance from Franny's death, approach it objectively. "But how can they be sure it wasn't suicide?" she asked calmly.

Clay paused. He seemed distracted, at odds with himself, as if his mind were elsewhere. "As soon as they saw the—body, they ordered a complete autopsy. There were signs, or rather the absence of signs associated with death by gas poisoning." Again he hesitated.

"Go on."

"When death is caused by carbon monoxide inhalation, the face, particularly the lips, become deeply reddened, the pupils of the eyes greatly dilated."

"What did the autopsy show?"

"No carbon monoxide in the lungs," he said. "It was determined that she died from a blow on the back of her head."

"But there was no blood, Clay. I saw her. She wasn't bleeding."

"She was struck by an object covered with something that prevented a break in the skin."

"You mean whoever killed her tried to make it look like suicide? They turned on the gas to make us think—"

"That appears to be the case."

She wanted to ask if Lieutenant Carney had questioned Roper, the one person on the premises with a criminal record. "Have they picked up any suspects?" she asked.

"They're looking for her boyfriend, one Chip Waggoner. He works for one of those used-car outfits in North Charleston. He's from Durham," Clay added.

"Have they questioned Duncan?"

"The fellow downstairs? Yes. Last night and this morning."

"Anyone else, Clay?"

"They want to talk with Elise," he said, "but I asked that they wait until this afternoon. She's a little under the weather." Seeing Sage's look of surprise, he elaborated. "They have to question everyone who had access to the house. Elise, as you know, has keys to both doors." He was staring at her but she felt his thoughts were not there. "And, of course," he went on, "the lieutenant spent considerable time with Roper Chalfont."

When she opened her door to Lieutenant Carney an hour later, she saw him appraise her with obvious pleasure. She also noticed that it gave her no satisfaction. He looked like Warren Beatty with wider spaces between his front teeth. Except for his tie, even Elise couldn't have faulted his appearance. "Miss Eliot, I apologize for bothering you," he said in a pleasant, deep voice.

He loved the house. "I've never been in one of these old places before. Good lord, look at the height of those ceilings!" He waited until she was seated, watching with admiration as she sank gracefully, if wearily, onto the sofa. She had expected to be grilled, led into traps, but he relaxed at once and told her how glad he was to be living in Charleston. "I didn't know cities like this existed in our country," he said. He told her how much he liked being on the seacoast, the friendliness of southerners. "It's a far cry from New Jersey," he grinned.

He told her about being an orphan, growing up in a series of foster homes in Hackensack. Almost wistfully, he asked her about her own childhood. She found herself giving an autobiographical sketch, beginning with the death of her parents. She couldn't help but be warmed by the attention in his steady gray eyes. Though she'd been taught never to discuss money with anyone but family she admitted to the house being a financial drain.

"It's a good thing you have those rental units," he said, "though I expect being a landlady presents problems."

Sage smiled. "My sister and brother-in-law don't trust my judgment." Immediately she sobered, realizing that Elise and Clay must feel entirely justified.

"You strike me as a person of excellent judgment," said Lieutenant Carney with charming candor. Sage looked at him gratefully. "It's just too bad," he added, "that Franny Barth didn't use better judgment."

"You think her boyfriend—my brother-in-law said you were looking for him—you think he—"

"I think, in this case, there were more than one. The fellow downstairs, McFee, says he's seen a couple of men leaving her apartment. One fit Chip Waggoner's description. We're not sure about the other. McFee says he saw a tall man, who limped a little, leaving just a few nights ago."

"But that must have been Clay, my brother-in-law. He wasn't leaving Franny's apartment! I saw him going through the gate that night just as I started up the steps. He'd obviously come by to see me about something. Why should Duncan say such a thing?"

"He implied there might even be others."

"He's just being spiteful," said Sage, "because Franny wouldn't go out with him. And when I think of how nice she was to him! Franny was a kind, decent person." Sage felt the sting of tears. "Dammit, she even let him do his laundry. At first when I saw him in there, I was upset, then I realized it was the way

Franny was, you know, really sweet and thoughtful."
She told him about the kitten.

The lieutenant must have seen her tears. He waited
a few seconds before he went on. "I'm going to meet
with your sister this afternoon. Your brother-in-law
said she's the only other person with keys to both your
doors. I hope she won't mind talking to me. It's routine to check with anyone who had access to the
house." He leaned back. "You know," he said, "I've
never liked the idea of anyone else having a key to my
place. I live alone and in case I lose my key I leave one
with this friend across the hall, but I don't feel good
about it. I mean, I trust him, but I don't know anything about his friends."

"I know what you mean." Sage found it comforting to talk with him. "My sister lost her keys, including the ones to this house and I got a little frantic."
Before she knew it she was telling him about the
sounds she thought she'd heard at night. Because he
seemed only mildly interested in this, she omitted
mentioning the incident of the fur coat. But he did ask
her if she remembered exactly when she'd heard the
sounds. She could be certain of only three dates, one
a few nights earlier, the night she'd fallen. "Of course,
I could have imagined it," she said, "and fortunately
Elise found the keys under the front seat of her car.
But not before I'd had the keys duplicated and suffered an attack of acute paranoia."

He laughed with her. "Paranoia?"

"Oh, you know, thinking of the party where she
thought she'd lost the keys, beginning to suspect that
one of those poor old souls—"

He laughed again. "Poor old souls? Where was this
party? At a nursing home?"

"It was at my aunt's." Spurred by the glint of amusement in his eyes, she told him about Octo and the Readers and Writers. She gave what she had to admit to herself was a colorful description of the group. He found this so entertaining that she almost told him about the cards Octo had left around the house to bolster her self-esteem but stopped, remembering her promise to her aunt.

When he finally rose to go, she noticed it was with some regret. "I'm afraid we may have to bother you again," he said, "checking out a few things up here. We did some preliminaries yesterday, in the back hall, but—"

"The back hall?"

"The steps that lead from the laundry up here, the door into the kitchen and this room. I hope you don't mind. Your brother-in-law met us here. As I said, it's just routine. You see, whoever had access to Miss Barth's apartment also had entry to the main house. And vice versa."

"When I told Franny she could use the laundry room that didn't occur to me. I wasn't very smart."

"But you were kind and thoughtful," said the lieutenant with a smile.

She saw him to the door, going out to the piazza steps with him as if he were a guest. He shook hands, thanked her sincerely. Halfway down the steps, he turned for another glance, another smile.

She remembered something and started to call him back, but he was through the gate. No doubt he already knew that Duncan had a key to Franny's apartment.

A grayness muted all the new color in the garden. Hers was the only car parked in the yard. The door and windows of the carriage house were closed. Her feeling of desolation was sudden. Twenty-four hours ago she'd been with Roper at Edisto. A few hours before that she'd lain in his arms as if it were the most natural thing in the world. Briefly, traitorously, her body quickened. For one night, transformed by the promise of what could be, she had found herself at the very center of life. She forced herself to think of the little boy.

Octo called, minutes later. She sounded out of breath. "Sage, I've been trying to reach you all morning at Elise's. Bea said that you were to stay there last night. The phone rang and rang. Then when I called a minute ago Etta said you hadn't stayed but—" There was a great deal of noise; distant clinkings and clatterings, dominated by a voice braying in the background.

"Aunt Octo, what's going on there? All that noise!"

"Noise, dear? Oh, that's what I called about. Eldredge and I are making a Lady Baltimore cake."

Sage realized at once that her aunt had not yet been told that Franny had been murdered. "A cake," she murmured.

"For the anniversary," said Octo brightly.

"Anniversary?"

"The twenty-fifth anniversary of the Readers and Writers! Tomorrow. We're using St. Philip's hall and we've invited over a hundred and twenty people, even some of the Poetry Society. Sage, didn't you get an invitation? Oh, it's going to be marvelous. We're having a regular program. Meta Marsh's nephew on piano, Deirdre on cello, and Stephanie Burroughs on harp; while Eldredge reads from the *Rubyiat,* Juani-

ta's daughter, Alice, will do an interpretive dance."
The braying had risen to a high whinny.

"Octo, what in heaven's name is that?"

Octo paused, listening. "Eldredge. I believe he's
into the big tenor aria from the last act of Puccini's
Turandot. Sage, please tell me you'll come."

"Aunt, I'll try," said Sage weakly.

"And if you could manage a dozen tunafish sandwiches—"

"I'll do my best," promised Sage.

"I know you will, Sage. Incidentally," Octo lowered her voice, "you haven't seen David Raeburn,
have you?"

"David? No. Why?"

"Oh, it's just that Peter was by earlier this morning, looking for him. He seemed a bit grim." Octo
chortled. "But then Peter's not exactly a barrel of
laughs, is he? I reminded him of the party, and suggested they might bring a few deviled eggs. You don't
think that was out of order, do you, Sage?"

"No, Aunt."

"Eldredge insists you stay with us tonight. He's
made a seafood chowder."

"Thanks, Aunt, but I told Elise I'd stay with her."

"All right, but you won't forget the party?"

"No. Aunt Octo," she said, "have you learned any
more about Eldredge? I mean, his background or—"

"No, dear. There hasn't been time." Octo's tone
was indulgent. "And you must remember, Sage, he's
a very private person, quite shy really, something of an
introvert." Sage heard a crash, followed by a distant
roar of frustration. Octo hung up.

She took off the yellow robe and put on her old
clothes. To distract herself she cleaned the kitchen

while the kitten sat on a counter watching her. She tried to eat a bowl of Octo's gumbo. She distracted herself with a fantasy, to force herself to stop thinking about Franny, Franny so young and full of life, suddenly lifeless. She saw herself discovering the key to the whereabouts of Elizabeth Benford's diamond parure. She imagined going instantly to the hiding place, a safe concealed in the paneling of the library. She saw a worn velvet box with a satin lining, the sudden blaze of jewels. Even more vividly, she saw herself writing checks, Octo's house resplendently painted and with handsome iron grills over the windows, her own house swarming with industrious workmen making repairs, including two hundred feet of new guttering. She saw the carriage house empty again, herself older and far wiser, ready to face the future. The thought of this last sent her running upstairs to her work room to scan the diaries again. Two hours later she was still bogged down in Charlotte's misguided passion for the obnoxious Reverend Gill. She was further depressed by the realization that she'd been just as misguided as Charlotte.

When the phone rang again she decided she'd better answer. Elise's voice was not soothing. It was barely under control. "Sage, where have you been? I've called three times!"

"Maybe I was in the tub."

"For three hours?"

"Cleanliness is next to godliness, Lise."

"Sage, don't get funny with me! Do you realize what you've done? Didn't Clay warn you?"

"Warn me about what?"

"That police lieutenant! Good lord, did you have to tell him everything you could think of?"

"What are you talking about? He was very pleasant. By any standards, he's a gentleman. He's—"

"He's a pro, you idiot! Did you have to tell him about the keys? Do you know what he's doing right now? He's gotten a list of everyone who was at Octo's birthday party. He's questioning each of them, all those flaky old poets, all our relatives—"

"But—"

"Clay says under no circumstances are you to talk to that lieutenant again unless he's present. And he thinks you should stay with us until this awful thing is settled."

"I'm staying with Octo," Sage lied quickly.

"Good. Under no circumstances are you to stay there alone," said Elise sternly. "Someone murdered that girl, and whoever they are, they're still walking around."

After she'd hung up, Sage sat looking at Auralee's watercolor of a wren in a mimosa branch. Lord, how she envied Auralee, born into that quiet era, preoccupied with her birds and the great Mr. Audubon. She looked more closely at the timid rendering of the wren, thought of Charlotte, thirty years later, finding her aunt's paintings "bold" and "unlovely." She wondered how Charlotte would have reacted to the brilliant and dramatic pictures "Jostle" painted. Poor Charlotte. Sage imagined her getting the news that the Reverend Gill had married the belle from Savannah. Did she cry? Did she cringe with shame over her dead dreams? Or did she shove it all under the rug? There was no entry in the diary to mark the occasion.

Suddenly Sage was aware of the magnitude of her own idiocy. She saw herself running around like some addled ninny; she reviewed what she'd told Lieuten-

ant Carney. In an effort to charm the policeman, she'd
managed to cast suspicion on Duncan, Clay, the
Readers and Writers and most of her relatives.

The day darkened too quickly. By six o'clock she
was turning on lamps, closing windows, because it
looked like a night of rain. She checked the doors to
be sure they were locked, going down to the laundry
room to make certain of the door to Franny's apartment. She hurried back up the steps, then stood in the
drawing room, aware of shadows, the weakness of the
pools of light. I'll call Octo, she thought. I'll spend the
night there. Then she thought of Octo and Eldredge
being questioned by the police, of what she'd done to
them and everyone else. She considered drinking some
of the bourbon that Bea had brought, and passing out,
but decided that this could set her on the road to al-
coholism. She'd passed out two nights ago at Roper's. She'd had more to drink in the last five days
than in all the rest of her life combined.

She took the dog outside at ten and saw that her car
was still the only one parked in the yard. When she
went back inside, she couldn't find the kitten. She
called again and again, her voice echoing through the
house. She searched under chairs and sofas, looked in
closets. Finally, carrying a poker and followed by
Major, she went up to bed. As she reached the upstairs hall the kitten came mincing down the steps from
the top floor.

Sitting propped up in bed, fully clothed, Sage was
chagrined to realize how much she must look like
Octo. She sat rigid, waiting.

The house where she had spent most of her life had
become alien territory. It had been violated by murder. Even the air seemed different, charged. Her eyes

burned. Every sound was magnified, the rattle of a windowpane, the loose shutter on the top floor, the scuttling inside the walls. She held her breath, certain she'd heard footsteps overhead, a dragging sound. Oh God, she thought, if only Roper—

When the phone rang she started with terror. Still clutching the poker, she unlocked the bedroom door and went into the hall.

"Sage, it's Clay."

"Oh." She couldn't believe how glad she was to hear his voice. She didn't care if he scolded her for not being at Octo's, for spilling the beans to the lieutenant.

"I've got good news," he said. "I didn't want to wait until morning to tell you. The police have picked up Franny Barth's boyfriend, that Chip Waggoner. They won't admit it yet, but they're pretty sure they've got their man. His fingerprints are all over her apartment. They even found them on that back hall door that leads into your drawing room."

"The back hall—"

"Oh, he made some lame excuse, said that one night while he was waiting for Franny to come back from a meeting he just slipped upstairs for a look. Sage, you aren't missing anything, are you? You'd better check."

"No. No, I'm not." There was no point in mentioning that she had heard Chip Waggoner prowling through the whole house. It would only prompt a lecture from Clay. The nightmare was over.

"Apparently," said Clay, "this Waggoner fellow has a record. Car theft when he was a juvenile. Heaven knows what he's been up to since then. I just wanted to report this, to put your mind at rest."

"Thank you, Clay."

"I hope all this has taught you a lesson."

"It has, Clay."

She crawled back in bed and lay reveling in her sense of relief. Obviously, it was Franny's boyfriend who had been going through her house at night, looking for something to steal. He'd come in through the laundry room, once Franny was asleep. Then Franny had found out and he'd... She'd been living with panic for weeks, as if with some illness. It had not only set her nerves on edge but impaired her judgment. She thought with regret of her behavior at Mille Fleurs. She'd fled like a frightened child instead of dealing with the situation. She clung to the feeling of relief. But it was ephemeral. Deep down she still was profoundly ill at ease. Her life seemed encircled by secrecy, by people who were all concealing some part of their lives. She knew this was true of Elise and Clay. Even Octo wanted to hide the fact that she'd been robbed. The relationship between David and Peter Larson was an enigma, their behavior unnatural. There was something odd about Duncan. Bea was a masquerade. And Franny, poor Franny with her secret love. Roper. He had more to hide than anyone. Now all his ugly secrets had been revealed. Or had they? Was there worse to come? She detested him, hated him for what he'd made her feel. She tried to fix her mind on hating him.

The sound of the phone ringing made her nerves jump. She looked at her watch. Who would be calling at eleven o'clock?

Bea didn't sound the least apologetic. Undoubtedly she kept unorthodox hours. "I thought you'd want to know," she said. "I just talked to my friend again, the one with the FBI lover. When I saw you the other day, I had a little info—oh, we were interrupted, weren't we? Anyway he finally got the whole story. Are you ready for this? It seems our pal David concocted a whole fiction about himself. He never taught in a boys' school, never even got a graduate degree." Bea's voice had the urgency of a sportscaster. "What's more, there never was any tragic car accident, no months of recuperation in a hospital. But there were plenty of months someplace else—a loony bin! He's been in and out for years. Sweetie, our David is a real psycho. Has been for most of his life. Lots of weird incidents with Mama covering up afterward. The last was the worst, a girl up in Boston, almost beaten to death. He was picked up by the cops, charged, then miraculously all charges were dropped. Mama again with the big bucks. The girl's living in a condo in Lauderdale. Look, Sage, I hate to spring all this on you, but—"

"That's all right, Bea." She couldn't say more. She replaced the receiver, then sat without moving for a long time. She felt as if someone close to her had died. Slowly, with a dull ache of grief, she found her whole, blurred relationship with David coming into focus. She knew why he had brutalized the girl in Boston.

Images of him rose to crowd her mind, the gentle, handsome man who'd first attracted her, their dinner together when he'd said, "You're so different from the women I've known," their walk on the battery and his enthusiasm about starting a school. Enthusiasm for a fantasy. His whole life had become a fragile fantasy. She'd helped it along, reinforced with the vision of himself he saw in her eyes, a man who was infinitely attractive, a man who was whole. She knew now why he'd struck her that day at Mille Fleurs. He'd asked

why she'd never married. Trying to show some so-
phistication, she talked about being a free agent,
women's lib, no long-term commitments. She remembered his look of shock, her nervous laughter, his
slapping her. She'd decided the slap was to keep her
from becoming hysterical. She'd been wrong. He
slapped her because she threatened to destroy his fantasy, his vision of her.

Thinking of him, she couldn't see a demented person, a violent person. She could see only the beautiful, sensitive young man, irreparably damaged,
looking for some shred of life that matched his dream.

As she waited for sleep that night, she tried to con-
sole herself with a feeling of safety. They'd found
Franny's murderer. There was no more mystery about
the night prowler. For some reason she kept remembering Bea's words, blithely spoken but oddly disqui-
eting. "We're all incognito."

FOURTEEN

SHE WALKED OUT of her house into a dazzling morning. She'd slept late. Of course, there had been no night sounds, not even a bad dream. Her sense of safety was reclaimed. Most important, she'd come to terms with what she'd learned about David. David's tragedy was part of the real world, a bewildering, often menacing world in which she knew she must finally learn to live. Even though she wore Amanda de Vries's face and Elise's green linen dress, the woman inside had a new identity, viewing life with a wiser eye, unclouded by delusions and unrealistic expectations.

She had almost reached her car when Roper walked out of the carriage house. He saw her, paused for a few seconds, then walked over to her. It was the second time she'd ever seen him in a business suit. The rugged barbarian was obscured. He looked older, unfamiliar, surprisingly distinguished. There was no glint of humor in his eyes, no teasing smile.

"I was going to call you," he said. "I wanted to let you know that I'll be leaving. My lease specifies a month's notice but I can make it earlier if you like."

"That won't be necessary." She was taken aback for a moment. "I mean, if you—"

"I've found a house on Beaufain Street, pretty much what I've been looking for, the right size, a big yard."

"I see." They stood stiffly, locked in formality. His face gave her no clue to what he was thinking. She felt as if she were wearing a tight mask. "Don't worry about the lease," she said. "Whatever you decide will be fine."

For her the pause was awkward, but he didn't seem to notice. He was staring up at her house. "I talked to someone I know at police headquarters," he said. "He told me they picked up the man they think murdered your tenant."

"Yes."

"You're still staying alone there?"

"Of course."

"Is that a good idea?" He was looking at her now, his face unreadable.

"Why not? What happened was between him and Franny. It has nothing to do with me. Besides, the man's in custody."

"If they don't have enough evidence or if bail is posted, he could be released."

"I'll take my chances." She opened her car door, then turned without meeting his glance. "Thank you for your concern."

Driving to her sister's she congratulated herself on her lack of feeling. She quickly discarded the thought that it was numbness prompted by a need for self-survival. She concentrated on the golden clarity of the morning, accenting the lines of the tiled roofs, porticos, Palladian windows, setting the gardens behind filigrees of wrought iron ablaze with color. She was anxious to tell Elise of the decisions she'd made, first a job, then graduate school, the big decision about the house.

Etta met her at the door. "Just see you now," she beamed at Sage. "Honey, I had to look twice. Got yourself up real sweet!"

Sage hugged the old woman. "Etta, I thought your oldest girl said you had to quit. Didn't Debra say that—"

"That Debra," laughed Etta, "big lawyer lady. I tell her, what she want me to do? Watch the soaps? Lose my Social Security on bingo?" Etta's rich laugh filled the hallway, echoed up the stairwell. "I tell her things are just too interesting around here for me to retire now."

"Where's Lise?"

"Cooking up a storm. Callie, she quit. I tell Lise not to hire that Callie in the first place. Callie stay two, maybe three week then she hightail it outa here. Says she'd been browning with fat-back and cooking in English for twenty-five years and she's not about to clear-i-fy butter and talk to her pots in a foreign tongue."

Going through the dining room Sage noticed that the table gleaming with silver and crystal was set for twelve. "Putting on the dog tonight," chuckled Etta.

Elise was wearing an old caftan. Her hair in strings, her face shiny with sweat, she stood among her Bazaar Français cookware, Swedish appliances, and counters overflowing with vegetables, fruits, herbs, and spices. She greeted her sister with an anxious, "Sage, try this." She dipped into a copper pot and held out the spoon. Sage took a taste and rolled her eyes. She was surprised and pleased that Elise wasn't using a caterer.

"*Magnifique,* Lise."

Etta took her turn and smacked her lips. "Always been partial to tripe."

"Sweetbreads," corrected Elise. "Etta, I have not spent the last three hours creating *ris de veau à la crème et aux champignons* just to have you stand there and call it tripe. What's more, you've spent the whole morning in here giggling and making me feel like a jackass.''

"You'd best get outa here," suggested Etta, "and do something about your hair."

"And you'd best check the towels in the powder room and see to the glasses on the bar."

"Tripe is tripe," insisted Etta.

"Etta—"

"I'm gone."

"She drives me crazy," said Elise, picking up a bunch of asparagus, then putting it down again.

"I thought Debra said she had to retire."

"I'd die if she did." Elise brushed back a strand of hair. "She teases me, puts me down, reminds me daily of how she used to change my diapers but—" Elise half smiled, "nobody else in the world calls me Sugar Baby."

"Lise, there's something I want to tell you."

"Let's go out on the piazza, Sage. I've been chained to this stove all morning."

Elise's piazza was ready for the long summer. A new straw rug had been laid, all the white wicker freshly painted, the green and white slipcovers laundered. Flowering pots of impatiens hung between pillars. Beyond, in a garden designed fifty years earlier by an Italian landscape artist, plants, shrubs, and trees, clipped, shaped, and espaliered, bloomed in perfection.

Elise slumped in a chair, rubbed her eyes. "God, Sage, I can't get that girl out of my mind. I mean, right in your house."

"Clay said the police are sure it was her boyfriend. I just wonder what could have driven him to—unless it was jealousy. Duncan told Lieutenant Carney that—"

"Jealousy! Why do people always assume it's a crime of passion? He could have been forcing her to steal drugs from the medical university, the hospital—"

"Lise, she was a secretary! She didn't have access to drugs."

"And then," said Elise, ignoring this, "she wanted to quit, get out of it. Maybe she threatened to go to the police and confess."

Sage stared at her sister. She'd never seen her so on edge, almost haggard. "Lise, are you all right?" she asked quietly.

Elise glared at her. "Of course I'm all right. For God's sake, don't you start in, too! I've had Etta fussing at me all morning." She straightened her back. "You said you had something to tell me."

"I do. I'm going to get a job."

"A job?" Elise looked blank. "Where?"

"I know. You're thinking nobody in their right mind would hire me. But I'm determined." Sage pulled a newspaper clipping from her purse. "I've been checking the classified ads and the possibilities are endless."

"Such as?"

"Listen to this one: 'Bachelor would like to share home in exchange for light housekeeping duties, with an attractive, fun-loving redhead, age twenty to thirty-five.'"

"You're not a redhead." Elise smiled in spite of herself.

"But I'm fun-loving."

"Try again, Sage."

"'Go-Go Girls, daytime hours. Top pay. Apply in person. We train amateurs and beginners.'"

"My dear, Go-Go girls all have great big—"

"I'll buy an enormous bra," said Sage firmly, "and fill in the gaps with after-dinner mints." She was delighted to hear her sister burst out laughing. "Lise, I'm going to let Clay have the house," she said.

Elise looked stunned. Then her face cleared. She sighed. "Sage, I think you're doing the right thing. Honey, I know how much the house means to you, but—"

"I was just being stubborn, putting it off. I knew I couldn't keep it forever." Sage decided the hollowness she felt was due to having skipped breakfast. "I hope Clay will be pleased," she added.

"You know he will. And, as Clay told you, anytime you want it back, anytime you're in a position to live there again—"

"No." Sage was surprised at the sharpness of her own voice. "I won't be living there again. Tomorrow, I'm going to enroll in a secretarial course; then I'm going to look for an apartment. It's taken me a long time, Lise, too long, but I think I've finally grown up. No more unreasonable hopes—"

"I know what you mean," Elise broke in, then paused, her eyes bleak. "Believe me, I know." She got up, moved to the railing, and plucked a dead leaf from one of the hanging plants.

"Sage, that man at your debut party, the one who wrote all over your dance card, then had a phone call and didn't come back—did you ever see him again? I mean, during the years after the dance?"

"You know," said Sage, "I think mints are a bit passé. I might stuff my front with candied ginger."

On her way home she bought the makings of her contribution to the Readers and Writers celebration, including an extra can of tuna for the kitten. When she pulled into her driveway Major was no longer in the garden where she'd left him. She decided he must be on one of his rare but thorough tours of the neighborhood. The kitten, too, had disappeared. There was no response even when she climbed the steps and called from the upstairs hall. As she made the sandwiches, carefully cutting off crusts, she thought of how much Major loved such sinfully fattening scraps and put some aside for him.

After setting off for Octo's, she changed her mind and headed for the church hall. She couldn't face a discussion of the murder with Octo and Eldredge. She didn't want to run the risk of seeing David. She'd drop off the sandwiches and make a quick getaway. She had no plans to attend the celebration, but knew she must have an interesting reason. Octo abhorred banal excuses. She'd tell her aunt that she'd started a poem about love and death and lost track of time.

The church hall vibrated with activity. A covey of ladies were laying a white cloth over five card tables pushed together. A banner with the group's motto, *Sic Iter Ad Astra,* was being nailed to a beam by Juanita Whipple, who stood on a spindly ladder braced by Mary Virginia Kemmelwright. A fat youth was banging out something discordant and faintly oriental on an upright piano. Juanita's daughter, Alice, her gray hair pulled into a ponytail that hung to her fanny, her ample curves encased in a black leotard and tights, rose up in a writhing motion, banged her fist against her brow, then sank to the floor again. Viola Spinner, sitting in what looked to be a discarded bishop's chair, stared into space. At her feet two small girls were blowing up balloons. Sage thrust her tray at a young man in clericals who sat at a side table, fashioning commemorative rosettes out of purple ribbon, and fled.

On her way home she concentrated on imagining herself in the world of working women. She imagined getting up while it was still dark, dressing to achieve a look of attractive efficiency, eating a cup of yogurt and wheat germ, then going off to a beautifully appointed office where a distinguished doctor, lawyer, or bank president would say, "Miss Eliot, I don't know what we would do without you." Sternly she presented herself with a more likely picture—the cramped, evil-smelling office of a sleazy loan company, with a potbellied, cigar-smoking boss saying, "This letter's all wrong! Whadya think I'm payin' you for, lady?"

After she'd parked the car in the yard, she sat staring at the carriage house. She allowed herself to think about Roper. She realized that here her outrageous tendency to fantasize had reached new heights. She'd reinvented him, stamped him with the qualities she longed to find in a man, an unreal combination of tenderness and strength. Her numbness had deserted her. Once again she felt aching loss. Let him go, she told herself. Some day you'll wake up and be able to remember him without any pain at all.

She spent the rest of the day going from room to room, deciding what to keep. She knew she wouldn't have space for all the books she wanted. An efficiency apartment wouldn't have a bedroom big enough for her four-poster and the pier glass. She made two lists and then tore them up. She ate the tunafish sandwich she'd saved and drank some milk. She was sitting in the drawing room looking blankly at the portrait of Thomas Benford when she realized that it had gotten dark. She opened the front door to see if Major had come back, but the piazza was empty. So was the yard. There were no lights burning in the carriage house or in Duncan's apartment. She called to the dog several times and then went back in the house. Major had stayed away overnight several times, once for two days. The kitten was still in hiding. She was quite alone, but it didn't bother her.

Before she went to bed she sat with the newspaper and made a list of apartments that were in her price range. First she'd enroll at business school and then find a place to live. Clay could handle the sale of the house. As she climbed the stairs she thought of all she'd lost and was yet to lose. First Gran, followed by all her own destructive illusions. Now the house. She ignored the sudden lump in her throat. And Roper.

Be positive, she ordered. There's one thing you should be grateful to lose—fear.

FIFTEEN

THE SOFT CRYING, distant at first, grew sharper. Lifting her head Sage thought hazily of baby swifts, newhatched and nesting in the chimney. She sank back on the pillow. The sounds came again, thin plaintive wails, much closer now; a mewing inches from where she lay. The kitten. Without opening her eyes she patted the bed, calling, "Come on, kitty, come up here, come on, kitty." But the kitten didn't jump on the bed and curl up beside her. The crying persisted. She tried to ignore it, to fall back into the pit of sleep.

The mewing became a howl of distress. Sage fumbled at the bedside lamp, turned it on. She looked under one side of the bed, then the other, glanced around the room. The kitten was nowhere in sight. The cries continued. As her mind cleared she discovered that the sounds came from directly behind the headboard of the bed. With a groan she realized what had happened. The kitten was inside the wall. In its exploration of the top floor it had found the one opening between roof and eaves that led through the network of walls in the house. Mice and squirrels had found it before. Sage remembered Gran's old tabby, Cleo, screeching from the wall of the dining room. By the time they'd reached the storeroom Cleo had managed her own escape and sauntered forth to greet them.

Sage got out of bed and put on her slippers. Padding across the hall and up the steps she couldn't help but enjoy the fact that after months of dread she now could move about her house in the middle of the night quite normally. Franny's murderer, Chip Waggoner, had prowled the rooms, rooted through boxes, moved books, but as far as she knew he'd taken nothing. Briefly, thinking of the incident with the coat, she shivered.

When she switched on the top floor light she paused for a moment to look at her great-grandmother's square piano, its top piled high with boxes.

The kitten was wailing now from the opposite wall. Calling loudly, Sage went to the door of the northeast storeroom and turned on the light. In the merciless glare, the jumble of trunks, boxes, and plaster trash bags filled with old clothes greeted her like a reproach. She picked her way across the room, then stopped at the small door leading to the narrow space between the wall of the room and the outer wall of the house. She'd wondered how Thomas Benford could be certain of a servant skinny enough to crawl in and go out to the balcony to open and close the high window above the stairs. She shoved aside Gran's steamer trunk. "Kitty," she called. She wished she'd brought a flashlight, considered going downstairs for one, and abandoned the idea. Cats could see in the dark. As soon as the kitten saw her it could come toward her.

Firmly putting aside her wariness of rats and spiders, she squeezed through the opening. It was pitch black, narrower even than she remembered. There was barely room to crouch. The dust was thick, plastic flaking where she brushed against it. Her back to the outside wall, she touched the beams and looked toward the pitch of the roof into darkness. "Kitty," she called. She reached upward, hoping the cat would see her hand and come down. She reached still farther, straining, calling. She was touching something. Glass. Bottles, there in the beams, between the partitions. She remembered Octo telling her that wines used to be stored between the attic and the eaves, "just as in the days of Horace and Maecenas." She pulled down a bottle, set it beside her, pulled down another. When she reached again something came toward her like a landslide. With both hands she caught it, braced it before it hit her full in the face. She felt a dry roughness, some kind of cloth and the weight of whatever it covered. She relaxed her hold and it moved heavily toward her. She felt a keen thrill of discovery. Someone had hidden this. It must be of value. And it was so big. Grabbing it in both arms, dust flying in her face, she eased it down until it wedged between her and the inner wall. She sneezed, sneezed again. It was much more unwieldy than she'd expected, but gradually she was able to shift her body to one side. On her hands and knees she pushed her bulky find toward the lighted square of the opening and shoved it through. Blinking at the sudden brightness, she crawled after it.

She knelt on the floor, looking down at her find. It was a large nondescript bundle wrapped in heavy canvas, securely tied. It can't be the parure, she thought, then realized the stupidity of this assumption. The parure could have been wrapped and hidden with other valuables. Clumsily, her fingers shaking, she untied the cord, picking at the knots. It seemed to take forever. Finally she pulled away the canvas.

The first things she saw were the neat bundles of letters. Underneath lay four huge leather-bound volumes. She searched carefully. There was no velvet box lined with satin, no blaze of jewels. She almost wept.

She looked at the address on one of the letters:
Thomas H. Benford, Esq. Charlotte's father. That
explained the wine bottles. Madeira. "Remember the
Madeira," he told her. She sighed. Then she couldn't
help smiling. Once again she'd expected life to be true
to fiction: "Local Girl Finds Family Heirlooms."
Something soft rubbed against her ankle, and looking down she saw the kitten.

Tomorrow she'd go through Thomas Benford's letters and papers. There might be something of interest
to add to the family history. She piled the bundles of
letters on the steamer trunk. She'd have to find somewhere to store the volumes. They were far too big for
the library shelves. Idly, she opened the top one,
turned the heavy page, marveling at the pristine con-
dition of the paper. She looked at the title.

THE
BIRDS OF AMERICA

from Original Drawings by

JOHN JAMES AUDUBON
Fellow of the Royal Societies of Edinburgh and
of the
Linnaean and Zoological Societies of London
Member of the Natural History Society of Paris,
of the Lyceum of New York

Published by the Author
1827-30

She read the words, then reread them. She had
trouble breathing, her body went hot, then cold. She'd
found a treasure beyond her wildest hopes. The last

time she'd read about an Audubon folio, it was val-
ued at over a million dollars. She stared down at the
title again. She turned the page. The great bronzy bird,
a wild turkey, rose regally against a background of
delicately rendered bamboo. She kept on turning,
seeing the Yellow-Billed Cuckoo, Prothonotary Warbler, Purple Finch. When she reached the sixteenth
plate she looked at the Duck Hawks, one with a
bloody bill, both feeding on the entrails of other dead
birds, and something clicked in her mind. She remembered Charlotte describing Auralee's bird pictures as "too bold and unlovely" to hang. The pictures
Charlotte spoke of had not been painted by Auralee.
They were here before her. Surely this was Auralee's
wedding gift, bought at a private sale, giving the girl
such pleasure because her father had remembered how
much she'd wanted it. Sage lost all track of time,
turning page after page. When she reached the plate
showing the Long-Billed Curlew against a view of
Charleston harbor she thought of Maria Martin
painting backgrounds for the artist. Had Auralee
watched and listened while Maria and Jostle considered appropriate settings for the birds? Sage thought
of the house on Rutledge Avenue, of Audubon, Dr.
Bachman, and Maria working in the room where the
bird skins were prepared and studied, poring over their
specimens, discussing them, with Auralee perhaps
sitting in a corner, quiet as a mouse. She closed the big
volume, laid her hand on the leather binding, imagining Auralee's delight when she opened her gift, the
four volumes that must constitute a complete set.

Suddenly she was in darkness. For several seconds
she sat, disoriented, then realized what had hap-

pened. The bulb had died. It didn't matter. The darkness no longer threatened her. She took time to catch her breath, revel in the staggering enormity of what lay before her, a fortune. At last, still trembling with excitement, she got up from the floor. She stopped. The thought hit her then with a sharp chill. There was no light in the hall. She knew she had turned it on. Both bulbs couldn't have burned out at the same instant. Her throat constricted. She scoured the darkness for the paler shapes of the windows, found the one on the north side of the room, opaque, gray. The eastern window was partially blocked. In the meager light from the upper half of the window, more an absence of darkness, she saw the outline of a head, featureless, almost silvery. A pale head.

Part of her rushed to reject it. The murderer, the prowler had been caught, the nightmare ended. The worst was over. She gaped, unbelieving, at the dim glow of the head, refusing to trust her eyes. Then something clutched at her mind like an icy hand. She was back at Mille Fleurs, waiting behind the door, listening to his footsteps coming up from below. Then she was seeing Franny, lying dead in Roper's arms.

As her mind grappled with terror, her hand was already reaching for some defense, some makeshift weapon. Her fingers closed on the knotted top of a bag of shoes, froze. For the briefest moment she doubted her senses; then the head, pale in the blackness, moved. With a great wrench she lifted the bag and threw it across the room. It hit with a thud, the bag breaking, shoes scattering. But she was already scrambling toward the door, losing a slipper, hands stretched to find her way in the dark. She reached the door, started for the steps; then her foot caught on a

box and she tripped over it. She hit the floor and lay
there stunned. She sensed him coming though there
was no sound. Like an animal she scuttled, half
crawled, half rolled under the old piano. Trembling
she pressed herself against the wall. Then with a desperate cunning she pulled off her other slipper and
easing toward the end of the piano, threw it toward the
stairs. She heard the soft but distinct sound as it
landed somewhere below.

She waited, barely breathing. She heard a step
creak, knew he had gone on down. He would expect
her to head for the front door. When he found it
locked he'd search the downstairs. She had time. She
could creep back to her bedroom, go out on the piazza, and scream for help. No, she'd go to the back
stairs and slip down to the door by the laundry room.

She lay level with the top step, could see it almost
plainly. The high window reflected the greenish glow
of a street lamp. She inched toward the end of the piano that was closest to the steps, started to crawl out,
then stopped. The faintest stirring of the air tore her
gaze from the stairs. She looked to her right and every
nerve in her body jumped. The dark legs were no more
than two feet away. Before she could think or move
he'd dropped to his knees and was reaching for her.

She opened her mouth to scream but no sound
came. She was grabbed, dragged out, lifted like a
bunch of rags. She hit out at the dark body, too terrified to look at the face, her blows ending in air. An
iron hand clutched her hair, another closed around her
throat. Choking, fighting for breath, she arched her
back and with a gigantic effort kicked upward. She
heard the gasp, felt the yielding softness, loosening
hands. She tore free, stumbled toward the steps. She'd

reached the railing when the hands closed again, gripping her arms, lifting, pushing. Bent backward over the banister, she saw a face, half in shadow, glittering cold eyes. She knew she'd fall the second he let go of her. It would kill her or break her back. He stretched above the railing, dragging her upward and over. But as she fell she clung to him. He clawed at her hands but she pulled him with her, hurling them both to the stairs below.

At first it seemed like a dream of falling, the coat thrown, the rank smell and feel of it. She felt pain. Her bones ached, rang. She was alive. It had happened again. The coat had saved her. She tried to move. Her head throbbed. She felt the firmness of the body under her. It was not the coat. With a spasm of revulsion she threw herself sideways, grabbed the stair rail. Slowly, agonizingly, she pulled herself to her feet. She made herself look at him. In the dim light from the telephone table across the hall she saw the odd angle of the body, the head face down. She had pulled him with her and his heavier body had broken her fall. She saw no sign of life.

She moved, wincing with every step, watching, in the big mirror opposite, the girl in a nightgown, staggering like a child learning to walk. She picked up the phone then stood uncertainly. She'd never called the police before. Should she dial the operator? No, she must go outside and call for help. But what if neither Roper nor Duncan was there? What if the streets were empty? She dialed the operator, still watching herself in the mirror, gazing at her own shocked eyes.

Her glance trailed to the middle of the hall. Listening to the voice on the phone, the brisk "May I help you?" she couldn't utter a sound. From the greenish darkness of the stairs a darker form was rising, a silvery white head moving upward. Slowly, relentlessly, swaying ever so slightly it came toward her. She couldn't tear her gaze from the mirror, dared not turn. Paralyzed, she looked at the image of the face behind her. No masklike features, no silvery blond hair, no Peter Larson. It was a hairless head, unearthly, inhuman. The eyes burned with a crazed fire. She turned, watched the dark arms climb the air, saw the black gloved hands reaching for her. Then the house exploded with a crashing sound, a bellow of rage from behind her. The work room door flew open. Roper stood for a fraction of a second, then flung himself forward, crashed into the dark form and pinned it, thrashing, to the floor. Sage felt her legs giving way and then she felt nothing at all.

SIXTEEN

SHE WAS IN HER BED, Elise stretched out beside her. Though sun streamed through the windows and the alarm clock said five after eight, the lamp on the bed-side table still burned. Across the room Clay sprawled in a small armchair, sound asleep. He was wearing wrinkled pants, a sweatshirt, and sandy sneakers. His hair stood on end and he needed a shave. He smiled in his sleep.

Sage turned to her sister. Elise looked as unlike herself as Clay did. She was dressed in jeans and one of Clay's old shirts with the tails hanging out. Eyes closed, lips slightly parted, her hair a tangle on the pillow, she'd never looked more beautiful. The kitten slept in the curve of her arm.

Sage sat up, aware of a painful stiffness, a ringing in her head. From downstairs came the sound of voices. Someone was moving about in the rooms overhead. "Lise," she spoke softly.

Elise stirred, her eyes opened. She pulled herself up, looked at Sage anxiously. "Honey, are you all right?"

"I hear voices downstairs."

"It's just Lieutenant Carney's people. They've been swarming all over the house."

"How long have I been asleep?"

Elise glanced at the clock. "Hours. We had Dr. Rhame come by and check you over. He gave you a mild shot."

"How did you know what had happened? How did you—?"

"Roper called us last night. I think he's still downstairs with the lieutenant."

Sage took a deep breath, looked down at the sleeping kitten. "Lise, did I dream it, or was it really—"

"It was Bea Bonham," said Elise. "My God, the whole thing's incredible! The woman's got to be crazy. And then Roper Chalfont, of all people, zooming in like Superman. I just can't believe—" Something in Sage's expression stopped her. "You know," she said lightly, "I never thought Bea's hair was real. All those scarves and turbans! Taking off her wig was a pretty effective disguise."

"Lise, she fell at least fifteen feet, with me on top of her!" Sage could feel the shock returning. "How could she get up and come after me again?"

"No one's got an answer to that. When they took her away, she could barely walk. Her getting up after the fall must have been sheer willpower. She had quite a career, Sage. Clay talked to some people at police headquarters and a man he knows in the solicitor's office. They'd run a check on Bea and all the other nonlocals at Octo's birthday party. Do you know, Bea was no more a novelist than you or I. They think it was some kind of cover, that she was a professional thief, going after antiquities."

"A professional—"

"She's been held for questioning a couple of times, once in Richmond and another time in Atlanta. In each case she either was the house guest or friend of the people who were robbed. Of course, they never had evidence to—"

"But why did she come to Charleston? She didn't know anyone here."

"Not in the beginning, Sage, but it didn't take her long. And, good lord, when you think of all the opportunities here, all the tours, people opening their houses. She could go in, look around, see what was of worth."

Sage thought of Bea pretending to be interested in the diaries as a novelist and then realizing she'd hit the jackpot, finding the reference to Jostle, knowing it was Audubon. She remembered Bea at Elise's party, wandering around upstairs, inspecting the eighteenth-century prints with a magnifying glass.

"Listen, Sage," Elise brushed a strand of hair from Sage's eyes. "Lieutenant Carney's very anxious to talk to you but I know he'll understand if you want to wait a bit."

"I'd rather get it over with." Sage sat on the side of the bed. "Lise, does Octo know?"

"Clay called her at the crack of dawn. He didn't want her to hear it on the radio. He also told Eldredge to keep her at home. Sage, that Audubon folio—do you have any idea what you found? Why, Clay says it's worth at least—"

"I know. I still can't believe it."

"Just think what you can do with all that money— fix up the house, travel. You'll have a whole new life."

"We're going to share it, Lise, you and I. That's only fair."

"We certainly are not! God knows, Clay and I don't need it. Sage, you can have practically anything you want."

Sage gave her a blank look, stood up.

"Tell me," she said, needing to change the subject, "why are you and Clay dressed like that?"

Elise glanced over at her sleeping husband, grinned. "We hadn't gone to bed when Roper called. We came as we were."

Sage opened her armoire, pulled a skirt and blouse from their hangers, found a pair of shoes. "But you and Clay were having a dinner party last night." She turned, mystified, as her sister stretched, then beamed at her.

"I'll explain," said Elise, "in good time."

Sage was enormously relieved to find that Roper had gone. She couldn't face him, especially knowing that he'd saved her life.

Lieutenant Carney took her arm and led her into the drawing room as if he expected her to fall to the floor in a heap. They watched two plainclothesmen go through the hall and start up the stairs before he spoke. "You must have some questions," he said.

"Yes. The last thing I remember—I saw her there, behind me—" She shivered. "Then I heard this great crashing sound."

"That would have been your tenant, smashing through the French doors to get in. You're one lucky lady. It seems Chalfont got home from Edisto about twelve. He'd been sitting up reading and went out to his car to get something, not bothering to turn on the patio light. He saw someone going in your basement door, thought it was you, and went back into his house. Then he remembered that your car had been in the yard earlier and he hadn't heard it go out or come in. It was one-thirty in the morning and there was a light burning on your top floor. He wasn't sure what was going on but, thinking about the murder and the fact that Miss Barth's boyfriend hadn't been charged yet, he called me. I told him then about the sounds you'd been hearing at night, and the fact that Waggoner had a firm alibi for the last night your mentioned hearing them. Chalfont didn't wait for me. He knew he had to get into the house. Apparently he'd rented an extension ladder to work on his roof. He dragged it across the patio and set it up against the side of the piazzas. Good thing it didn't take him any longer." The lieutenant looked at her expectantly, but she made no comment. "It would be a big help," he said, "if you would tell me exactly what was going on inside the house."

She tried to remember everything, beginning with the sound of the kitten crying in the walls. When she finished, the lieutenant was still writing in his notebook. Finally he looked up. "We couldn't figure out what she was doing in your house, why she'd attack you. It was Chalfont who suggested we take a look on the top floor, because of the light he'd seen. He went up there with us. He was the one who spotted those big books on the floor. You know, he told us they could be worth well over a million dollars." The lieutenant whistled under his breath, shook his head. "And you found them in that crawl space, looking for your cat. How long do you suppose they'd been there?"

"Since August of 1863." She told him about the diaries, Auralee's connection with Audubon in the 1830s, Charlotte hiding the folio with her father's papers thirty-three years later, thinking the pictures not only worthless but unattractive.

"How the devil did that Bonham woman know they were hidden in the house?"

"She read both diaries," said Sage. "A lot of people read them, but Bea was the only one who knew what Charlotte had hidden. She's good at research." Sage thought of her conversation with Bea the day she went to Mille Fleurs. "The unexplained, the inscrutable drives me up the wall," Bea had said.

The lieutenant consulted his notebook. "She had keys to your basement door and the front door. She used the basement entrance because she was less likely to be seen. She didn't count on running into Franny Barth. Either Miss Barth heard some sound or came in to use the laundry. I gather she kept odd hours."

"The keys—Bea—"

"We figure she took your sister's keys the day of that party at your aunt's, and had them duplicated."

"My sister found her keys. They were under the seat of the car."

"Where Miss Bonham planted them once she'd had them duplicated. My men searched her place after we'd made the arrest. They found some stuff locked in a closet—a TV set, an antique clock, some odds and ends of silver. Chances are she had started picking off different houses in town."

"No," Sage said. "Those things were taken from my Aunt Octo's. I think it was Bea's way of getting me out of the house. She thought if I was worried enough about Octo I'd go over and stay with her. As it turned out, one of my aunt's friends moved in. I only spent one night there."

"Miss Eliot, I know you must feel beat. Why don't we leave the rest of this until later? You had a long night."

Sage watched him tuck the notebook into his pocket. "Even when I saw that it was Bea," she said,

"I couldn't believe it. I was so certain it was Peter Larson."

"Larson?" Lieutenant Carney was surprised. "You mean the fellow who looks after David Raeburn?" He shook his head. "Larson's a masseur; he worked for Raeburn's mother. He doubles as a kind of keeper. Raeburn's—"

"I know."

"You never suspected Miss Bonham?"

"No. And I still don't believe Bea meant to kill Franny, not at first."

"What about you?"

"No," she said stubbornly. "Hurt me maybe, scare me into fainting or—"

"Look, Miss Eliot—"

"She was desperate by then. But she wouldn't—" Sage broke off, too dazed, too heavyhearted to say the words. "I liked Bea," her voice was almost a whisper. "She was my friend."

The lieutenant laughed, then at once became apologetic. "Forgive me, Miss Eliot, but how long has Miss Bonham been in town?"

"I can't remember. Less than a year."

"And knowing nothing about her, you and your aunt accepted her, made a friend of her?"

"She was interesting! She was fun to be with and she loved the town."

"She also was a stranger." Suddenly he grinned at her. "Before I came here," he said, "I was warned that Charlestonians are the worst snobs in the western world. I was told that they are clannish, elitist, and make everyone born beyond the city limits feel like a peasant. So you see, you're something of a revelation." He stood up. "Just for the record, that lady is a thief and a murderer. What would it have taken to put her beyond the pale?"

Sage didn't try to answer this.

"Do you suppose a lowly but well-behaved lieutenant from Hackensack might dare at some future date to invite a daughter of the old south to split a pizza?"

"He might," Sage smiled.

It was another half hour before the lieutenant and his men packed up their gear and left. Sage and Elise stood on the piazza and watched them go. Clay walked with the lieutenant to the street, deep in conversation. The light in the garden had turned from rose to gold. Elise put her arm around Sage's shoulder. They watched a tiny blue gray gnatcatcher perch on the branch of a towering pecan tree. "Sage, you're sure you're all right?"

"I'm fine. I just want to take a bath."

"I want you to come to dinner tonight. It's important. And I think you ought to stay with us until—"

"I'll come to dinner. I won't stay."

"You're so damn stubborn."

"How was your party last night?"

"Party? Oh, we didn't have the party. Clay called everyone and told them it was canceled."

"*Clay* called them?"

"We packed some sandwiches and a bottle of wine and went to the beach. It was beautiful! We walked by the water for hours and talked and talked. Sage, we haven't talked like that for years. Clay was like a different person. When I think of the way he's been knocking himself out, trying to give me all the things he thought I wanted. And me! Determined to be the perfect hostess because I thought—"

"Clay canceled a dinner party!"

"I'll expect you around six-thirty, Sage. I'm going to invite Octo and Eldredge. Do you suppose he has a dinner jacket? I don't want him to be uncomfortable."

"What are you talking about, Lise?"

"There'll just be the five of us, but Clay and I want to dress up. Wear something pretty, Sage, that white voile, maybe."

"Lise—"

"Six-thirty, Sage."

Mystified, she was still staring at the gate after Elise and Clay had driven away. She turned to the carriage house. Roper's car was in the yard. She knew what she had to do and she'd better face it at once. If she waited, her courage would ebb, she'd find excuses for herself. He'd saved her life. Despite what she'd told Lieutenant Carney, she remembered the wild, lost look in Bea's face; Sage had been brushed by death. She had to thank him. With a pang of shame she admitted that she was, in some mean and ungenerous way, trying to figure out how to show gratitude without abasing herself. Before she could take a step she heard the phone. Reprieved momentarily, she ran to answer it.

The minute she heard Octo's voice, she knew her aunt had not called until she had her emotions under control. "Sage, I've been told what happened. Are you all right, dear?"

"Yes, Octo. Elise and Clay just left."

There was a pause but the old lady spoke calmly. "I won't say I'm not shocked. I would have trusted Bea with my life." She cleared her throat. "It's just so difficult to understand. You know what I mean?"

"I know."

"And, Sage, terrible as this is, we cannot harden our hearts. There's no telling what causes people to— We really know very little about Bea's life."

"That's true, Aunt."

"Or anyone else's," said Octo glumly.

There was another, longer pause. When Octo spoke again her voice sounded distant. "David Raeburn has gone. The Pullams, across the street, said they saw David and Peter packing their car early yesterday. They just up and left, without a word."

Sage couldn't speak. She was filled with sadness for David.

"I'm shocked!" Octo's voice had gained vehemence. "But then a lot surprises me. I just don't understand people anymore. I've always enjoyed newcomers. They add spice to life. A lot of the Readers and Writers are from away, you know that, Sage. Even Eldredge."

"I'm sure you can trust Eldredge, Aunt."

"I'd like to trust everyone."

Sage had no answer to this. She pictured her aunt sitting in the dim hallway by the telephone, confused and heartsick, not knowing what to do next. "Aunt Octo," she said, "I think it would be an act of charity if you send a few things over to Bea, a change of clothes, a toothbrush." It was an outrageous suggestion but, predictably, not outrageous to Octo.

"A pie!" she said brightly. "I made a pecan pie for you, but if you don't mind, Sage—"

"I don't mind, at all."

"It will be a welcome change from bread and water or whatever they give them." Octo sounded almost cheerful. "Speaking of food, Elise has invited Eldredge and me to supper tonight; she said you'd be there, too. Sage, about the pie—where should Eldredge take it?"

"To police headquarters, Aunt. Tell him to deliver it to a Lieutenant Carney."

"But will it get to Bea? Will he understand?"

"Yes," said Sage, "I'm sure Lieutenant Carney will understand."

She didn't give herself time for further thought. She must go to the carriage house at once. But when she opened her front door, Roper's Aunt Janet stood before her, holding out the blue sweater Sage had taken to Edisto. She still wore her old sandals but she'd put on a faded cotton dress, and neatly pinned up her hair. "Sage, I hope I haven't disturbed you," she said, "but I just dropped Charlie at the dentist's a few blocks from here, and I thought I'd bring by the sweater you left the other day."

"Please come in," said Sage. Much as she liked Janet, she dreaded discussing what had happened the night before.

"I can only stay a minute." Janet followed Sage into the house, looking around with interest. "Wonderful old place."

Sage realized that Janet had no idea what had been going on in the wonderful old place. She and Gabe had a phone but no radio or TV, probably didn't even get a newspaper. Sage decided not to tell her. Later, after she'd learned what had happened, Janet might think this odd, but Sage had a feeling she'd understand. "Would you like some coffee?"

"I would, but I don't want Charlie to come out to the waiting room and find me gone.'

"Won't you sit down for a minute?"

"No, I'd better not." Janet laughed. "You know, driving to town with Charlie this morning, I had a real attack of déjà vu. Then I remembered I'd taken his daddy to the dentist once, when young Louis was about Charlie's age. Big Louis and Mary had left both boys with us when they went to New Orleans. I recalled giving little Louis a stern lecture about sweets—"

"Janet—"

"He always had a candy bar melting in his back pocket. Mary tended to spoil those boys. It's a wonder—"

"Janet," Sage broke in, "did you say Louis? Did you say Charlie's father was Louis?"

"Yes, of course."

"But I thought—I was sure—" Dumbfounded, she stared at Janet.

Janet looked at Sage in confusion, then her face cleared. "Oh, my God! You thought he was Roper's! But didn't Roper explain?"

"He never explained anything."

"I have to sit down." Janet backed up to a chair, sank into it. "That jackass!" she said. "When I saw you together—well, to be frank, when I saw the way you looked at each other I just assumed that—oh, hell, knowing Roper, I should have realized."

"Realized what?"

Janet hesitated, then she stood. "Sage, you'd better ask Roper. I have no right. Look, I've got to get back to the dentist's."

"As far as I know, Roper is a convicted criminal. I also assumed that Charlie not only was his illegitimate child but that Roper had abandoned the mother, that his whole life had been one despicable, dishonorable—"

"Dishonorable!" She turned on Sage like a tigress. "Lady, the word *honor* might have been coined for Roper!" She closed her eyes for a second, unclenched her fists. "The hell with it," she said. "God knows he deserves something, and if you're what he wants—" She stopped, then went on. "What's happened to feminine intuition nowadays?" she asked bitterly. "Don't girls like you have any clear perceptions of people? For years I've prayed that some really splendid woman would find Roper and know him, instinctively, for what he is. He deserves that."

"I wish you'd tell me—"

"All right, I'll tell you." Janet took a quick look at her watch. "Eight years ago, Roper's sailboat was picked up in Bull's Bay, loaded with drugs. Louis and a friend were aboard. Of course they were arrested. Louis called Gabe, trying to find Roper. Roper had come down from Washington, where he worked, to visit the family. Louis admitted everything to Gabe. He was scared witless. Anyway, Gabe finally located Roper at some party. The next morning we heard that Roper had given sworn testimony that the drugs were his, that Louis knew nothing about them and had borrowed the boat without asking. Roper said he'd had a rendezvous off the coast the night before with a Bolivian trawler. He was the middleman and planned to meet with the dealer later that night, on Wadmalaw Island. Going to the party was an attempt to establish a partial alibi. A pretty lame story but the agents believed it."

"You mean he took the blame for his brother? He actually—"

"It's very simple. Louis was in his final year of law school, with an outstanding record. He was married, had a young child, and he was the pride of old Louis's life. Young Louis was brilliant, but he was weak, and though he was the eldest, Roper always fought his battles for him. In Roper's mind there was no alternative. He took the blame, served the sentence. When he was released he traveled for a few years. Last year, after Louis and his wife were killed in an accident, the maternal grandparents took Charlie. Roper offered to take him but they refused. Now they're simply too old and infirm. Roper adores that boy." Janet handed Sage the sweater. "I'm sorry if I've been rough on you. It's just that I'd hoped—well, Gabe says I always hope too much." Briefly, she touched Sage's shoulder. "I've got to go." At the door she turned, elegant in her faded dress. "Do you know what Gabe calls Roper? The last of the knights, the last of the Round Table." She managed a smile, and then she was gone.

Sage called the bank and arranged for them to put the Audubon folio in a safe place, then she carried the four heavy volumes and Thomas Benford's papers to her workroom. She sorted the letters into two stacks, personal and business. Twice she went to the window and each time found that Roper's car was not in the yard. She was remembering their conversation on the way back from Edisto; Roper saying, "I suppose Janet explained about Charlie," thinking that his aunt had told her the boy was his brother's child. She, having assumed the worst, had coldly replied, "Yes, she did."

Wave after wave of shame rolled over her as she thought of what she'd lost through her own hard-headed stupidity. Words she'd once read kept coming back to her: "We see ourselves most clearly in the eyes of the beloved." She remembered David being attracted not to her but to the image of himself reflected in her eyes each time she looked at him. Her perception of him, wrong as it was, had nourished him. The thought of looking into Roper's eyes filled her with grief. She couldn't face what she'd surely see. It was David who'd spoken of words like honor. It was Roper who lived them.

She made herself concentrate on the folio. For several hours she sat studying each plate. She hated the idea of selling it. It was part of the family history, of Auralee. Then she thought of Alfred Freeman holding forth at Elise's cocktail party about backward Charlestonians. "They're mired in the past," he said, "reveling in the glories of their ancestors. It's their whole identity."

She thought of the way she'd tried to lose herself in the diaries, to find an alternative world or to fashion her own to fit another era. Like putting David Raeburn in a satin waistcoat or a Confederate uniform. Like fearing and misjudging Roper because he looked too much a man of the future. She'd dreaded facing him before Janet had told her the truth. Ashamed and heartsick, she found it impossible now. She remembered his remote, expressionless face when he'd told her he was moving, the formality that denied everything that had happened between them. Inevitable, justifiable. One day in the future she'd be able to talk to him. One day when time had dulled her shame, his terrible disappointment in her. But not now. Not now.

She wrote the letter three times and each time tore it in half and threw it in the wastebasket. At last, realizing there was no way to express herself with any grace, she compromised.

"It's hard to thank someone who has saved your life. Lieutenant Carney says I was truly lucky and he's right. Someday I hope I'll have the courage to face you and thank you again. Right now, I'm too ashamed. Your aunt came by today and we talked. She told me everything. All I could think of was what I said to you on the way back from Edisto, ranting about duty and honor like some priggish fool. I had a chance to believe in you in spite of everything. I missed it. Your aunt says she prays that some really splendid woman will find you and know you instinctively for what you are. I hope her prayers are answered."

It sounded hopelessly disjointed, groveling, even maudlin, but it said what she felt. She put it in an envelope.

Later that afternoon a man from the bank came to collect the folio and put it under lock and key. Major arrived a few minutes later, dirty, unrepentant, and ravenously hungry. By six o'clock Sage was ready to go to Elise's and Clay's for dinner. She found irony in the fact that just as she had decided to adapt herself to the world of the present, the pier glass reflected a girl from another century, in white voile with a flowering skirt and high lace collar; a romantic Godey print except for the desolate face.

Before she left, there was a call from Lieutenant Carney. "You were right about Miss Bonham," he said. "We made a thorough search of her place, especially her papers. She'd put together quite a file on the Benford family, including Xeroxed excerpts from the diaries. One, dated August of 1863, describes some letters, papers, and pictures being hidden in the house.

And the important stuff was in the earlier diary of an Amalie Benford."

"Auralee Benford."

"That's right. She mentioned a wedding gift from her father, something he'd bought privately from a Dr. Geddings. Well, clipped to this entry we found a notation of 'The Double Elephant Folio,' a book that describes the creation of the folio, subscribers, and extant complete sets. The notation singles out this Dr. Geddings, who had a complete subscription, but whose folio was never found. It says his library burned during the Civil War. It looks like your ancestor bought the folio from him some years earlier."

"Yes," said Sage. "Once Bea suspected that Auralee's father had given her the folio, all she had to do was check and see if Dr. Geddings had owned one."

"Miss Bonham had a real talent for organization. Under a file marked 'Madeira,' she has a card on each room in the house, listing possible hiding places. At first that had us stymied, then I went back to Charlotte's diary and found the place where she says her father told her to 'Remember the Madeira.' You told me you found some bottles of wine, hidden beside the folio—"

"Bea was way ahead of me in her detective work, lieutenant."

"Are you all right?" he asked suddenly. "You sound kind of—"

"I'm doing fine."

"I hope you haven't forgotten that we're going to split a pizza someday."

"I haven't forgotten."

She made herself think about the evening ahead, which she gathered was to be a celebration of some kind. She climbed to the top floor, picked up a bottle of her great-great-grandfather's Madeira, dusted it off, and took it with her. As she was leaving she was relieved to see that Roper still hadn't returned. With a sense of finality she slid the letter under his door.

SEVENTEEN

AS SHE DROVE TO her sister's, she kept thinking of the letter. She saw him finding it, turning it over curiously, and then reading it, his face expressionless. She saw him crumpling it in one big fist and throwing it in the fireplace. Then an ironic smile, perhaps, a shrug. She wondered if he berated himself for poor judgment, for being a romantic fool. She knew for certain that he'd begun to fall in love with her, allowed himself, against all odds, to trust her feelings for him. Would he grieve, as she grieved now, for what was lost? No. That wasn't his style. He'd learned to handle far worse tragedy than this. He'd leave it all behind, move on.

She drove around an extra block before she felt that her smile could pass muster, that somehow she could get through the evening, celebrate whatever she was being called upon to celebrate.

When Etta opened the door, she was grinning like Christmas morning. She grabbed Sage in a bone-cracking embrace, then stepped back for an admiring inspection. "Do God, just look at you! I declare, child, but you are a sweet sight. That dress is even prettier on you than on Lise." Sage looked around the hall, glanced into the dining room and drawing room, and saw daffodils, tulips, and daisies massed in vases everywhere. "They're waiting for you," said Etta, still grinning, "in the library. So you hurry on up there."

Sage heard their laughter as she climbed the stairs. When she walked into the library she saw more flowers, an extravagance of azaleas on the Georgian mantel, more on the coffee table, and still more on the handsome Sheraton desk. Even the dark paneled walls seemed to glow. Elise, in chiffon the color of a Pink Perfection camellia, rushed over to hug her. Clay, resplendent in evening clothes, grinned like Etta. Octo held up her face for a kiss. Eldredge, rising from his chair, greeted her with a charming bow. "Lovely lady, come and sit here," he invited in the rich tones of a Shakespearean actor.

Sage turned to her sister. "What's going on here? Is Clay going to run for governor?"

Elise laughed. "Oh, Sage, can't you guess? Surely, you've guessed by now."

Sage watched Clay take a bottle of champagne from the big silver cooler and pop the cork. "Lise! Oh, Lise, you don't mean that—"

"We found out yesterday," said Elise, "right after you left. Dr. Hooper called. I'd taken the home test weeks ago and it was positive. But when Dr. Hooper did the first blood test it was negative. I had to wait almost a week before I went back for another test, then wait another twenty-four hours for the results. I'd put off having the test for weeks. I was so sure we'd be disappointed."

"You're going to have a child," breathed Sage.

"A child!" Octo leaped to her feet and ran to hug Elise.

"A child," echoed Eldredge. "Now this really is something to celebrate!"

Clay turned to Sage, his face suddenly years younger. She saw an appeal not only for celebration but for something that she and Clay had never managed to share, kinship. Without words she went to him, kissed him, held him tightly. "Oh, Clay," she said, finally. "Oh, brother!"

There was no talk of what had happened the night before, no mention even of the Audubon folio. As always, in times of great stress or happiness, they reminisced. Elise teased Clay about being sent home from dancing class for dropping a roach down her cousin Corinne's fat little neck. Clay remembered Elise losing her petticoat as the first angel in the Ashley Hall Christmas pageant. Memories of long past parties, games, jokes were pulled out and dusted off with nostalgic delight. Sage knew that Elise and Clay were already seeing their child running across the field at East Bay playground, singing in the choir at St. Michael's, sailing in the harbor on hot summer days.

"Elise was one of the prettiest babies I've ever seen," said Octo. "Etta would take her every day to White Point Gardens in that big wicker carriage. Do you know that your mother was wheeled in that carriage, Elise?"

"I know, Octo."

"Sage, it must be there in the house. I'm sure it's there."

"It is, Aunt. I'll get it out first thing tomorrow."

"Eldredge, where were you raised?" Clay spoke to the old man, who had been listening raptly.

"I?" Eldredge laughed, coughed nervously, then pulled a handkerchief from his pocket and patted his face. "Nowhere as splendid as this, I'm afraid." He undid the button of a dinner jacket so old it had a greenish cast. "I grew up in Pittsburgh, which in those days was far from being a garden spot." He looked at Octo, then looked away. "My father was with U.S. Steel."

"I ran into a fellow from U.S. Steel at a meeting in Atlanta," said Clay companionably. "I believe his name was Speers."

"I'm afraid I don't know him."

"I guess the company's changed a good deal since your father's day."

Eldredge took a big swallow of champagne, as if giving himself time to make a decision. "My father worked on the open hearth," he spoke in a flat tone, all resonance gone. "We lived in a four-room row house a stone's throw from the mill. My grandfather operated a coal barge on the Monongahela River."

Clay refilled Eldredge's glass. "That's interesting," he said. "The first Hillman who came to Charleston was a dock worker from Liverpool. He signed up as a bonded servant."

"One of my forbears," Octo chimed in, "toiled in the phosphate mines of Surrey."

"Cornwall," amended Clay gently.

"En route to this country," Octo continued blithely, "he worked in the sugar cane fields of Bermuda."

"Barbados, Aunt."

"Clay," said Octo, "if I could wish two gifts for your blessed child, the first would be a soaring imagination, free from the dreary bondage of fact."

"Supper is on," summoned Etta from the doorway.

"And the other?" beamed Clay.

"Why, your teeth, of course. I've always said the Hillmans have the soundest molars and the brightest bicuspids south of Calhoun Street."

They sat down to the dinner prepared for Elise's canceled party. Looking around the table, Sage thought, how beautiful they are, Elise's and Clay's faces still struck with wonder, Eldredge amazed to find

imself unquestionably included, Octo, tiny and quite
mart in a blue lace dress she'd worn to the annual
Colonial Dames banquet for six years.

Octo was delighted when Etta passed the *ris de veau
la crème aux champignons*. "Elise, what a treat! I've
lways loved tripe." Sweeping around the table, Etta
aught Elise's eye with a look of sheer triumph.

After they'd assured Elise that the breast of guinea
vasn't too dry and exclaimed over the pear meringue,
Eldredge got to his feet and lifted his wineglass. "If I
nay, I would like to propose a toast—to the event we
elebrate and to the good fortune of the child born to
uch gracious and loving parents."

There were more toasts and reminiscences. They
inished dinner and went up to the library for coffee.
Sage produced the bottle of Madeira and proposed a
inal toast to the child with the wine of its forebear,
which tasted a little strange but, amazingly, had not
gone sour. Then Clay opened the tall French windows; they all gathered to enjoy the fragrant night air
and look down at the garden lit by a three-quarter
moon.

"This city—this wonderful city—" breathed Eldredge, but for once words failed him.

From behind him, Clay spoke softly:

*"'They tell me she is beautiful my city,
That she is colorful and quaint, alone
Among the cities. But, I who have known
Her tenderness, her courage and her pity,
Have felt her forces mold me, mind and bone.'"*

"DuBose Heyward," murmured Octo. "He wrote
that over sixty years ago. Remember the last of it,
Clay?"

> "'Hers are the eyes through which I look on life
> And find it brave and splendid. And the stir
> Of hidden music shaping all my songs
> And these my songs, my all, belong to her.'"

The evening ended. Their good-byes were quiet, al most ceremonial, as they moved through the fron door, across the piazza; Octo, Eldredge, and Sag went to their cars. Sage took one last look at Elise an Clay, arms around each other's waists, wanting t hold this picture of them as long as she lived.

Driving home along empty streets, she tried to sh out her own misery, to think of Elise's and Clay child. The news of the child changed everything. I erased the horror, made her uncertainties about th future seem petty and selfish. It made clear some thing she'd sensed but never understood, the mystery of her people and her town, the aura Alfred Freema had perceived as snobbery, ancestor worship, smug ness. There was no mystery at all, simply lives live with an unbroken connection across centuries. It wa not pride of ancestry but the comforting knowledge that one didn't have to establish or create an identit because one already was known. Few people were s fortunate. Most of them lived in a world where noth ing was permanent. They changed jobs, moved fron one town to another, and with each change of addres were forced to rewin acceptance. Here, belonging is birthright, she thought gratefully. It's also one tha can be shared as it had been shared that night with Eldredge. In time, even if the truth was never know about him, it would be restored to Roper.

To Sage the narrow streets weren't empty at all. On Tradd Street, she saw Charlotte, her face hopeful under a shabby bonnet, hurrying to one of Rosa Bridge's soirées. A block away, Auralee, carrying her drawing pad, paused to listen to the night call of a warbler and think of her friend, Mr. Audubon. Elias Benford limped down Meeting Street in the parade that marked the end of the Revolution. On Church Street, William Eliot, his uniform in rags, took the last few steps of his long journey from Appomattox, home at last. In the background, like distant music, Sage seemed to hear the sound of roller skates, a bat hitting a ball, a child laughing somewhere in the future. They were all around her, those who had gone before. Like them she'd survive. She wouldn't rot here as Barbara Jane Thorpe had predicted. She'd not only survive, she'd make a life for herself. She'd get rid of the foolish expectations that had weighted her down for years. She was already letting them go, tossing them through the car window like so many stones. She dropped several at the Exchange Building, more by St. Philip's churchyard, a handful at the Old Powder Magazine.

She parked her car on the street by her house instead of going in the driveway. She couldn't face meeting Roper. Not yet. Not tonight. When they met it would be with a protective civility, a tacit understanding that only the most trivial things would be discussed, the weather, the tourists, the new guttering for the roof. Soon he'd be moving to Beaufain Street and if they saw each other at all it would be only to wave or nod.

She fled up the steps on the street side like some furtive, wounded animal. She tried to avoid looking

at the carriage house but the glow of lights stopped her
on the landing. Lights and music. Every window was
lit. Music poured through his open front door. On the
patio, the card table was covered with a white cloth
and set with two places, silver, china, a champagne
cooler, candles.

At first she simply froze with astonishment. Then
she stood stricken. What she saw was totally out of
character for Roper. Roper is a man for shrimp and
beer, she thought, the blunt statement, not a Lo-
thario who sets up romantic trysts. It occurred to her
that there was a side to him that she didn't know at all,
undoubtedly a side that enabled him to leave behind a
blighted love and move at once to greener fields.

She was torn between wanting and not wanting to
see the woman who would sit with him at that table.
She was sure the woman would be beautiful, loving,
trusting, everything Janet had prescribed. She turned
away blindly and headed for her door.

"Sage!" His voice rang out, stopped her at once.

Halting, uncertain, she went back to the landing.
Roper, wearing white tie and tails, stood just outside
his doorway. Almost casually he walked toward her,
waited, smiling up at her. The music swelled. It wasn't
Bach, nor Mozart. Without willing it, she found herself walking slowly down the steps. They were facing
each other. He regarded her with great care. His gaze
moved lingeringly from the top of her head to the hem
of her dress and back again. "There's something you
owe me," he said solemnly. From inside his coat he
pulled a card, let her see it, turned it over. It was a
worn dance card and the name Roper Chalfont was

scrawled across both sides. It was then that she recognized the music, the old song, "Tenderly."

With a courtly formality he touched her elbow, led her to the enclosed patio. Suddenly she was back at her debut ball, shy, miserable, not daring to meet his glance, torn between longing and fear.

"Sage?" he said.

She wished passionately that she'd behaved differently, defied reason, never lost faith in him. It was several seconds before she could bring herself to lift her head, look in his eyes. Mirrored there she saw not the timid debutante, nor the bitter prig ranting about nobility and honor. There was no trace of the woman unable to forgive herself. She saw, with a great rush of unexpected joy, someone transformed, quite splendid, someone both loving and unconditionally loved.

His smile was full of mischief. "I'm back," he said. "Sorry to have kept you waiting so long."

She gazed at him, hardly daring to believe what was happening. When she finally spoke, her voice was steady, almost nonchalant. "Was it long?" she asked, managing a lift of the eyebrow. "I hardly noticed."

Their laughter filled the garden, echoed in the street, sent a startled mockingbird from the mimosa tree to the carriage house roof. Roper held out his arms. With the spring night proclaiming all things new, all dreams possible, they danced.

A SUSAN WREN MYSTERY

THE WINTER WIDOW

First Time in Paperback

CHARLENE WEIR

SHE'D BEEN ONE OF SAN FRANCISCO'S FINEST—SEMI-HARD-BITTEN, CYNICAL AND HAPPILY UNATTACHED...

Until Daniel Wren blew in like a tornado, sweeping Susan off her feet and back home to Hampstead, Kansas, new bride of the small town's police chief. Ten days later Daniel was killed by a sniper.

Susan was an outsider—a city slicker, a woman, and worse, personally involved in the case. She was also Hampstead's new police chief... hunting for her husband's killer.

"Nonstop action and harrowing suspense." — *Publishers Weekly*

WORLDWIDE LIBRARY ®
™

CHASING AWAY THE DEVIL

A MILT KOVAK MYSTERY

First Time in Paperback

SUSAN ROGERS COOPER

HEAVEN CAN WAIT

On Friday night, Sheriff Milt Kovak of Prophesy County, Oklahoma, proposed to his longtime ladylove, Glenda Sue. She turned him down. On Saturday morning, Glenda Sue is found brutally murdered.

Kovak begins a desperate search to find the killer, well aware he's a suspect himself. When he discovers a first-class, one-way ticket to Paris in Glenda Sue's belongings, it's pretty clear she had been keeping secrets—deadly secrets.

"Milt is a delightful narrator, both bemused and acerbic."
—*Publishers Weekly*

Available in October at your favorite retail stores.

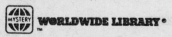

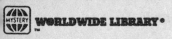

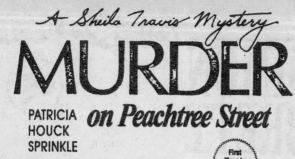

A Sheila Travis Mystery

MURDER

PATRICIA HOUCK SPRINKLE

on Peachtree Street

First Time in Paperback

NO MORE MR. NICE GUY

Prominent television personality Dean Anderson was as popular as he was respected, but he had incurred a good deal of animosity among family, friends and co-workers. Though the police are willing to rule his shooting death a suicide, his old friend Sheila Travis is not.

Because of meddling Aunt Mary, Sheila gets involved in finding Dean's killer. No easy task with a long list of suspects that includes a resentful ex-wife, an enraged daughter, a jealous co-worker, a spurned admirer, a mobster with a grudge. The truth goes deeper than either Mary or Sheila suspects. And it may prove equally fatal.

Available in November at your favorite retail stores.

WORLDWIDE LIBRARY®